"What do they wa
asked.

Twisted Hair shrugged, thought about the question for a moment, then said, "I think they want to trade with us. They tell us that there are other white men to the north—they call them British—and say they, too, are traders, but that the Bostons are more generous in their trade."

"What do they have to offer us?"

"I don't know. They showed us some things, but said they were just gifts, things they brought with them to show their goodwill to all the peoples they meet on their journey."

"What peoples had they met? Did they tell you? Did they meet the Blackfeet, and are they friendly to the Blackfeet?"

"They say they want to be friends with all peoples. They had met the Blackfeet and had no trouble with them."

"Then how can they be friendly to us?" Broken Arm asked. "How can they be friends to us?"

"How can friends of our enemies be our friends, too?" This question was addressed not to Twisted Hair, but to the other chiefs gathered around the council fire.

BOOKS BY BILL DUGAN

WAR CHIEFS

Chief Joseph
Crazy Horse
Geronimo
Quanah Parker
Sitting Bull

Published by HarperPaperbacks

Chief Joseph
WAR CHIEFS

BILL DUGAN

HarperPaperbacks
A Division of HarperCollinsPublishers

HarperPaperbacks
A Division of HarperCollinsPublishers
10 East 53rd Street, New York, NY 10022-5299

A previous mass market edition of this book was published in 1992 by HarperCollins*Publishers*.

ISBN 0-06-100388-3

HarperCollins®, 🔥®, and HarperPaperbacks™ are trademarks of HarperCollins Publishers Inc.

Cover illustration by Jim Carson

Revised HarperPaperbacks printing: March 2000

Printed in the United States of America

Visit HarperPaperbacks on the World Wide Web at
http://www.harpercollins.com

❖ 10 9 8 7 6 5

THE BEGINNING
1805–1806

Chapter 1 ===========

Clearwater River Valley—1805

IT WAS SEPTEMBER, and the camas fields were ready to be harvested. The long stems, their flowers now faded, were through waving at the sky like so many blue fingers. The lakes were starting to change, their deep blue and blue-green waters taking on the grays of autumn. Already, the high passes through the Bitterroots were clogged with early snow. The men, most of them, were gone, eastward through the mountains to the buffalo grounds of Montana and south across the Blue Mountains to punish the Bannocks for a raid on the horse herds. They would not be back until the spring, maybe even the late summer.

Sometimes the hunts lasted for eighteen months and sometimes they lasted for years. While the warriors were gone, the Nez Percé camps belonged to the women and children, a handful of old men, and a few warriors. But there was little to fear. The Blackfeet would not try the passes until the spring. The Shoshone were, if not friendly, at least distant, content to stay to the south, except during trading season, when they needed horses or the camas cakes and salmon the Nez Percé had to trade. And the Bannocks were on the run, with Broken Arm in hot pursuit. Secure in their homelands, the Nez Percé could pay attention to the only business that mattered, getting enough food to see them through the winter and tending to the huge herds of spotted horses.

Tu-eka-kas, like the other boys, would help, but not just yet. His mother was already in the camas field, poking the soft earth with a sharp stick to turn over the fat, fleshy tubers one by one. He was supposed to be helping, but he was late. Still, he was often late, and his mother would not yet be worried.

Squatting in a stand of pines, watching the cold, clear water of the creek tumble over the stones, sucking in the pine-scented air, he realized there were too many things to distract him. Since he was not yet ten, work was still optional for him, and as long as he helped a little, no one would pay much attention to how much.

Something darted out from behind a rock in the water, something brown, probably a trout, he thought. Moving closer, leaning over the fast-moving brook, he reached down into the water. It was cold, and made his fingers feel stiff, as if they had turned to stone. The brook bottom was sandy, dotted with stones the size of his fist, the size of his father's fist, and even larger. Not much sun made it through the trees, but the occasional splotches of light made it even more difficult to see. The trout took advantage of the shade. He saw it again, darting from one rock to another, even larger. It stayed almost motionless, its fins moving just enough to keep it in place against the cold current.

He was leaning out now, canting his head, trying to look through the gloss of light that came and went whenever the wind swayed the crowns of the tall pines. When the gun went off, he lost his balance and fell on one knee into the cold water.

Blackfeet, he thought. It must be. They got guns from the east, from the Sioux and the Hidatsa. But if the Blackfeet had come over the mountains, it could be for only one reason—a raid. And most of the warriors were gone.

Tu-eka-kas scrambled out of the creek, ignoring the chilly water still trickling down his legs, ignoring the numbness that made his legs feel wooden and useless.

He looked up the slope, trying to see through the dense ranks of the pines, but he saw nothing unusual. He had to find out who had fired the gun. He started up the mountainside, using the larger pines for cover. With the movement, feeling returned to his water-numbed limbs, and he realized he was breathing hard, harder than the zigzagging run required. With a shock, he understood what it was—it was fear, an intense fear he hadn't felt for many years.

He stopped now, trying to put his thoughts in order. They were all confused, tangled in the clinging threads of his fear that covered them like vines, made them hard to move, hard to sort out.

There had been only the one shot, and it made him wonder what the target had been. If a war party of Blackfeet had stumbled on some of his people, there would have been more than one shot. He would have heard war cries, too, horrible yelps and howls that would have thickened his blood and made his heart stop. But after the gunshot, its echo had slowly faded away. And the silence had returned. Now all he could hear was the slowly receding muttering of the brook as he left it behind, and the scratch of breath in his throat. Leaning close to a large pine, wrapping his arms around it for a moment, he could hear the beating of his heart, a distant thunder in his ears. He could feel the throbbing in his chest, like a small fist pounding on his rib cage, something trying to get out.

He realized that the birds had fallen silent. For a moment he thought they had gone, then he looked up and saw them, perched on their limbs, their heads cocked, listening. He cocked his own head, as if in imitation, but could hear nothing but the brook.

Taking a deep breath, he started up the mountainside again, taking care now to let the thick carpet of needles cushion the fall of his moccasins. His hands were trembling. His mind, ordinarily so active, could concentrate on only one thing. In its eye he saw a gargantuan Blackfoot warrior, blood dripping from his lips and from the gore-darkened blade in his right hand. The eyes were full of fire that seemed to spin, and when they fell on him, he felt his heart stop for the second time.

Once more he stopped to listen. He imagined he could hear voices, but they were low and he just wasn't sure. He would have to get closer. As he darted from tree to tree, almost as afraid of stopping as he was of pushing on, his nostrils twitched. Smoke! He looked up, expecting to see thin gray tendrils drfting through the tall, arrow-straight trunks of the thick pines, but he saw nothing unusual—just the dark masses of the crowns of the massive pines, the bright patches of blue and occasional white where the sky seeped like water down through the forest canopy.

But it was smoke, all the same. He was sure. In the shade of the forest, it was getting cooler as he climbed. The wind whispered fitfully and the limbs of the pines bent slightly, sending a thin shower of needles sifting down through the branches, hissing like water on a hot rock as they scraped from limb to limb then plummeted. Some of them pelted his neck and shoulders, stinging like small, harmless bees.

The smell of smoke was getting stronger now. He stopped once more, this time to listen for the crackle of the flames, the pop of exploding bubbles of sap, the sudden rush as a spurt of flame licked up along a branch full of dry needles. He wondered if he had been mistaken. Maybe his imagination had been playing tricks on him. Maybe it wasn't a gunshot at all, but a clap of thunder. Maybe lightning had struck a dead tree far up the mountainside, sending flame lapping down along the dry and brittle bark of the trunk and a shower of burning needles cascading down onto the forest floor.

But it hadn't been loud enough for that. It couldn't have been thunder. The sky was too clear, the wind too gentle. It had been a gunshot, and nothing else.

Then he heard the first pop of the flames and, behind it, voices, soft, as if whoever spoke knew he was there and didn't want to be overheard. Above him, the ground curved up, then bellied down into a small hollow. It was still three hundred yards or

so until he would be close enough, and he realized
he should circle around so that he could look down
into the hollow without running the risk of expos-
ing himself.

Moving to the left, his eyes pinned to the lip of
the hollow, Tu-eka-kas tripped over a small boulder and went sprawling. The loose needle carpet
dug into his flesh as he skidded several feet downhill, with a sound like snow avalanching from the
treetops in springtime. He held his breath and
fought off the urge to cry out. Getting carefully to
his knees, he plucked the needles that had stabbed
into his thighs and chest. It reminded him of when
his mother would pull pin feathers from a duck or
the old men would pluck tail feathers from a captive eagle to make their warbonnets.

Every needle burned as he pulled it free, and he
could feel the fire of the resin squeezed under his
skin. When he had the last needle out, he ran his
fingers over his skin and felt the hard pebbles, as if
he had been bitten by a swarm of mosquitoes. He
knew the bumps would be red and would well out
like small hills, but there was no time to worry
about it now.

So absorbed in ridding himself of the stinging
needles, he forgot to be quiet. He held his breath
when he realized it, and cocked one ear uphill.
Still, he could hear the crackle of the flames, and
the tang of smoke was stronger now. Under the
wood smoke was the scent of something else—
meat. It made him hungry, and his stomach turned
over once, then growled at him.

Starting uphill again, he made a wide circle to
the left and promised himself he wouldn't stop

until he could look down on the man who was cooking the meat, and the man or men he'd been talking to. He was used to the slopes and sprinted easily. Knowing where they were, he was less worried about running into them. His curiosity had pushed the fear aside, but it was still there, tugging at the back of his mind the way he tugged at the back of his mother's dress when he wanted her attention.

Tu-eka-kas was even with the hollow now. Another hundred yards up the mountainside would bring him to a point from which he could observe the bowllike depression in the pine-covered slope. All he'd have to do then was move carefully back to the right, a hundred yards or a little more ought to be enough. He was far enough below the crest of the mountain that the forest was still thick. There would be plenty of cover, as long as he was careful.

As soon as he was high enough, he stopped once more to listen, and to catch his breath. Again he could hear the muttering: three voices, maybe more. The men were keeping their voices low, but they didn't sound as if they were afraid. And he could hear enough to know that it was not the hated Blackfeet below him. But who could it be? It wasn't Cayuse or Shoshone that was being spoken. And it wasn't Umatilla or Spokan or Flathead. He'd heard those languages many times. Whoever these people were, they were of a kind he'd not encountered before.

The needle carpet was loose, and he took care in placing his feet. He crept now, from tree to tree, often waiting nearly a minute beside each tree before daring to slip from behind the rough trunk

and make his way to the next. He could see the
firelight now, not bright, because sunlight still
spilled through the trees, but it was there, a faint
orange wash on the trunks of the pines, and there
was smoke in the air now, too, smoke he could see,
the gray-white smoke of burning pine. It coiled
straight up along the tree trunks, then spread out in
a thin cloud where the wind made it swirl and ripple. Whoever these men were, they were not concerned about being seen. He knew that now,
because the smoke would have been a dead give-
away. Either they were men who had no fear, or
they were stupid enough to think they had no reason to be afraid.

Ten yards away, a small cluster of boulders, their
rounded backs humped like turtles, bulged out of
the needled floor. He ran to it, skidding on his rump
behind the largest rock. After listening patiently to
make certain he hadn't been discovered, he turned
on his belly and crawled up over the rock, keeping
his head down to avoid detection.

There were six of them, men he'd never seen
before, men like no others he'd ever seen. They
wore thick layers of clothing and had hair on their
faces. And they were busy butchering a horse, a
gelding that belonged to Broken Arm. They used
metal-bladed knives to skin the horse, and as he
watched they cut great hunks of meat from the carcass, then sliced them into thick steaks and spitted
them for the fire.

Some were already cooking over the flames,
dripping fat in great gouts that burst into bubbles of
yellow flame when they landed in the fire. Each
gout hissed like a diamondback for a few seconds,

then the burst of flame died down and the noise stopped until another glob of fat fell into the fire.

He listened again, but understood nothing. He didn't know who these men were, but he knew they had guns, and he knew they had killed a horse that did not belong to them. There was only one thing to do. He had to run to the camp and tell Twisted Hair.

Now.

Chapter 2

BUT TU-EKA-KAS WAS PARALYZED. He didn't know whether to stay and watch the strange men butcher the horse or run back to the village. He counted them once more, even creeping a little closer to make certain he saw everything important, then backed away from the boulders and turned to run. Moving away from the strangers, he was less afraid, and ran with abandon, his legs pumping like pistons, his moccasins slipping on the shifting carpet of needles.

He didn't stop until his chest felt like the slowly building fire inside it would burn him to cinders. Gulping air, he skidded to a halt beside the same brook where he had been watching the trout. He bent over, cupped his hands, and swallowed several mouthfuls of the cold, clear water. He was worried now, because Twisted Hair's camp was a long way away. There was no point in running to the camas fields, because only women were there. If the strangers meant trouble for his people, it would be important to have warriors—and weapons. The strange men weren't Blackfeet, but they had guns like the Blackfeet had. He'd counted three or four of the long guns, and there might even be more. There might even be more men, for all he knew.

But there was no time to wait, no time to count. No time to do anything but run.

The fire in his chest had died down, and he took one more scoop of cold water before breaking into a trot, then a fast run. He wished his father were in camp, but there was nothing to be done about it now.

It was nearly five miles to the nearest village—a small one, at that—on the banks of the Clearwater. Twisted Hair was even farther away, but he wanted to tell someone what he'd seen, someone older, someone who already had a *wyakin* to turn to, to ask for help, for guidance. He struck the bank of the Clearwater a mile later, then headed downstream, keeping to the edge of the water where the travel was easiest. It would still take him an hour, but there was no getting around that, just as there was nothing to be done about his absent father—or the strange men butchering a horse that did not belong to them.

Tu-eka-kas tried to plan what he would say when he reached the camp. He thought over all the times he had stayed with the other boys just outside the reach of the campfire, listening to the chiefs talk. They were always so careful about what they said. Everything fit together. Everything made sense. What was important was said first; then, as the chiefs and the warriors argued about what to do, the little things were added, until everyone knew enough to make a decision.

Not everyone would agree with that decision, and that was all right. The people were free to do what they wished. But they knew that there was strength in numbers, and that if the village stuck together, or, if the emergency was great enough, if all the villages stuck together, then they would be strong enough to deal with it. It all seemed so simple to him now. So he planned what he would say.

He would be just like his father, and like Twisted Hair and Broken Arm and the others. Maybe it was time for him to go off alone, he thought, time to learn about his own *wyakin*. It was important, in times like these, to know where to turn. But it was a big step, and he needed his father's advice for something so important.

His legs turned to lead as he ran, and sometimes his feet slipped on the smooth grass, but he kept on running. By the time he reached the village, his thoughts were jumbled, and as he staggered into the clearing he no longer knew what to say first. What was most important? he wondered.

Concentrating on his thoughts, he stumbled over a pile of pine boughs and fell headlong, narrowly missing a fire where one of the old men was boiling the horns of a bighorn sheep to soften them so they could be shaped to make a bow.

A woman heard the commotion and came running from one of the doors to the long lodge. He didn't know her name, but recognized her face. She was friendly with his mother and knew his name.

"Tu-eka-kas," she said, trying hard not to laugh. "What's wrong? Have the Blackfeet tried to steal you away?"

The boy scrambled to his feet. He wanted to tell her, but all he could do was shake his head. He couldn't breathe, and the fire in his chest was licking its way through his ribs, threatening to consume him. He opened his mouth to explain, but could only gasp.

"What is it, then? What has happened? Why are you running?"

Tu-eka-kas doubled over, gasping for air. "I . . . they . . . the men . . . they had guns . . . strange men . . ." He stopped, panting, and dropped to his knees again.

The woman looked at him with alarm. "You're not making this up, are you? You saw something, didn't you?"

He nodded his head, then doubled over and threw up. The woman gathered him in her arms and picked him up as lightly as if he were an empty wicker basket. She ran to the lodge, calling out to those inside. Several women poked their heads out, and as they saw the woman with her burden they ran toward her, calling to others that something had happened.

The woman ducked her head and stepped down into the lodge. She lay Tu-eka-kas on a woven mat, then sent another woman for water. Brushing the hair, soaked with sweat, little beads of which glittered in the light of a small fire, out of his eyes, she cooed soothingly, "It'll be all right, Tu-eka-kas. You're safe now."

The boy shook his head wildly, rolling his shoulders with the energy of his denial. He tried to sit up against the pressure of her hands, but she was too strong for him, and held him down against the mat.

The woman sent for water was back now, carrying a small, densely woven basket full of cold water from the creek above the camp. The woman who knew his mother held the bowl to his lips, and Tu-eka-kas clasped his hands around her strong fingers. He could feel the coolness of the basket in the spaces between the woman's fingers and gulped the water down.

He was beginning to regain his composure. The woman sensed this and let him sit up, but held her hands ready to haul him back in case he should try to bolt. Looking back over her shoulder, she said, "Go get Too-hool-eka." Two young women dashed out of the lodge in search of the chief.

While she waited for the headman she continued trying to calm the boy. "Just relax. You're all upset. It couldn't have been that terrible, could it?"

Once more he gave his head a vigorous shake in the affirmative. She nodded as if in agreement. "All right, then, when Too-hool-eka gets here, you tell us what happened. In the meantime, try not to get upset again." The boy nodded and lay back, this time of his own accord, on the woven mat.

Moments later, the headman, who was a chief but no longer young enough to go on the buffalo hunts or war parties, entered the lodge. His hands were still sticky with the fish glue he had been using to bind deerhide to a new bow he was fashioning for his son. He nodded to the women, and they made way for him. Kneeling beside Tu-eka-kas, he reached out to pat the boy on the shoulder. Tu-eka-kas could feel the tug on his skin as the old man's hand came away.

"What's wrong?" the old man asked.

The boy gulped, swallowed hard, and shook his head. "The men, strange men. They killed a horse. Broken Arm's horse, I think, I'm not sure . . ."

"All right, tell us about the men, first. Blackfeet?"

Tu-eka-kas shook his head.

"Shoshone?"

Again the negative shake of the head.

The old man nodded as if to himself. "Snakes, then?"

"No," the boy said. "They had white skin. I never saw men like them before. They did not dress like us. They did not dress like any men I have ever seen. And their skins were white. They killed the horse and they were butchering it. They were cooking the meat over a fire. They ate like they were starving."

"White-skinned men? Are you sure?"

The boy nodded.

"How many?"

"Six . . . at least, I saw six. Maybe more. I don't know. . . ."

"Where?"

He told them about the depression near the top of the mountain, about the fire, and about how far he had run. The old man rubbed his chin with the glue-thickened fingers. In the silence, everyone could hear the ancient skin rubbing against itself and the soft crackle of the lodge fire. And they could hear the old man grunting to himself, and his breath, which was growing more rapid, as if he were disturbed.

Finally, he straightened. Looking down at Tu-eka-kas from his full height, Too-hool-eka said, "Rest. In a little while you will show me the white-skinned men. We need to talk to Watkuweis. Where is she?"

"She is in Twisted Hair's village," one of the women said.

"Good. We will need Twisted Hair to go with us."

"Why Watkuweis?" the woman asked.

"She has told us many times about white-skinned men. A long while ago, after she was taken by the Blackfeet, she lived for a time far away among men with white skins. She can tell us again about them. It will be a help. Send someone to Twisted Hair and tell him to bring Watkuweis here with him. Don't tell him anything else, just that it is important that he come here with Watkuweis. He will know what to do."

The old man then shooed the rest of the people away. He stamped his foot and waved his arms until everyone had moved to the far end of the long lodge. Then, folding his arms, he sat down beside the boy. "You were very brave," he said.

The boy chewed at his lower lip. "I wanted to tell everything just right, like in the council, but . . ."

"You did well."

"No, I didn't know how to say what was important. I wasn't clear. When you and my father and other warriors talk in the council, it's different. I wanted it to be like that, but it wasn't."

"Tu-eka-kas," the old man said, patting him on the knee, "the important thing about the council is that everyone know what they need to know to make a decision. That is the way we do things, and that is just what you have told us. Someday, when you are older, you will speak as a chief before the council, and you will see then that what I say is true."

"Then why did you send for Twisted Hair?"

"Because if you are right, then things are never going to be the same for us. Not ever again."

"But why?"

"Where do you think the Blackfeet get their long guns?"

The boy shrugged.

"From people to the east, but where do you think *they* get them?"

He shrugged again.

"From the white-skinned men. And if they have found their way to us, others can, too. And others will. And already we need guns to protect ourselves from the Blackfeet and the Snakes. Soon we will need more guns, and maybe bigger guns. That is important to know. And that is what you have told us. Just as I would have told it in the council. You have done well. It isn't your fault that the news you bring is bad."

"What will Twisted Hair do?"

It was the old man's turn to shrug. "What is there to do?"

Chapter 3 ═══════════

TWISTED HAIR PUSHED the boy forward. "Go on, Tu-
eka-kas, show me where you saw them."

The boy started to move, but his limbs seemed to
have a mind of their own. He kept looking back at
the chief, feeling the trembling in his arms and
legs. This was not how it was supposed to be. He
had already seen nine winters, and it wasn't right
that his body should betray him like this. Twisted
Hair gave him an encouraging smile, but still the
boy's legs rebelled.

The chief walked to the boy, patted him on the
shoulder, and then knelt beside him. "I have an
idea," he said. "I'll go first. If I make a mistake, you
tell me. All right? Can you help me?"

The boy nodded, relieved of his burden. "Yes,"
he whispered.

"Can you do that?" the chief asked, giving him
one more chance to change his mind. He knew he
could find the place the boy described, but it
would take time. It was better to be shown the way.
Time was too precious to waste now.

Tu-eka-kas nodded his head and pointed
upstream. "That way," he said, his voice clear and
strong for the first time since the chief had arrived.

Twisted Hair nodded and stood again, looking

upstream the way the boy had pointed. He started slowly, letting the boy get used to the idea, then picked up his pace almost unnoticeably. He could see the prints of the boy's moccasins in the grass, and followed them, glancing back once in a while to reassure Tu-eka-kas and give him a chance to correct the course, if necessary.

The four warriors followed the boy. Their faces were immobile, their dark eyes flitting from place to place along the watercourse, occasionally darting to the far bank, just to make sure they weren't being flanked. Tu-eka-kas was feeling more confident now and soon moved up beside the chief, but said nothing. He knew better than to engage in idle chatter. It was important that they all be silent, in case the white-skinned men had somehow followed him, or stumbled this way by accident. If they had found the river, they would certainly follow it, since the going was always easier along the banks of a stream.

Soon Tu-eka-kas was bouncing along ahead of Twisted Hair, looking back now and then and waving one small bronze hand to hurry the chief and the warriors after him. He watched the trees, sometimes the ground, but mostly the sky, as if he expected something terrible to appear there, something that would swoop down on them all and carry them away in its awful talons. He didn't know quite why, but he had sensed some apprehension in the adults, as if they feared the same thing and had somehow communicated it to him without words.

Watkuweis had told them something about the white-skinned men she had seen in the east. She said they were kind to her, had strong medicine, and many things that were too wondrous to be described or, if described, too strange to be believed. But she had done little to reassure the chief. He was concerned about the weapons the intruders carried. He had seen firsthand what guns could do, when a party of Blackfeet with three of the long guns had attacked a small hunting party. Three of his people had been killed and two more badly wounded, one of whom died a few days later. The rest had been lucky to escape with their lives.

He knew that his people needed guns to protect themselves, but knew, too, that it would be far better if no one, especially the Blackfeet, had the deadly weapons. Bows and arrows were enough and no one made a better bow than the Nimipu. Everyone knew that, even the Blackfeet. The bows were highly prized and often traded for a high price at the Dalles, the trading places on the Columbia River or over the mountains to the east.

When the boy turned to the east and started into the pine forest, it grew cooler, and Twisted Hair wondered whether it was just the deep shade of the trees or something else that made him feel the chill. They moved easily among the trees, but were more tense now, more watchful. The closer they came to the place where the horse had been slaughtered, the more cautious they became. Twisted Hair sent Tu-eka-kas to the rear of the line now, but the boy pouted and the chief relented. Instead, he took the boy by the hand and held a finger to his lips to cut off the protest forming on the boy's lips.

They were heading uphill now, a steep slope through the trees. Underfoot, the pine needles whispered under the weight of moccasined feet. The forest was silent, except for a few birds that darted among the tall trunks, looking more like bats than anything else in the shadows high above them. Patches of sunlight, few and far between, dappled the forest floor.

As they drew near the place of the butchery, the smell of smoke hung in the air and the scent of charred horseflesh. Twisted Hair called a halt for a moment and listened to the silence. Even the birds grew quiet and the air seemed to thicken around them like glue hardening in a pot.

When he heard nothing, the chief ordered his warriors to stay behind with the boy, then moved on alone. He flitted from tree to tree now, instead of threading his way through the ranks of dark columns that seemed to reach all the way to the sky. Three hundred yards above him, Twisted Hair saw the lip of the bowl the boy had spoken about, and smiled at how accurate the description had been.

Approaching to within one hundred yards, he stopped once more. The silence was still perfect, and he bent into a crouch to cover the remaining distance. Creeping up under the rounded lip of the depression, he flattened himself against the nee-dled floor, here studded with rocks and cushioned by an inch-deep layer of fragrant moss.

Using a few of the larger rocks for handholds, he negotiated an angle across the bottom of the bowl, then crept up behind one of the largest boulders. His nostrils twitched as the odor of burnt flesh grew still stronger. He lay still for a long time, motionless and silent as the moss beneath him. Satisfied at last that no one was there, he crawled up and over the lip.

Far behind him, the warriors of Twisted Hair tightened their grips on their bows. Tu-eka-kas grew very still. Only his lip trembled and he squeezed it with two fingers to make it still. Then Twisted Hair reappeared, standing on the lip of the bowl and waving for them to join him.

The warriors heaved a collective sigh, then sprinted uphill, one hoisting the boy to his shoulder and carrying him several hundred yards, taking a detour around the bowl to avoid the steeper part of the climb.

The remains of the fire could still be seen in the bottom of the bowl. It had been covered with a thin layer of dirt to make sure it was extinguished. Twisted Hair walked over to the slight mound and kicked some of the dirt away. Squatting, he reached out with one hand, holding it palm down, then lowering it to gauge the heat.

"Still warm," he said. "They have not been gone long." He looked at the stark remains of the carcass, the bones covered with bloody strips of gristle and tendon, stark smears of white showing where a knife had sliced through. It glistened under the chitonous jewels of scurrying insects. Then he looked up at a nearby tree, where huge slabs of partially cooked meat hung from a rope almost twenty feet off the ground.

"Either they are coming back . . ."

"Or what?" asked one of the warriors.

"Or more are coming." Twisted Hair licked his lips and crooked his head to one side, trying to relieve the tension at the back of his neck. His shoulders felt stiff, the muscles pulled taut as a bowstring.

Twisted Hair looked once more around the small depression, first at the fire, then at the meat suspended above him, and finally letting his eyes linger on the ruined carcass, already teeming with ants and beetles. Flies buzzed in the quiet as he reached into the pile of warm embers. Grabbing a hunk of charred wood, he turned it over and over in his hand, still staring at the stark remainder of the horse. Casually, almost thoughtlessly, he tossed the charred wood at the bones and watched as a swarm of insects ballooned out, swelling almost to the former dimensions of the animal before settling back down to their work.

It seemed to him that something had changed, that something beside the horse had died here almost unnoticed. He couldn't put his finger on it, but he couldn't push the thought from his mind.

Sighing, he walked over to Tu-eka-kas and squatted down. "Can you find your way home?" he asked.

The boy nodded, but said, "I want to go with you."

"Go where?"

"To find the white-skinned men. I know that's where you are going. I found them first, and . . ."

"This is not like finding a pretty stone in the creek, Tu-eka-kas. This is not something that you can own. You have done well, but it is best if you go home."

"Will you fight them? Will you kill the white-skinned men?"

"That is up to them," Twisted Hair said. "We have to see why they have come and ask them what they want here. If they come in peace, then they will be made welcome, as all peaceful visitors are, and they will leave in peace."

"And if not?" This time it was one of the warriors speaking.

Twisted Hair looked up at him and shrugged. "We'll do what we have to."

The warrior nodded. "You should let the boy come with us."

Twisted Hair looked sharply at the warrior. "Why?"

The warrior thought for a moment, then said, "He saw the white-skinned men first. He should know what this discovery means. Only if he is there will he truly know."

The chief sucked on a tooth, then nodded. "All right," he said. Then, turning to the boy: "Tu-eka-kas, you will have to do what I say if you come along."

The boy nodded gravely. "I will," he whispered.

This time they were concerned with speed. Twisted Hair took the lead. The trail of the white-skinned men was not hard to follow. It seemed to the chief that either they wanted to be found, or they did not care if they were. Either way it could mean they meant no harm. Time would tell.

At the river, the trail crossed at a shallow point and turned downstream. It continued to be easy to follow, and Twisted Hair allowed himself to hope that the warning he had seen in the bones of the horse was misplaced. The intruders must have been tired, because they were moving slowly. If he hurried, Twisted Hair thought he could catch up to them before they caught sight of the first village, where Watkuweis, Spotted Elk, Too-hool-eka and the rest waited to hear what he had seen.

After an hour and a half, the chief knew they were getting close. The signs on the riverbank were still very fresh. Places where the damp earth had been disturbed had still not had time to dry, despite the warm sun. Twenty minutes later, they caught their first glimpse.

Twisted Hair held up a hand and called a halt. Creeping to the edge of the stream, he peered out through some undergrowth and watched as the men, six of them, struggled down a slippery slope, just above a small waterfall. They seemed intent on their descent, and if they were worried about pursuit, they gave no sign. They were talking among themselves, he knew, because he could see their mouths moving, but any words were drowned by the small thunder of the cascade.

Moving into the open for a moment, he signaled the warriors to follow him, then headed away from the stream to avoid the densest growth along the bank. They were sprinting now, anxious to close the gap. When they reached a point abreast of the white-skinned men, some one hundred yards to their left, they started toward the river, stopping just below another, smaller waterfall.

They huddled together, like newborn rabbits in a warren, and watched the intruders slip and slide on the slick grass at the edge of the falls. When the last of them had reached the bottom, Twisted Hair stepped into the clearing, not thirty yards ahead.

He held one hand in the air, conscious of the tautening bowstrings in the brush behind him. He saw knuckles tense around the long guns, then the tall one in front smiled. He laid his gun on the ground and stepped forward with one hand extended.

"Hello," he said.

Twisted Hair's eyes squeezed slightly as he tried to understand the greeting. Another man, a small one with red hair, stepped up beside the first. He, too, held out a hand. In garbled Shoshone, he said, "Greetings." Twisted Hair recognized the tongue, but did not speak it. He started to sign welcome and the red-haired man smiled broadly, nodding his head in approval. The chief returned the greeting, and the others put down their long guns. The big one, obviously the leader, extended a hand again. "William Clark," he said.

Chapter 4

THE FAR-FROM-FLUENT Shoshone of the two men was barely enough to explain that Clark and his men needed food and shelter for a few days. They were being followed by several more men and had left the remainder of the horsemeat, for which they offered payment, to the trailing party.

Twisted Hair was reluctant to bring the men to his village, but custom required that strangers be received with hospitality. People, regardless of skin color, deserved respect, and got it, until they proved to be undeserving. Twisted Hair wondered whether that would happen with these exhausted men, and how soon. But the rules of courtesy were unequivocal.

It took nearly an hour to reach Twisted Hair's village, and along the way they passed Too-hool-eka's village, and Twisted Hair sent a warrior over to pick up Watkuweis. He hoped the old woman would be able to help him assemble the pieces of this strange puzzle in some way that made sense.

He was pleased about one thing. In his camp there was a Shoshone man who had married into the village named Broken Blade. He should be able to make communication better. And according to the man who called himself William Clark, there

was a Shoshone guide with the rest of his party.
Communication would not be quick, and Twisted
Hair knew enough about language to know that it
would not be accurate either, but at least some reasonable conversation ought to be possible. There
was much he feared about these white-skinned
men, and much he wanted to know before he
would be able to put those fears to rest.

When they reached the village, after following
the riverbank for two more hours, the chief arranged
for Clark's men to be fed and had a small lodge of
saplings and woven rushmats constructed for them.
Reserves of food were meager, because it had been a
bad winter the year before, and camas cakes, berry
cakes, and dried salmon were all in short supply.
But in receiving guests, one did not stint on the
essentials, so the strange men were fed as well as
the village residents, then fell into a sound sleep.

But Twisted Hair did not sleep. He spent the
early part of the night talking with Broken Blade,
the Shoshone man, and Watkuweis, the woman
who had seen the white men in their own land, a
place she called Minnesota.

Long after Broken Blade and Watkuweis went off
to sleep, Twisted Hair sat staring into the fire.
Twice, his wife came out of the lodge to get him,
and twice she went back alone. He couldn't sleep,
he told her, so he might as well stay outside. The
fire was low, and the forest seemed to press in from
three sides, the shadowy forms of the huge trees a
dark gray wall that arched over him. Walking down
to the riverbank, he sat on the ground and leaned
against a flat rock. He could see the stars now and
closed his eyes for a moment, listening to the

sound of the water and, somewhere far across the river, an owl.

He wished he were not alone, but the other chiefs would not be back until after the spring thaw, if then. Until they returned, the awesome burden was his alone to bear, and he doubted that he was up to the challenge.

He entertained thoughts of gathering all the warriors he could summon, maybe even sending to the Cayuse and Yakima villages across the mountains, then falling on the visitors and snuffing out their lives. It would be a breach of custom, but it might be better than the chance of trusting these strange men who killed a horse that was not theirs without first asking to whom it belonged and whether there were any objection. He knew the men were hungry, and he did not blame them for that, but there were things one could do, and things one shouldn't do.

Twisted Hair was wise enough to know that William Clark's customs and his own were different, but still . . .

Around and around went the thoughts. Each solution seemed to create additional problems of its own. There was no clear way to solve the dilemma except to continue to do what he had been doing. It made him uneasy, but slaughtering men who had given no real offense would make him uneasier still. Perhaps when the others arrive, he thought, we can see what to do.

He hoped the guide he would send would not be harmed, but even that small uncertainty picked at him with its tiny claws. Perhaps in the sunlight, things could be seen more clearly. Perhaps. He closed his eyes again, letting the sounds of the night wash over him, but he did not sleep. He wondered if he would ever sleep again.

When the sun finally came up, he was still sitting there, his elbows on his knees, his cheeks squeezed between exhausted palms. He stared at the water, watching the fish dart in and out among the rocks, sometimes breaking the surface then vanishing with a flip of their fins.

He heard the footsteps behind him but did not turn around. He saw the shadow on the ground next to him, but continued to stare into the silvery water. When William Clark sat down beside him, he glanced at the leader of the white men, who smiled and nodded. Clark signed a greeting, then opened a leather box he held in one hand. Twisted Hair was surprised to see that the box only had one side. It was full of cream-colored leaves with strange markings on them.

Clark riffled through the leaves until he found what he was looking for, then shook his head in satisfaction. Aware of Twisted Hair's intense scrutiny, he closed the box on his thumb. "Book," he said. "Book. Bible." Then he pointed to the sky.

Twisted Hair looked up, but saw nothing unusual. The thick white clouds were still tumbling over one another as they raced eastward, but they always did that. The blue was already bleaching down to a blue white, and in the distance the mountains were shrouded with mist, their jagged peaks sawed off flat by an impenetrable haze.

The white man opened the book and pointed to some of the markings. "Words," he said, then signed.

Twisted Hair grunted. "Words," he said, trying

to imitate the sound that Clark had made. The chief smiled, but did not understand. He got to his feet, reached down to pat Clark on the shoulder, and went wearily back to the long lodge.

Twisted Hair had a difficult choice. It made sense to send Broken Blade as guide because there was another Shoshone with the rest of Clark's party. But that would leave Clark and the villagers all but unable to communicate except by signs. And if he sent someone who could not speak with Clark's party to guide them, there was the chance that many days would be lost. It was going to be difficult either way, but in the end, the chief knew he would have to send Broken Blade and hope for the best.

Two days passed with the agonizing slowness of thick glue wending its way down an upraised finger while Twisted Hair and Clark tried to bridge the yawning gulf between them. Sign language was so limited, and Clark's command of it was marginal. Even with its help, there was the real possibility that something would be misunderstood. Some signs were nearly identical, and when you subtracted those that Clark seemed not to understand, Twisted Hair felt as if he were talking to a slow-witted child.

But the days did pass, and it was almost at sundown on the third when Broken Blade hailed the village from across the river. Twisted Hair, nearly asleep in the long lodge, bounced to his feet and ran outside. Already, the women and children of the camp were milling around, their excitement ventilated in endless chatter that was as incessant and unintelligible as that of hornets driven from a nest with a sharp stick.

The Shoshone moved toward the ford, stepping

carefully to keep his footing, and he was followed by several more white men, most carrying heavy packs, and a handful of pack animals, all of which had gone a long way since their last decent meal.

Clark raced out into the water, ignoring the treacherous footing. Nearly halfway across, he slipped and went down, his head disappearing for a moment before he rose, foam streaming from his long dark hair, and danced like a madman the rest of the way across. The other white men stood on the near edge of the water and watched the greetings, then rushed together into the current to help their comrades across.

Altogether, there were twenty white men now and one man with very dark skin that looked like coal, and Twisted Hair grew even more uneasy. His warriors were outgunned and nearly outmanned. He thought once more, knowing it was far too late, that he should have fallen on Clark and the others when he had had the chance. He wondered whether his descendants, if they should outlive him, would spit when his name was spoken, or if it would be spoken aloud at all.

Pushing his apprehensions to one side, he walked out into the river until his knees were below the surface and waited for the two leading white men to stagger across. It seemed to take an eternity and yet it ended all too soon. There was no turning back now.

At midstream, Clark introduced the leader of the stragglers as Meriwether Lewis. Like Clark, he seemed open and friendly. Lewis smiled broadly and extended a hand. Twisted Hair grasped it in his own, and Lewis shook it with a strong grip.

Letting go of the chief's hand, Lewis turned to his comrade and the two white men sloshed across the river to the village.

Twisted Hair stood there up to his knees in the current as if paralyzed. One by one, the new arrivals plunged into the river and waded across, each one nodding to the chief as he passed. The last man in line was the Shoshone guide, who had a young boy with him. Broken Blade stood on the opposite bank, arms folded across his chest. Twisted Hair waved to him, but Broken Blade stayed where he was until all of Lewis's men had climbed out of the river and headed for Clark's shelter. Only then did the Shoshone step into the water. After three steps, he turned and looked up at the towering pines for a moment, shook his head, then joined Twisted Hair in the center of the river.

The chief looked at Broken Blade, waiting for some explanation, but the Shoshone said nothing. Instead, he clapped the chief on the shoulder, left his arm draped around Twisted Hair's neck, and urged him back toward the riverbank. There was something on the Shoshone's mind; the chief knew that, and knew that now was not the time to discuss it.

Twisted Hair watched as Broken Blade walked toward the lodge and stepped down inside. Leaning back through the doorway, he said, "Call me when you need me to help speak with the white men's guide." Then he disappeared.

The chief then set about the business of welcoming the newcomers. Wading into the crowd of the curious, all jabbering nonstop, he ordered additional shelters constructed and walked to Clark's lodge. He stood in the doorway until Clark noticed him and waved him inside.

Lewis looked up at the chief, signed his thanks, and lay down to sleep. Clark got up and walked outside, tugging Twisted Hair along with him. Both men stood to one side and watched as the villagers, assisted by Clark's men, who were better rested, staked and lashed two more lodges. Only when the frames were assembled did Clark go back to his own lodge. Twisted Hair remained watching, his arms folded across his chest. He felt like a stranger in his own village now. As the rush mats were lashed in place he finally turned and walked to the long lodge. Inside, Broken Blade sat by the fire, staring into its dull orange flicker with his hands folded in his lap.

Twisted Hair sat down beside him. "There is much to talk about," he said.

Broken Blade nodded. "When you're ready. "

"Tomorrow, after they are rested," the chief said. He looked up then, and saw Tu-eka-kas watching him, leaning forward to hear what had been said. He waved for the boy to come to him. Tu-eka-kas looked as if he'd been surprised with his hand in another's possessions, then, staring at the ground and occasionally kicking the dirt floor, he scraped his way around the fire to stand beside the chief.

"You must watch and listen to everything, Tu-eka-kas. "

The boy nodded.

"Many things are going to change now. Do you understand?"

Again Tu-eka-kas nodded, but Twisted Hair knew the boy did not understand. He didn't understand it all himself. Things were rushing now, out of control. Many seeds were being planted that might not sprout until after he was gone. But he knew it was important that someone see, that someone remember the way it was now, and see how it all had changed. Only then would the Nimipu have a chance to save themselves from a future they no longer controlled.

Chapter 5 ═══════════

THE FOLLOWING MORNING Lewis and Clark sought an
audience with Twisted Hair. Using Broken Blade
and the explorers' Shoshone guide and a Shoshone
woman, Sacajawea, for the complex interpretations,
the white men explained that they were traveling
as far west as they could go, to the western ocean, if
possible. Villagers crowded around the small cluster of speakers, and more continued to flood in
from other villages along the Clearwater River.
Clark had taken to calling the villagers Nez Percé,
because some of the men and women wore small
spiral shells through their pierced noses.

Spreading a rolled skin out on the ground, Clark
showed Twisted Hair where he had come from.
Lines in black and blue showed where rivers even
greater than the Columbia ran, and far to one edge
was another great ocean like the one to the west.
The sheer size of the country Clark represented was
overwhelming. Sacajawea and Broken Blade tried
to explain why the white men had come, but it all
seemed too strange.

But one thing was clear. Clark's people were
very powerful. They had many wonderful things
with them, samples of things that were as nothing
to Clark but that took the chief's breath away. One,

a long, gleaming tube, Clark held to his eye, then handed to Twisted Hair and gestured for him to do the same.

Warily, the chief raised the shining wand and put one end to his eye. Everything suddenly grew large, and Clark's face swelled up like the belly of a bloated deer. The white man's blue eye was the size of a fist, and Twisted Hair lowered the tube, staring at it as it lay there in his hands.

"Spyglass," Clark said. "You keep it."

Clark presented Twisted Hair with a medal showing a likeness of the president of the United States, whom he called the "Great Father in Washington," and tried to explain how the great western plains, the mountains to east and west, and the land beyond the western mountains, all the way to the sea, had been purchased from France by the Americans. The concept was not readily rendered into either Shoshone or Nez Percé, and Clark, sensing the difficulty, quickly moved on to other matters.

He noticed blue and white beads decorating much of the clothing of both men and women. Knowing they had been manufactured in the east, he asked where they had come from, and Twisted Hair explained how there was a great trading place on another river, where people came from all over with their goods. The Nez Percé horses were much in demand, and it was not difficult to obtain anything they needed.

"There are white-skinned men west of the trading place," Twisted Hair said. "Or so I have been told. You are the first white-skinned men I have ever seen."

Excited, Lewis called for some treated skins, and asked if the chief could draw a map. It took some time to explain what he wanted, but eventually Lewis got the chief and several of the warriors to collaborate on a reasonably detailed sketch of the waterways, starting with the Clearwater. Twisted Hair indicated rapids with cross-hatching, and difficult passages where portage would be necessary with squiggles parallel to the watercourse.

Despite their exhaustion, Lewis and Clark determined to push on, thinking to make it all the way to the mouth of the Columbia River. Two hours spent in negotiation for supplies were concluded when Clark presented Twisted Hair with an American flag for Tunnachemooltoolt, whose name, it was explained, meant Broken Arm. The Indians would safeguard the explorers' horses, and would store saddles, powder, and shot until the white men returned.

The rest of the day, and all of the next two, were spent constructing canoes for the long river voyage. The villagers, still awed by the appearance of the strange men, continued to gather in curious throngs, sometimes pitching in to help with the construction, or teasing the white men, who, despite the language barrier, understood they were being made sport of.

When they were ready to leave, Clark oversaw the burial of the powder and shot and the storage of the saddles in a weather-resistant lodge constructed especially for that purpose. Lewis took charge of loading the canoes and the assignment of men to each. And, finally, they were ready.

Word of the white men had continued to spread

from village to village, and on the morning they pushed their canoes out into the Clearwater, the banks were lined with cheering onlookers who then began to race along the river's edge, following the canoes and shouting encouragement and wishing the explorers well.

For miles along the river, knots of waving Indians seemed to appear almost out of thin air, only to vanish as soon as the canoes had slid past. Twisted Hair and two of his warriors rode along as guides, but there was no opportunity for further conversation in the narrow canoes. The grunt of tired men digging their paddles into the current and the slap of wood on water would have drowned out any but the most strenuously shouted exchange.

Watching the familiar banks slide by on either side, the chief waved from time to time when he recognized a face or someone shouted his name, but he was thinking about other things, and his waves became more distracted as time went on.

For three days, people continued to dot the riverbank, and when one of the canoes failed to negotiate a treacherous rapids and split open on a rock, spilling men and goods into the swirling water, the Indians on the bank pitched in to save almost everything. That night, white men and Indians celebrated, one of the whites sawing on a fiddle that had made the long trip from his home in the Virginia mountains, the Indians supplying rhythm on drums and melody on hand-carved wooden flutes. But even these festivities failed to reassure Twisted Hair. The Shoshones, frightened by the accident, or perhaps using it as an excuse for more inchoate fears, decided to leave the party.

Pushing on the next day, Lewis and Clark reached the confluence of the Clearwater and Snake rivers. Far ahead lay the broad river the white men knew as the Columbia, but there was a rugged, winding route still to be traveled. The crowds thinned then evaporated altogether as the Snake roared through steep canyons, sometimes bobbing the canoes like corks on its foaming rapids, sometimes treating them with even less respect.

Each night, arm weary and stunned by the sheer beauty of the country and the welter of new experiences, Clark wrote in his diary, detailing the habits of the Indians encountered, mapping the terrain, and trying as best he could to control the flood of sensory impressions, channeling it onto the page the way the rugged rock walls channeled the Snake itself.

For Twisted Hair, though, the nights were empty. As tired as the rest, he slept little. He tried to sort out his feelings, partly to understand what was happening to him and to his people, and partly just to keep from being overwhelmed. It was as if each new thing had to be paid some attention, however scant, before he could digest it and push it aside to concentrate on the next.

A week later, they finally reached the Columbia, the deep, fast current of the Snake blending into the broader blue of the great river. Ahead lay the trading center at the Dalles. From this point, the explorers needed no guidance, so Twisted Hair and his warriors, after one final conference, of necessity conducted in sign language, stood on the banks of the Columbia and watched the white men slowly drift out toward the center of the river, where the current would save their weary arms and shoulders a little effort.

On the way home, Twisted Hair spoke very little. His warriors, knowing his mood, made small talk among themselves, trying from time to time to engage their chief in idle conversation, but to no avail.

When the three men finally reached their village, Twisted Hair disappeared into the lodge and lay down to rest. He was no longer young, and the trip had been strenuous. Each of his sixty-five winters had taken its toll on him, but none so much as this eventful autumn.

He slept fitfully through the night, waking several times only to find that the sound he'd heard had been someone moving in the lodge, or an owl skimming close to the ground after a mouse, its wings almost silent, not enough to cover the squeals of the frightened rodent.

He woke early, and as he stepped outside he saw that the sun would not be up that day. During the night, a mass of clouds had moved in. Most of the mountain peaks in the distance had been cut off, their jagged tips flattened to tabletops, as if someone had sliced them off with a sharp blade. Already, the first flakes of snow were sifting through the trees, hissing as the wind drove them against the sides of the lodge. They blew off the slanted roof, whispering over the rush mats and collecting against the base of the lodge.

It was early for snow, but he had expected it. The white men had told him that the mountain passes were already clogged with head-high drifts, and that it snowed almost every day on the spine of the Bitterroots. He watched the snow sift through the branches, already starting to cover the ground. The stacks of camas cakes, berry cakes, and kous cakes on their platforms were covered with skins, and safe from the weather, but the supplies were small, maybe not even enough to last the winter. If spring came late, the villages would be hard-pressed to feed everyone.

And with the snows already heavy in the mountains, the hunting parties were cut off until the spring thaw. He would have to send the remaining warriors out for as much meat as they could find, try to fatten the larder as best they could while the weather still allowed. Ducking back into the lodge, he roused the warriors one by one, trying not to wake the women and children. The men rose quickly and filed outside, where they collected around the remains of the campfire.

Once he had the party assembled, Twisted Hair pointed to the sky and explained what he wanted them to do, and how little time they had in which to do it. He didn't want to alarm them, but he knew they needed to be goaded into their work. Food was ordinarily fairly plentiful, and many of the young warriors weren't old enough to remember the last time it had been short. Twisted Hair knew that the memory of an empty stomach would work on the women and the older men, but neither group was able to track elk and bighorn sheep into the high meadows where they would be looking to hole up for the winter.

Once the hunting party had been dispatched, Twisted Hair gathered the women and children, explaining that they would have to ration their food.

Some of them, inclined to superstition, wondered aloud whether the white men were responsible for the change in their fortunes. The chief knew better, but he also knew their fortunes were in for a more drastic change than something as simple as short rations.

Sending the women off in groups to make one last search for berries and camas roots and trout, he cautioned them to keep one eye on the storm. If it got bad, he told them, make sure they allowed themselves time to return home. "And be certain you allow yourselves some daylight. If you go too far and get lost, we won't be able to find you until morning. If it gets colder, the morning might be too late, especially for the children." Instructing each party to take a horse loaded with extra robes, he watched as they made hasty preparations.

The chief tried to keep himself busy, but it was hard not to think about what had happened. And as the snow continued to drift against the lodge, he found himself thinking about past winters, even the harsh ones. He used to look forward to the cold and the snow. The quiet of the forests, the brilliant sun flashing off the high peaks, the snowy owls falling like feathered avalanches out of the trees, and the white rabbits, like snowdrifts come to life, had been so soothing to him.

Walks in the valley after a sudden snow had been the most peaceful events of the year for him. They were times when he could put his concerns behind him, let himself recover his energy from the hard work of the summer and fall. But all that was behind him now. This winter was the first of a new age.

And it was going to be a long one.

Chapter 6 ═══════════════

THE WINTER WAS HARD. Cut off from the rest of the world by the Bitterroot, the Blue, the Wallowa, and the Salmon River Mountains, the Nez Percé villages had nothing to do but wait for spring and the return of Lewis and Clark. Stretching the food supplies proved to be more of a challenge than Twisted Hair had first thought. The snows came frequently, a few inches at a time, and the cold seemed to fill the valleys like water in a bowl.

Hunting parties made forays into the forests whenever the weather permitted, but there was little game, and what there was was thin to the point of starvation. The thick snow blanket kept everything but the huge pines on the mountainsides inaccessible. Twisted Hair himself tracked a deer, and found it lying prostrate, exhausted, its jaws still full of the bark of a small willow sheltered at the base of a rock wall. It wasn't much, but he killed the animal, dressed it, sectioned it, and hauled the strips of bleeding venison home on a travois pulled behind his horse.

The horse herds were hard hit, too. The younger animals could barely move in the shoulder-deep snows, while the mares and the stallions pawed incessantly, trying to clear away the snow and get

46

to the grasses entombed beneath it. All the meadows were marked with huge trampled clearings, ragged nubs of grass poking through the thin crusts, stubbling them like unshaven cheeks. And then it would snow again, and even this meager forage would be hidden.

Even firewood was scarce, but the chief kept his spirits up, knowing that it was the only thing he could do to get his people through. In the back of his mind was the thought that spring might come late and that food would be difficult to come by the following year. And the spring floods would make fishing all the more treacherous. But it was the only way of life he knew, and he wouldn't change it if he could.

There had been harsh winters before, and they had taken their toll on the people. But they had survived, they had come back even stronger. It took courage, but they had more than enough of that. Occasionally, Tu-eka-kas would come to visit, snuggle down under a buffalo-skin robe, and listen while Twisted Hair told stories of other severe winters. Often the boy would lean forward, his eyes bright with firelight, his breath held for long periods while he hung on every word.

Other boys, too, would gather around Twisted Hair in the lodge. As he watched their faces during his narrations he wondered about their futures, whether one of them would someday sit before another fire in another lodge and tell tales of this winter. He wanted to think so, but the oppressive weather had given him too much time to think, and he was anything but certain about his own future, let alone that of the circle of enthralled young children at his feet.

Sometimes, late at night, he would take out the medal Clark had given him, run his fingers over the likeness of the man etched in the metal, closing his eyes and trying to compose a proper speech should he ever meet the man whose delicate features were slowly wearing away beneath his restless finger-tips. What would he tell the Great Father? And would the Great Father understand him?

The white men had come from so far away it was impossible to imagine what their villages were like. Watkuweis had said they made great buildings of wood and stone, that they had very strong medicine, and that they were as numberless as the camas flowers in the summer meadows. He couldn't imagine such numbers of men, and he couldn't imagine his people surviving such a flood if the white men were to take it into their minds to come this way to stay.

Every day, it seemed, he thought of a new question to ask Clark when he returned in the spring. Sometimes, he tried to imagine what Clark's answer would be, but it was useless. He didn't know enough about the white men or their ways. He didn't even know whether all white men were like Clark and Lewis. He supposed there would be bad men among the whites, just as there were among the Nez Percé and the Cayuse.

And he kept thinking of the Heavenly Book. He could still see Clark pointing to the cumulus-filled blue expanse, sitting there by the side of the Clearwater, the Heavenly Book in his lap, and pointing to the strange markings, telling him what they meant. He wondered if there were more such books, and if having one of your own gave you strong medicine. He wished he had one, to keep his people safe from the Blackfeet and the Bannock . . . and from the white men, too. He wondered if Clark could get a book for the Nez Percé, and decided to ask in the spring, when Clark came back.

It was March before the weather finally broke. It snowed all night long, but Twisted Hair knew by the consistency of the flakes that it was not going to last. Huge puffs, like exploded milkweed pods full of fine white silk, hung from the branches, and a thick layer of the fluffy white lay on the frozen crust of the winter's accumulation, but by sunrise, the sky was blue and the snow was already melting.

The mounds on the treetops melted quickly, falling in zigzags as they slipped from the crowns of the pines and blew apart in the air. A handful weighed nothing, could barely be felt on the palm, and did not even feel cold to the touch.

Soon the rivers would thaw, and as the snow higher in the Bitterroots began to melt, the ice would grind and clatter as it broke up and then the streams would overflow their banks, filling the channels with turbulent milk as they swept down toward the Clearwater, then the Snake, and finally flooded into the Columbia.

The food was almost gone, and it would be weeks before they could begin to replenish their stocks. In the meantime, rabbits and squirrels would have to supplement the dwindling rations. Flash-frozen carcasses of deer and elk, antelope and bighorn sheep would turn up higher on the slopes, and the meat would be edible when it thawed. Twisted Hair sent out a search party and several small bands of hunters, including some of the older boys, those who would seek their *wyakin* this summer, to look for meat and to try to salvage as many of the diminished herds as possible.

Then, going back into the lodge, he went to the woven rush hamper he used to store his valuables and opened the lid. There, still neatly folded, the brightly colored cloth still frozen to the touch, was the United States flag Meriwether Lewis had given him to keep for Broken Arm. Lewis had shown him how to fly it from a sapling stripped of branch and bark, and Twisted Hair thought it would be a good thing to fly it now to celebrate the coming of spring.

Holding the flag almost reverently, the way Clark had held his sacred book, he walked out into the bright spring air. The sapling Lewis had used for his demonstration lay on one of the drying platforms with the last of the dried salmon, and Twisted Hair slogged through the melting snowdrifts to retrieve it.

The villagers started to gather around him as they saw him drive the sapling into a drift and pack the snow around its base with his feet. Then, attaching the flag by its woven cord, he shook it loose, let the stiff spring breeze work the folds free, and tugged the flag to the top of the sapling. Stepping back, he watched the tricolored cloth flap in the cool air. It would be good, he thought, for Broken Arm to see the flag when he returned. It would still be several weeks before the passes were usable, but he wanted to be sure the flag was up when the other chiefs returned.

Walking back toward the lodge, he was conscious of the snap and crackle of the thick cloth in the stiff breeze. He resisted the urge to turn back and take down the flag, knowing that it would change nothing. It was far too late for so simple a gesture to change what was already so firmly implanted in his mind.

As the spring continued the snows began to melt more quickly. In two weeks, the meadows already showed broad patches of brown and green where the thin snow of the last clearings trampled by the herd melted through. The edges of the clearings grew outward almost daily. Much of the snow that remained was little more than slush a week later.

Every morning Twisted Hair would walk to the top of a rise behind the village. Under the crystalline blue, he would shield his eyes and stare toward the east, hoping to catch a glimpse of the returning hunters. The rest of the people seemed to discover some source of renewed optimism that so far had escaped him, almost as if their own sap rose in their veins as steadily as that of the newly revealed shrubs, the lengthening blades of grass.

Food was still scarce. The daily finds were not enough to keep pace with daily consumption, and the reserves continued to shrink. Twisted Hair hoped the returning hunters would be bringing enough meat to get them through until summer. He was worried, too, that there might not be enough to feed the returning white men, but the custom was unbreakable—you shared what you had with guests, whether you had enough for yourself or not. And at the moment it was all too clear that there was not enough.

It was Tu-eka-kas who spotted the returning warriors. In one of those symmetries that seemed to abound when you looked closely at the earth and its influence on human life, Twisted Hair was once again summoned by the excited boy, this time with the news that he had seen Broken Arm and his warriors coming down through the Wallowa Mountain pass. They would take a day to reach the village, but knowing they were close seemed at least to lift Twisted Hair's spirits.

The warriors would be exhausted, he knew as he summoned the village to prepare a feast for the homecoming. The festivities would not include much in the way of food, but it was the intention that mattered. And the additional men, whether or not the hunt had been successful, would mean that more food would soon be available.

And in the back of Twisted Hair's mind was the thought that the people would be safer with the warriors back. If food was scarce all over—and he knew from bitter experience that winter could be as cruel on the southern side of the Wallowa range and east of the Bitterroots as it had been in the relative shelter of the valleys—the Blackfeet and the Bannock, the Piegan and the Shoshone would be as hungry as his own people. Raids were not only possible, they were likely. With the warriors back home, it would be easier to fend them off.

For the first time in months, Twisted Hair slept well that night. In the morning, Broken Arm and Cut Nose would be back. The troubles of the people would be lifted from his shoulders and the younger chiefs would once again have the responsibility. More impulsive than he, less inclined to think things through to their bitter end, Broken Arm and Cut Nose would decide that the coming of the

white men, while a mixed blessing, was still a
blessing. They would believe that they could turn
it to the advantage of the Nez Percé. Trade and its
rewards would seem worthwhile. Things change,
and while old men knew it because they lived long
enough to see it with their own eyes, young men
tended to ignore the truth, confident that even if
they were wrong, there was nothing in the future
they couldn't handle.

Broken Arm was like that. And while he was a
courageous warrior, he was inclined to seek the
path of least resistance. Peace was cheaper than
war, after all.

Twisted Hair dreamed that he was under the
earth, a great weight pressing him flatter than a
worm, and no matter how he tried to wiggle out,
the crushing weight would not let him go. He
changed shape, stretching himself to the thinness
of a strand of a child's hair, so long he could not
see his tail, and still he couldn't get free. Then he
would swell his body like the cheeks of a frog, trying to throw off the weight by pushing it away, but
just when he could see the sun through a crack at
the edge of the world, the weight would crush him
flat again, all the air rushing out of him with the
hissing of a thousand snakes.

He tossed and turned, sometimes sitting up with
his eyes open, but the darkness around him was
from some other place, some other world, maybe
the world that Coyote had made, maybe the belly of
the great monster before Coyote killed him and cut
him into pieces to make the people of the mountains, the Nez Percé last, from drops of the beast's
blood.

He would sink back then, pull the robe around him, once even pulling it up over his head like a frightened child and rolling himself into a tight ball. But it did no good. The dreams would not leave him alone.

Yet, when he opened his eyes in the morning, wakened by the chirping of birds outside the lodge, he felt refreshed, quiet and relaxed, a man waking from a great fever. It was over, he thought. Now it is for someone else to worry about.

Chapter 7 ═══════════

Clearwater Basin—1806

AS THE SPRING STARTED to warm the valleys the
snows in the passes turned from crystalline white
to blue white, then became tinged with green. The
warming sun caused them to compress, then turn
to slush, and finally to melt altogether.

All up and down the river, from one village to
another, people exchanged stories in hushed voices.
Lewis and Clark were at the Dalles. Lewis and Clark
had been attacked by Bannocks and killed. Lewis
and Clark had decided not to come back at all. Each
story was imparted with all the solemnity of a whisper into the ear from the Great Spirit himself. The
tellers nodded sagely and the listeners, slack-jawed
with wonder, hung on every word.

When April came, no one knew what to expect.
If the big hearts of the east were to show up wearing fish and riding on grizzly bears, there would
have been one person to say, "I told you, didn't I?"

And then the news started to filter upstream.
They were coming, soon probably, although how
soon was still uncertain.

The chiefs tried desperately to keep their people
focused on the real concerns of the villages. Getting

enough food, the stores of which had been danger-
ously diminished during the long, hard winter, had
to be the first priority. Hunting parties were made
larger and sent out more often and for longer stays.
Fish weirs were made by the dozen to get ready for
the rush of salmon later in the year. Anything that
could possibly help stay the pangs of hunger until
stores were replenished was turned to its best
advantage.

The horses Lewis and Clark had left in Twisted
Hair's care were fed to the detriment of the Nez
Percés' own diminished herds. At a council in the
middle of April, Broken Arm and Cut Nose asked
Twisted Hair once more to tell them what had happened the previous autumn, what the white men
had said, and whether Twisted Hair thought they
could be trusted.

These were things that had occupied his mind in
the long nights since the explorers had left, and he
felt he was no closer to understanding than he had
been the morning he had left them on the banks of
the Snake River.

But he tried. He thought for a long moment, trying to find a place to begin, and when he realized
there was no beginning, he started to speak, slowly,
measuring his words, trying to remember his con-
versations as precisely as he could, sifting through
his recollections for nuances of meaning, for hidden significance in the exchanges, but he could
delay just so long.

Sensing that the chiefs were getting impatient,
especially Broken Arm, who was the most respected war leader, Twisted Hair cleared his throat and
began. "I think they are good men," he said. "They

treated us well and they told us many things about their country. They were courteous and respectful of our old ones and of our women. They were friendly to our children, especially Tu-eka-kas, who was the first one to see them."

"What do they want with us?" Broken Arm asked.

Twisted Hair shrugged, thought about the question for a moment, then said, "I think they want to trade with us. They tell us that there are other white men to the north—they call them British— and say they, too, are traders, but that the Bostons are more generous in their trade."

"What do they have to offer us?"

"I don't know. They showed us some things, but said they were just gifts, things they brought with them to show their goodwill to all the peoples they meet on their journey."

"What peoples had they met? Did they tell you? Did they meet the Blackfeet, and are they friendly to the Blackfeet?"

"They say they want to be friends with all peoples. They had met the Blackfeet and had no trouble with them."

"Then how can they be friendly to us?" Broken Arm asked. "How can friends of our enemies be our friends, too?" This question was addressed not to Twisted Hair, but to the other chiefs gathered around the council fire. It was greeted with muttering, and some of the chiefs leaned over to whisper in the ears of others. Twisted Hair felt as if Broken Arm were using him for purposes of his own, trying to manipulate the uncertainty of his answers into a caution to them all. The old chief would be the first to admit that there was much he did not know, and many questions he had not even thought of, even over the longest of his sleepless nights over the past winter.

Broken Arm knew this. He, too, had spent many sleepless nights, talking into the darkest part of the night, sometimes even until the first smears of gray appeared in the east. But the questions were very hard, and there was so little knowledge with which to answer them.

Cut Nose took the floor then. "I think that we will have to watch them closely when they come back," he said.

"You mean if they come back," another chief suggested. "I will believe they will come back when I see them with my own eyes."

"What are you all afraid of?" Twisted Hair demanded, turning Broken Arm's technique back on them. "You seem to think they are trying to deceive us for some reason. What reason could they have? They know as little of us as we know of them. They know of nothing that we have that they might want."

"Horses," Cut Nose said. "We have many horses. You said they had very few and they were not in good condition."

"Does Cut Nose bring all his horses with him when he goes to the buffalo country, or when he rides against the Blackfeet or the Bannock? Does Broken Arm carry all he owns on his back when he goes fishing?"

Cut Nose nodded. "That is a fair question."

"What is the answer?" Twisted Hair asked, leaning toward him. "Would you want your wealth to be judged by only a part? These men have traveled for many days before they came to us. They had little with them, that's true. But think how much they must have, to have even that much after so long a journey."

"I still think it is dangerous to be too friendly."

"I think it is dangerous to be unfriendly," Twisted Hair said. "We may turn away friends by being too suspicious. We can't have too many friends. Besides, they have guns, and can get many more. The Blackfeet already have more guns than we have. If we want to hold the Blackfeet back, keep them on the other side of the mountains, we will have to be able to fight them with weapons as good as they have. Can Cut Nose make a gun?"

The war chief shook his head. "Twisted Hair makes another good point. It is important that we not turn away friends before we know how much we might need their help."

Twisted Hair was feeling more confident now. The hard questions were helping him to clarify his own confused impressions of the white men. He didn't know whether he was forming the correct impressions, but he knew that it was always better to expect the best while preparing for the worst. As long as they were prepared, bad things could be seen and prevented. But if they were too suspicious and unfriendly, they might turn away good things before they even knew they were there to be had.

He was about to speak when a shout interrupted his train of thought. At first he didn't comprehend what was being said. But Broken Arm did. He jumped to his feet and cried, "The Blackfeet are coming!"

Without waiting for anyone to respond, the chief raced from the lodge. Cut Nose dashed out after him. Twisted Hair was the last man out of the lodge. In the distance, he could hear the war whoops of the Blackfeet. It sounded as if there was a large war party somewhere up above.

"The horses!" someone shouted. "They are after the horses."

Already, warriors were mounting up, urging their horses out of camp and up into the meadows beyond the trees, where the herds were grazing on the early grasses. The shrieks of the Blackfeet echoed down though the trees, distorted and made to sound even more inhuman than they were meant to by the distance and the thick forest.

Broken Arm was already on his horse and charging through the trees. Twisted Hair grabbed his own mount, swung aboard, and reached back for his bow. He withdrew an arrow from a rabbit-skin quiver and clutched it and the bowstring in nervous fingers.

The warriors were already responding to the Blackfoot challenge, venting shrieks and howls of their own as they charged through the trees, ready to do combat.

As Twisted Hair came through the last of the trees and broke into the open, he fitted the arrow to the bowstring and scanned the meadow above him. Two small bands of Blackfeet were near the top of the meadow, already driving two large groups of spotted horses ahead of them. They were yipping and yowling to keep the frightened horses on the move. A third, and much larger, band was well down in the meadow, arrayed in a half-moon, its concave edge toward the Nez Percé. This formation made it risky to charge up the middle, and difficult to outflank, since the middle warriors could swing in either direction and be ready to fire without risk of hitting their own men.

Cut Nose led a feint up toward the left end of the half-moon. A ragged volley of gunfire crackled and spat smoke in wispy plumes. Cut Nose counted the plumes as he charged, knowing that the Blackfeet could never hold back, and fired all their guns at once. Reloading was very difficult on horseback, and the best tactic was to charge straight ahead without giving the Blackfeet time to reload.

Several Nez Percé launched arrows, and Twisted Hair watched as the polished shafts arced high in the air and speared down toward the Blackfeet. One arrow struck a horse, and the animal whinnied in pain, reared up, then fell on its side.

The warrior astride it scrambled to his feet, shaking his fist at the charging Nez Percé, then turned and ran. The others returned fire, this time with bows and arrows only. Cut Nose urged his warriors on, knowing that shooting downhill was difficult and that if he were lucky, he and his warriors would charge under the Blackfoot volley and have the arrows land harmlessly behind them.

Broken Arm led a small band of warriors far to the right, where they began to charge across the meadow, trying to get in behind the Blackfeet warriors driving the stolen horses. If the thieves could be caught before they reached the first of the passes into the mountains, they would leave the stolen horses behind to run for their lives. But if they got the animals through the pass, it would be suicide

to follow them. They would have a nearly impregnable defensive position.

Broken Arm was well out in front of his band
and was closing fast on the Blackfeet. The stolen
horses were already beginning to scatter and had
slowed their captors down to a dangerous degree.
Sensing that he had the advantage, Broken Arm
urged his mount on even faster, and his warriors
plunged after him.

The Blackfeet veered off to the north, letting the
stolen horses career across the mountainside on
their own. The Blackfeet were getting desperate,
and they drove their ponies hard, heading for the
long, scree-littered approach to the pass. The half-
moon of Blackfeet collapsed in on itself, and the
invading warriors made a break for the pass, leaving three of their force behind. These three dismounted and worked feverishly to reload their
rifles, but Cut Nose rallied his men into a furious
charge.

The Blackfeet warriors were still trying to ram
the patches and balls down into their rifles as the
wave of Nez Percé bore down on them at a full gallop. A flurry of arrows showered the invaders. One
Blackfoot took an arrow in the chest and fell forward, driving the shaft all the way through until
the flint head protruded through his back. He lay
there twitching, propped up like a rude tent, slowly sank down along the shaft, and finally lay still as
the Nez Percé thundered past.

One of the Blackfeet got his rifle loaded, turned
to face the regrouping defenders, and aimed his
rifle as Cut Nose dropped his right arm and shouted for a second charge. The Blackfoot raised his

weapon, tried to sight in on the chief, but the skittish charge threw him off, and when the rifle discharged, Gray Elk, just behind and to the left of the war leader, fell from his horse, a bullet lodged in his skull.

Both surviving Blackfeet broke into a run, leaving their rifles and horses behind. They streaked for the trees, never turning to look back at their pursuers, as if terrified of what they might see. The rest of the Blackfeet roared down on Broken Arm's forces, overtaking them so quickly, the Nez Percé were startled to see their ranks broken by the hated easterners.

By the time they recovered, the Nez Percé were fifty yards behind, and the Blackfeet were well on their way to the safety of the pass. Satisfied that the attack had been repelled, Broken Arm called a halt to the pursuit. The Blackfeet, realizing they were home free, reined in then and turned to shake their fists and taunt the Nez Percé, acting for all the world as if they had been victorious.

Broken Arm's warriors were incensed, and several started to drift forward, as if ready to resume the pursuit. "No!" Broken Arm shouted. "They are beaten. They will go away now. Let them. See to the horses."

Some of the young firebrands were frustrated. Their appetites for combat had been whetted, not slaked, and they disliked enduring the insults of the Blackfeet without responding, but Broken Arm was adamant. "We want to protect what is ours, that's all. Suppose there are more Blackfeet who are just waiting for us to leave our villages untended?"

The young warriors grumbled, but they knew the

chief was right and turned their attention to the spotted horses, scattered in small groups all across the upper half of the meadow. The warriors eased their mounts uphill while a single Blackfoot stood at the entrance to the pass, shook his lance, then turned and raised his breechclout to insult his enemies one last time before mounting up and disappearing into the pass.

Broken Arm rode downhill to where Cut Nose sat on the ground beside the severely wounded Gray Elk. Even before dismounting, Broken Arm knew the wound was fatal. An ugly hole in Gray Elk's forehead, just in front of the temple, oozed blood and pink water. The warrior's eyes were closed, and his breath was shallow and intermittent.

Dismounting, Broken Arm joined his fellow chief, sitting on the opposite side of the wounded man. Cut Nose was chanting softly, a prayer to his *wyakin*, asking for guidance, for some medicine that would save the wounded man. Broken Arm knew it was a mere formality, that not even Cut Nose expected the prayer to be answered, but the Nez Percé believed strongly in their medicine, and it was not an empty gesture.

When Cut Nose stopped his incantation, he got to his feet and backed away, leaving the field to Broken Arm, who began a prayer of his own. Cut Nose then sent one of his warriors to the nearest village with orders to get word to Gray Elk's family that he was badly wounded and to alert the shaman that he was being brought home. Then he directed the construction of a travois, fashioned of saplings and quickly woven grass mats.

By the time the travois had been finished and

Gray Elk strapped on, the horses had been recovered. Some of the warriors herded them to their pastures while the others dismounted and followed along behind the travois as Gray Elk was taken to Broken Arm's village.

Alerted by the messenger who had been sent ahead, the villagers were already coming up the trail, their piercing lamentations wafting up into the trees and drifting in wave after wave of sorrow through the shadows of the forest.

Gray Elk was taken to a separate lodge, where the shaman was already waiting for him. The wounded warrior was left alone with the shaman; even the immediate family, a wife and two young children, as well as his mother, were taken to the main lodge to be comforted by the older women.

Twisted Hair had seen the wound and knew that it was fatal. He also recalled the medicine of William Clark and the Heavenly Book Clark had been reading that bright, chilly morning down at the river, and he wondered if Clark could save the wounded man. It was, after all, a white man's weapon that had wounded Gray Elk. It only made sense that the white men would have ways of treating such wounds, just as the Nez Percé had ways of treating wounds caused by arrows and lances.

It was true that many wounded warriors died of their injuries, that even the holiest of holy men could not save the men who suffered the worst battle wounds. But still, there might have been something Clark or one of the other white men could do.

He mentioned the thought to Cut Nose, who had acquired his name from a battle wound that had deformed his nose and nearly cost him his life. But

Cut Nose just shook his head, as if Twisted Hair were feverish and rambling.

Gray Elk died during the night, as nearly everyone had known he would, and everyone had hoped he wouldn't. And even before the body was cold, a runner carried word that the white men were coming. They had been sighted downriver, paddling against the swift current of the Clearwater, swollen with the spring melt.

The white men were still two or three days away. The runner said that some Nez Percé were traveling with the expedition, having joined it at the juncture of the Snake and the Clearwater. This time there was no great celebration all along the riverbanks as there had been the previous fall, but word was spreading rapidly, and the Nez Percé waited expectantly for the arrival.

Broken Arm made certain that the flag was flying and draped the medal Clark had left for him around his neck. Twisted Hair and Cut Nose donned their own medals and paced nervously the morning the travelers were expected at long last to reach Broken Arm's village. Last-minute hunting parties had been sent out to catch as much game as possible. Everyone in the valley seemed to be waiting with held breath.

But it was too late for Gray Elk.

Chapter 8

LEWIS AND CLARK WERE WELCOMED back like long-lost family. The expedition leaders were full of excitement about their trip down the Columbia, and their heads were spinning with the number of tribes they had encountered in the Columbia Basin. Tired from their long trip upriver, they spent the first three days in Broken Arm's village relaxing. On the morning of the fourth day, though, they were ready to talk to the Nez Percé, and the chiefs of the various bands had been drifting in accompanied by small bands of their people since the explorers' return. Among the headmen was a number of Cayuses. The two tribes had a long history of friendly relations. Their languages were closely related, and many of the people had intermarried.

When the council began, there were nearly two dozen chiefs in attendance. Most, even those like Twisted Hair who were certain that their lives would never be the same again, were favorably disposed to the white men, while others—Broken Arm, Cut Nose, and the Cayuse chief Red Grizzly Bear among them—came with open minds, but with more than a little skepticism.

These were men who had worked long and hard to attain their positions of responsibility. Some had led their people in battle against the Bannock and the Blackfeet, earning their respect with torn flesh and lost blood. Others had attained their positions by being thoughtful, even wise. It was a reasonable mix, even an essential one. Courage solved some problems, but not all. One had to think to survive when surrounded by enemies on all sides. And if one wanted to be left alone, one had to be prepared to defend one's conclusions with lance and bow.

They gathered out-of-doors, red men and white men both enjoying the warm spring air. The population of Broken Arm's village had swollen to five times its normal size, and groups of the curious dotted the riverbank like clumps of willows and the meadows above the village like early flowers. Despite the dwindling food supplies, the atmosphere was almost festive.

Clark sat cross-legged on the ground, Lewis to his left. There was a hush broken only by the shuffle of moccasins as the chiefs arranged themselves in a broad circle. Broken Blade sat on Clark's right to help with interpretation, and to his right sat War Eagle, a Shoshone who spoke reasonably good English, a product of his year at a missionary school in Canada. Sacajawea was also there, as she had been almost from the first.

"I want to thank you for your hospitality," Clark began, pausing for the translation, then continuing. "We have traveled far and seen much since we were last among you. But as I told you last year, the Great Father in Washington wants very much that your people and his be friends. He wants all people to be friends, all red men and all white men."

"That is a pretty thought," Red Grizzly Bear said.

"But we have learned that some people do not wish to be our friends. The Blackfeet like our horses, but they don't like us very much."

The chiefs laughed, and Clark smiled. "It doesn't have to be that way forever. Even the Blackfeet can learn to be your friends."

"Who will teach them?" Twisted Hair asked. The other chiefs nodded, and several grunted their approval. "We have known the Blackfeet far longer than you. We know they cannot be trusted. They do not keep their word, even when they give it."

"The Great Father can help them to understand why peace is important to all red men."

"Is the Great Father coming here to the Clearwater?" Broken Arm asked.

"No," Clark said. "But I can speak for him. I can speak to the Blackfeet and tell them what he would tell them if he were here."

"One can also talk to stones," Red Grizzly Bear said. This time no one laughed. "One can talk to trees and to the sky, but do the stones understand? Does the tree, or the sky? I don't think so. And I think this is what talking to the Blackfeet would be like, even for the Great Father in Washington. We have many times made peace with the Blackfeet. And many times the peace has been broken, always by the Blackfeet. Why do you think you will have more success than we have had?"

"That's a fair question," Lewis said.

"What is a fair answer?" Twisted Hair asked.

Lewis tugged on his beard. He looked at the old chief a long moment before saying, "We will visit the Blackfeet on our way home. We will tell them what we have told you. We will tell them that you wish peace, and that if they, too, wish for peace, then it will happen."

"And if it doesn't?" Broken Arm asked.

"I think it will. This land belongs to the Great Father now, and he wants everyone in it to live as a friend to everyone else."

"The land does not belong to anyone," Twisted Hair said. "The land is our mother, and we belong to her."

Clark cleared his throat before responding. "What you say is so. But it is also true that men rule the land, just as you rule your mountains and the meadows where you graze your herds. You rule th camas fields where you dig the roots that feed you, and the streams that give you salmon. The Blackfeet do not rule those places."

Mutters of approval ran like an electric current around the circle of chiefs. Some leaned toward neighbors to whisper, and Clark waited patiently until their attention returned to him. "But," he continued, "the land across the Bitterroot Mountains, where you go to hunt the buffalo, is different. You do not rule over that land."

"The Blackfeet don't either," Broken Arm argued. "That land is so great and the buffalo so many that it belongs to all men."

"Do the Blackfeet believe that?" Lewis asked.

Broken Arm hesitated, before saying, "No."

"But you hunt the buffalo there, don't you? You cross the mountains? And to the east, past the Blackfeet, the Cheyenne and the Sioux hunt the buffalo, too. There are more buffalo there than a man can count, a thousand for every star in the sky. Enough buffalo for all men forever. There is no reason the Blackfeet should try to stop you from hunting buffalo."

"Is there a reason they should steal our horses?" Red Grizzly Bear demanded. "Is there a reason they should take our children and kill our warriors?"

"No, of course not."

"But these things happen," the chief insisted. "They have always happened, and they always will happen. The Great Father can't change this any more than he can change the color of the grass."

Clark shook his head. "He can't change the color of the grass, of course. Only the Great Spirit can do that. But he can make the Blackfeet understand that they must stop stealing your horses."

"And the Bannock?" Twisted Hair asked.

"And the Paiute?" Cut Nose asked.

"All peoples in the land the Great Father rules can learn to live in peace," Clark insisted. "It will be so."

"And how will the Great Father do this? Will he bring men and guns and burn the Blackfeet villages if they do not? And if this is done, is not the Great Father no different from the Blackfeet or the Bannock or the Paiute?"

"Words are powerful things," Lewis said. "Words can make things change. Words can bring peace where the lance and the rifle cannot."

"Words like those in the Heavenly Book?" Twisted Hair asked. "Can we get a book? Can we learn these words, and how to use them to make peace?"

"Yes," Clark said. "All men can learn the things in the Heavenly Book. All men can learn how to talk to the Great Spirit in the same way. And the Great

Spirit can make men do what he wants them to do. He can make it thunder on a clear day. He can fill these valleys with snow in the middle of summer, or make it black as night in the middle of the day."

"We should learn these things," Twisted Hair said. "We should learn to speak to the Great Spirit the way you do."

"There are many things that we can teach you," Clark said. "In the east, there are great cities with thousands of people and thousands of buildings. More people than you have ever seen at one time. There are great ships that cross the oceans. There are rivers even mightier than the Columbia."

"Does the Great Father rule over all these people?" Broken Arm tilted his head, as if the question were a sly one, one that he expected Clark would be unable to answer.

But the explorer didn't bat an eye. "Oh yes," he said. "The Great Father rules over all that and much more."

"We will need time to talk these things over among ourselves," Twisted Hair said. "You have told us much that is new, and much that is hard to believe, but we think that you do not lie. We will meet again tomorrow."

Clark nodded. "Very well," he said. "And please, if you have any questions, if there is anything that you want me to tell you again, or anything that I did not make plain, tell me."

"We will talk among ourselves," Broken Arm said. "We are not afraid to ask questions. But we want to consider what you have said."

"I understand." Clark got to his feet and walked around the circle, extending his hand to each chief in turn. Some took it immediately and shook it firmly, in emulation of the greeting Twisted Hair had explained to them all. Others, though, were more cautious, as if they were not willing to commit themselves even to the formality of a handshake.

Lewis went back to his lodge, but Clark walked down to the river. The sun was high in the sky, and its warmth seemed to fill the river valley like an invisible liquid. He walked to a flat outcropping of rock that extended over the turbulent waters swollen with spring melt, and sat with his feet dangling over the edge.

There was something about the Nez Percé that moved him in a way he had never experienced before. Their courtesy and friendliness were unlike anything he had encountered among the dozens of Indian tribes he had met in the last two years. And there was some inner strength in them, not just the chiefs, but all of them, some dignity that was proud but not haughty, as if they believed themselves the equals of anyone, neither superior nor inferior. And with this pride came a relaxed confidence.

He lay back on the rock, leaving his feet out over the current a dozen feet below, and closed his eyes. He could feel the warmth on his face and chest, even through his shirt. The subdued rumble of the swift current was somehow soothing. He thought for a moment that he would fall asleep, but then a shadow fell across his face, and he opened his eyes.

Cut Nose was standing over him, looking down with some hesitancy. Beside him stood War Eagle, the Shoshone.

Clark sat up. "Is there anything wrong?" he asked.

"The chief says his daughter is sick," War Eagle explained. "He wonders if the Great Father in Washington has taught you medicine."

Clark looked at the chief. He wondered what he should do. He felt that he was close to winning their agreement to Jefferson's peace plans, and didn't want to risk undercutting the progress he'd made at the council. But he knew that to back away from a problem might cause as much difficulty as trying to accomplish too much. "Tell him I will take a look. Tell him I am not a doctor, but I will see if there is anything I can do."

"Doctor?" War Eagle asked

"Healer, doctor . . . tell him I have some medicine but not as much as many."

The Shoshone translated Clark's uncertain remarks, and the Nez Percé nodded. Without waiting for Clark to stand, he turned and started back toward the village. Clark scrambled up and hurried to catch the chief.

Cut Nose led the way to his lodge and gestured for the white man to enter. Clark ducked under the low doorway and stepped into the lodge. It was only dimly lit by a smoky fire and smelled of sickness.

A young woman who must have been Cut Nose's wife, sat on a buffalo robe. She had a woven water basket in her lap and rubbed the forehead of a small girl of seven or eight with a piece of doeskin she kept moistening in the basket.

Clark knelt across from her and leaned forward. Cut Nose stood behind him, bending over to watch as Clark felt the child's forehead. It was warm to the touch, some sort of fever, and her stomach was distended, as if she might be suffering from food poisoning, but there was no other indication of what might be wrong. Clark stood and said he would return shortly.

Hastening to his lodge, he prepared an emetic in a small wooden bowl and sprinted back to Cut Nose's lodge. Kneeling again, he lifted the girl's head while Cut Nose took the place of his wife and leaned anxiously over the child. It took some coaxing, but she finally downed the bitter medicine, which would force her to vomit. Clark took the child in his arms and carried her outside, still wrapped in a buffalo robe.

Cradling her in his arms, he carried her toward the Clearwater, cooing in her ear and patting the girl's back to reassure her that he meant no harm. He walked back to the rock outcropping and sat, holding the child in his lap while Cut Nose and his wife paced nervously, the woman wringing her hands and Cut Nose himself showing a rare tenderness.

The girl started to quiver, and Clark turned her toward the edge of the rock. Her body was racked by convulsive wretching. She choked and spewed by turns, then started to sob. Clark motioned for fresh water, and Cut Nose ran back to the lodge, returning with a water-filled skin, which he held to the girl's lips. She sucked greedily at the fresh water, and Clark continued to stroke her forehead, still cooing softly to her. The woman held out her arms, and Clark handed the girl to her.

Cut Nose signed his thanks, then draped an arm over his wife's shoulder and the two of them moved slowly back to the lodge. Clark lay back again to close his eyes, but caught a glimpse of an eagle high above him, its huge wings barely beating as it rode the warm currents of air rising from the river valley. It circled once, then twice, as if it had seen something of interest, then it seemed to shrink to nothing and started to fall like a stone.

It was a tiny speck of black now against the brilliant blue of the sky, slowly growing larger as it fell. Not until it was fifty feet from the water did it suddenly explode into a flurry of great wings as it descended, talons extended in a pair of gnarled fists, and struck the far bank. For a moment the huge wings fluttered furiously, as if they would tear lose, then settled into an even rhythm as the eagle started to climb, a huge rabbit limp in its claws.

Clark watched the great bird climb up above the tree line, then started as a shadow fell across his shoulders. He turned to find Twisted Hair and the Shoshone again.

"There are many who need your medicine," the interpreter said. "They say you are a healer who does not like to boast." The Shoshone grinned at him, and Clark shook his head as he climbed to his feet once more.

Chapter 9 ═══════════

DURING THE NIGHT, Lewis and Clark talked quietly, sitting by the river wrapped in buffalo robes to ward off the chill. Somewhere upriver, the sound of a flute drifted toward them, its plaintive notes barely audible above the dull roar of the current.

"Do you think they'll go along?" Lewis asked.

Clark shook his head slowly, scratched his cheek, and said, "I don't know. I hope so, but we're askin' a lot. They been on their own for a long, long time. And the Blackfeet have their own reasons for sayin' no. I reckon it's a long shot."

"I wish there was something we could do, some way to convince them, but I'm fresh out of reasons."

"I don't think it's a question of reasons, Merry. I think maybe it's all up there." He jabbed a finger toward the sky, and Lewis looked up at the brilliant points of light on the deepest, darkest blue he had ever seen.

Lewis pulled his arms out of the robe long enough to yank a tobacco pouch and pipe from his coat, pack the pipe, and tuck the pouch back out of sight. He thumbed a match and sucked the flame into the bowl. The light rose and fell, flickering over his bearded features and smearing shadows in the hollows under his eyes. When the tobacco was securely alight, he puffed twice to make sure, and wreathed his partner in blue-gray smoke.

"I don't think I've ever seen a tribe as decent as these people. They're different, somehow. They got a way about them. Dignity, I guess it is. And pride. I got the feeling that they'll do whatever they think is best for them, no matter what we say."

"I guess you're right. I just wish . . . aw, hell . . . no point in wishin'. But if all Indians were like these Nez Percés, I think it'd be a snap to get all the tribes to agree to some sort of general peace."

Lewis sucked on his pipe, then held it in the palm of his hand, to gesture upstream with the stem. "That's right pretty music."

"Sound's kind of sad and lonesome, to me."

"Nothing wrong with that, is there?"

"No." Clark lapsed into a long silence, and Lewis seemed content to suck the smoke into his lungs.

Finally, shifting his position on the cold stone, he said, "That there Twisted Hair is one smart old man."

"Seems to me like he's of two minds, Merry. What worries me is if they do go along."

"That's what Mr. Jefferson wants. Why should you worry about it?"

"Suppose they agree and we can't deliver? What do we do then?"

Lewis took a long drag on the pipe and held it for several seconds. "Let's worry about that when they agree." He exhaled a long plume of smoke that looked almost white against the mass of trees on the far bank of the river. Then he leaned out over the edge of the outcropping and tapped the upended bowl of the pipe against the stone. The glowing embers cometed into the current twelve feet below and winked out with a faint hiss.

"I think I'm gonna turn in, Bill. Want to be bright-eyed and bushy-tailed for the council tomorrow."

"You think they'll decide so soon?"

"Why not? There's no reason to drag things out, is there? We spoke our piece, and, most likely everybody from that Red Grizzly feller to your friend Twisted Hair has spoke his piece as well. Most likely, they'll sleep on it, palaver some in the morning, then tell us what they decided."

"You wonder what'll happen to them, ever?"

Lewis sighed. "Hell, I got all I can do wonderin' what'll happen to me."

"It bothers me some. They don't have any idea what's in store for 'em. This country is so beautiful, but it's only a matter of time before it all starts to change."

"Maybe we can spare them a little pain, then. Maybe if they agree, we can do something for 'em, something to make it easier for 'em."

"But I seen what happened back east. You look at it, all the tribes pushed off their lands, shoved around like they was so much furniture. Put 'em here until somebody wants that land, then shove 'em over there. Until somebody wants that place, too. It don't set right with me, Merry."

"There's nothing we can do about that, Bill. They got to fend for themselves, is all. Besides, it's a big country. There's plenty of room for everybody." Lewis shrugged. "You comin'?"

When Clark said he wanted to sit awhile, Lewis

said good night and headed to the lodge. Clark listened to the flute, wondering who was awake at that hour just to play music. After worrying it a bit, he decided he didn't care. The music itself was reason enough.

After listening for nearly an hour, he found himself drifting off to sleep despite the chill. He jerked himself awake and got to his feet. Folding the heavy buffalo robe over his arm, he paused for a few moments to listen as the flute ended its melody. In the silence that seemed suddenly so absolute, he muttered a prayer, then trudged off to the lodge for a few hours' sleep.

The village came alive early. The sun was brilliant, and the air clear and chilly when Clark awoke. He stepped outside to find the council already in session around a large fire to ward off the morning chill. He watched from a distance, unwilling to approach without being invited. When the chiefs wanted to speak to him, they would let him know.

Meriwether Lewis was already awake. He saw the taller man striding toward him from the river, several fish dangling from a line in his left hand. When Lewis was close enough, he held the fish aloft. "Breakfast," he said, grinning. "Give me a hand."

The two men spent fifteen minutes gutting and filleting the fish, tossing the heads and entrails into a pile beside their cookfire. The village dogs kept slinking up and whining, but Clark chased them with a clap of his hands whenever they got too close.

When the fish were ready, Lewis speared the fillets with a willow twig and held the slabs of pink meat over the fire until they turned white and the lower edges charred black. Most of the men were still sleeping, still exhausted from their long trek up the Snake, where their canoes had been useless half the time.

Lewis snapped the willow twig and handed one half, dangling several pieces of fish, to his partner. They ate the fish right off the stick, crumbs sticking to their beards and juice running down their wrists and into their sleeves.

Clark still had one piece left when he saw Twisted Hair approaching.

The old chief signed for the white men to follow him, and led the way back to the council circle. The interpreters were already there, and Twisted Hair pointed to a gap in the circle just large enough to accommodate the two white men as he stepped back into his own place and sat down.

"We have decided," Broken Arm said. The chief waited for a long moment, and when neither Lewis nor Clark said anything, he continued. "We are willing to try to make peace with the Blackfeet and the Bannock. But they must agree first, and we want to hear it from the lips of their own chiefs."

"Good," Clark said. "That's very good. I think you will not be sorry."

"I am not so sure. Most of us are not sure, but we trust you, and we believe that you will not lie to us."

Clark nodded. "We will talk to the Blackfeet on our way home. We will cross the Bitterroots and head straight for the Blackfeet country. We will tell them what you have said, and we will ask them to send word to you if they are willing."

"I do not believe they will be," Broken Arm said. "Red Grizzly Bear does not believe it either. Many of us do not believe it, but we will wait and see what happens. Tell us again why it is important to you."

"As I told you," Clark said, "the Great Father's people will establish trading posts. I can show you where later, on the maps we have made. This will make it possible for your people to get many of the goods made in the land of the Great Father, things that you will want and need. In exchange, you can provide to us things that we want and need. Everyone will benefit."

"Will you trade guns to us?"

Clark hesitated, but just for a moment. "Yes, of course. As long as they are not used for making war."

"We are not interested in making war unless others make war on us," Cut Nose said. "In that case, we will use the guns in war. But this will be of no concern to you, because once we have traded for them, they will be our guns. We will not tell you what to do with the things we trade to you. That is fair, is it not?"

"Yes, it is fair."

"And if you trade guns to the Blackfeet and the Bannock and the Paiute, you must trade guns to us, too. If our enemies have guns, we must have them to protect ourselves."

"I understand. But the Great Father wants all people to live in peace. He will not permit others to make war on you as long as you don't make war on them."

"We will see."

"What about the Heavenly Book?" Twisted Hair asked. "There is great medicine in the Heavenly Book. We would like to have one for ourselves."

Clark smiled. "I will see to it."

"Then there is nothing more to discuss," Broken Arm said. "The Cayuse people and the Nimipu will forever be friends to the Great Father and his people." He nodded to Cut Nose, who held a long wooden pipe in his hands. It was stuffed with a fine lichen the color of dark bronze. He got to his feet and moved close to the fire, used a slender straw to light it, then took a puff and passed it to the chief on his right.

"We learned this from the Hidatsa in the east," Broken Arm said. "It was not always our custom, but if we are going to make peace with all peoples, then it is a good thing, and we will do as they do to signify it."

When the pipe reached Clark, he took one quick puff, nearly choking on the strong smoke, and passed it to Lewis, who had less trouble. When the pipe had made a complete circuit, Clark said, "I have many things to show you. I'll be right back."

Getting to his feet, he sprinted to his lodge and returned with a deerskin bag. Sitting on the ground again, he loosened the drawstring and took out two pieces of dark metal. Placing one on the ground, he slowly brought the second piece close to it until it jumped and spun, joining the second with a sharp click. A murmur of amazement went around the circle.

"Dancing stones," Twisted Hair said.

"Magnets," Clark explained. "Watch." Pulling the magnets apart again, he once more placed one on the ground. Once more he brought the second one close, but this time the one on the ground quivered in the dust then started to slide away from the one in his hand. The faster he closed the gap, the faster the magnet on the ground slithered away. Then, with a twist of his wrist, he reversed the poles and the first magnet leaped off the ground and once more clicked home.

The chiefs were crowding in around him now, jostling one another to see who could get closest. "Here," Clark said, handing the magnets to Twisted Hair. "You try it."

The old chief knelt on the ground, the two magnets in his palm, and stared at them as if he were afraid to touch them. Clark took them from him, separated them, and dropped one into the dust. Handing the other one back, he said nothing as the old man examined the dark metal in his palm for nearly a minute. Then, with trembling fingers, Twisted Hair grasped the magnet and slowly lowered it over the one in the dirt.

The magnet on the ground swiveled one hundred and eighty degrees then jumped to rejoin its mate. Twisted Hair, his face frozen in awe, handed the magnets to Red Grizzly Bear as Clark reached into the deerskin bag a second time. This time he withdrew a magnifying glass and a piece of paper. Placing the paper on the ground, he trained the glass on it, moving it nearer then backing it away until he had the sharpest focus. After a few seconds the paper blackened at its center and a wisp of gray smoke curled away. A spit of flame jumped as the black hole disappeared and the charred circle grew larger and larger while Clark lowered the glass.

Another amazed murmur rippled through the fascinated throng. "Strong medicine," Cut Nose said. "Does the Great Father have many such things?"

Clark nodded. "A thousand things you have never seen, and more."

"Will we trade for such things?"

"If you wish."

Over the next three weeks, the explorers were constantly besieged with requests to show the dancing stones and the fire-breathing glass. When the snow clogging the high passes finally melted enough for the white men to make it through, the Nez Percé were convinced that the great medicine Clark had shown them was a sign from the Great Spirit.

When the expedition was ready to head out, Clark thanked the Nez Percé for their hospitality and promised the Blackfeet would send word if they were willing to accept the general peace. The Indians crowded around them on the morning of their planned departure, and Clark, seeing Twisted Hair in the crowd, presented him with a copy of the Bible. The old man's lips quivered, and a tear formed in the corner of one eye.

As the white men headed up through the meadow leading to the nearest pass, Clark looked back once and saw the old chief standing there still, the Bible clutched in both hands. He waved, but Twisted Hair either did not see or did not know how to respond. Clark turned his eyes eastward, heaved a long sigh, and wondered what the future would bring to the proud and gentle people he was leaving behind.

THE BEGINNING OF THE END
1836–1847

Chapter 10 ══════════

Green River Rendezvous, Wyoming—1836

THE WAGON LABORED up the hill, its wheels squeaking and snarling like cats in a burlap bag. Dr. Marcus Whitman, as was his way, squirmed nervously on the seat, his black suit pants snagging repeatedly on the rough wood. Beside him, his wife, Narcissa, sat primly, her hands in her lap and only occasionally grasping for the side when the wagon jolted or when it leaned into a rut.

They were in the middle of the pack train, and dust swirled around them in choking clouds, hissing against the canvas cover of the wagon and coating their cheeks and necks with a fine silt that felt almost like talcum to the fingertips. Their clothes were dusty, and their throats were dry.

It had been a long trip from St. Louis, but it was almost over, or so Whitman wanted to think. He knew there was one more leg, and that one the most uncertain, but he wasn't sure Narcissa was ready to think about that yet, so he tried to keep her focused on a more immediate goal.

Hearing the clop of hooves somewhere ahead, he leaned out to peer through the dusty swirls. Materializing out of the cloud, the way he imagined an archangel paid a visit to John the Baptist or Mary, Tom Fitzpatrick, the wagon master, appeared to him first as a dark shadow in the pale beige haze, then as something more substantial but not quite solid. Whitman recognized the horse before the rider, and then Fitzpatrick swung in an arc and pulled up alongside the wagon. Nodding to Narcissa, he said, "Ma'am, Dr. Whitman, won't be long now. The Green River's just over the next rise. It's a long run, maybe five miles, but we'll be there in a snap."

"Thank you, Mr. Fitzpatrick," Narcissa said. "That's the best news imaginable. You have no idea."

Fitzpatrick laughed his throaty laugh, coughed, and turned aside almost daintily, to hawk a dust-thickened gob that was almost mud back behind his mount. Then, smiling by way of apology, he said, "Trail's a mite dusty this year."

"How much longer, Mr. Fitzpatrick?" Whitman asked.

"Three hours, if we're lucky."

"A man doing God's work doesn't need luck, Mr. Fitzpatrick," Whitman said. There was no trace of humor in the remark, and Fitzpatrick just grunted. Whitman continued, "You're sure we'll be able to arrange for the rest of our passage at the rendezvous?"

Fitzpatrick nodded. "That's the way it's done. You ain't the first, you know, God's work or no. I'll be heading back east in a week or so, but there's sure to be plenty of folks heading your way. You can hook on with 'em easy enough. Probably have to wait around, though, for the end of the rendezvous. That'll be a week, or thereabouts. All depends . . ."

"Depends on what, Mr. Fitzpatrick?" Narcissa asked.

"On how the trappin's been, on how much whiskey there is, on how many redskins show up, and—"

"You don't mean there's likely to be an Indian attack, do you?" Whitman interrupted.

Fitzpatrick laughed. "Hell no," he barked, then touched the brim of his hat for a second to apologize for his French, as he characterized it. "That's no problem. Too many people there. Them mountain men eat wild Injuns for breakfast, and most of the tribes in these parts like the rendezvous. Most of 'em are friendly, at least most of the time, and it's the best place for them to get white man's goods. Especially guns and ammunition."

"I'm not sure it's such a good idea for them to have modern weapons, Mr. Fitzpatrick, but it doesn't seem to bother you."

"Why should it? If somebody's gonna shoot me, most likely he'll be a white man. And you got to realize that a gun is becoming a necessity out here. Most of the wild redskins already have 'em, thanks to the British, and the peaceable ones need 'em just to protect themselves. It makes good sense to see to it that as many friendlies as possible are armed. They take care of the mean ones and it don't cost even a drop of white blood. That's a good deal, seems like to me."

"God isn't in favor of anyone shooting anyone else, I'm sure, Mr. Fitzpatrick," Narcissa suggested.

"Maybe not, ma'am, but if He's not, there's somebody who is. And meaning no disrespect, there's enough shootin' going on to suggest he might have some influence of his own, whoever he might be."

Narcissa smiled. "That's precisely why Marcus

and I are here, Mr. Fitzpatrick. Perhaps we should start a mission for the white men, while we're at it."

Fitzpatrick smiled broadly. "Best way I know to have an empty building, Mrs. Whitman. Not too much time for church out here."

"Maybe there should be, Mr. Fitzpatrick."

The wagon master tilted his hat back, rubbed his five days' worth of whiskers, and said, "Maybe so, at that, Mrs. Whitman. But I don't reckon you'll make much headway with the Indians."

"That's where you're wrong, Mr. Fitzpatrick," Whitman said. "A delegation of Indians from the Columbia Basin journeyed all the way to St. Louis in search of someone who could arrange for missionaries to be sent to them."

"I know about that. They went east with a feller I know. And where are they all now?"

Whitman looked blank. Fitzpatrick waited a moment, then answered his own question. "They're all dead, Dr. Whitman, every last one of 'em."

"You're not suggesting that a desire for religion is responsible for that, surely?"

"Not religion, exactly, no. But it seems to me like white men are white men and redskins are redskins. Neither one better'n the other; they're just different, is all. The God you talk about don't mean nothing to the Indian. He don't look at things the same way you do."

"Minds can be changed, Mr. Fitzpatrick."

"Sure, they can be changed. I know that. But at what cost, Reverend? And who pays it?"

"I mean no harm to the Indians, Mr. Fitzpatrick."

"And that's the worst kind of harm, Dr. Whitman.

You mean well, and you're made welcome. But harm will result, all the same."

"I don't think so. I think the Indians are ripe for conversion. I have heard stories. There was even a preacher, Spokan Garry, who studied at the Episcopalian religious school in Saskatchewan. And there have been many others as well."

Fitzpatrick shook his head. "You don't understand. Hell, I don't understand the Indians either, not completely, but I know a damn sight more than you do about such things, and I'm here to tell you that no good will come of it in the end. The Indian thinks about religion in a real different way. He's more interested in the notion of having power against illness, power to keep the rain off his head and food on his table and, most of all, to keep his enemies at arm's length. That ain't the kind of power you mean to give 'em, now, is it? In fact, it ain't even in your power to give it to 'em if you wanted to. Is it?"

"No, of course not."

"Then what's gonna happen when he realizes he's been sold a bill of goods?"

"Is that what you think of religion, Mr. Fitzpatrick, a bill of goods?"

"Most often, yes, it is. Seems to me like most of your rules, or God's—"

"They're not my rules, I assure you, Mr. Fitzpatrick."

"Whatever. Anyhow, it seems like to me they're more honored in the breach. I seen enough to know that the last thing a angry man reaches for is his Bible, and he sure as hell don't turn the other cheek." He glanced at Narcissa, who seemed too absorbed in the argument to have noticed the escalating profanity, so he didn't apologize for fear of calling attention to it and giving offense where none had been taken.

"That's not the way I see it, Mr. Fitzpatrick. I see religion as a civilizing influence. It will give something to the savage that he lacks, something that he needs without even realizing it is missing in his life."

"What's that, Reverend?"

"Faith in God, of course, a connection to the Almighty. You have no idea how important that can be, how comforting in time of tribulation."

Fitzpatrick smiled again. "No, I don't. You're right about that, Dr. Whitman. I'll tell you what, though. You and I should talk again in a year or two, see who's right."

"I'm not a betting man, Mr. Fitzpatrick, or I'd make a wager right now."

"A talk'll do, Dr. Whitman. We'll see who's right." He touched the brim of his hat, then reined in to fall back along the wagons and heavily loaded pack mules as they passed one by one. Ten minutes later, he rode past again at a full gallop, heading for the head of the train. Whitman watched him go, ignoring the waved hand Fitzpatrick tossed his way. Narcissa, less stiff-backed than her husband, returned it.

It was nearly two hours later when the wagon lurched up and over the crest of a hill and canted downward. And spread out below, as far to the left and right as the eye could see, was a welter of tents, tipis, lodges, and lean-tos. The Green River rendezvous was in full swing, and the tiny figures teemed like ants on a slice of bread and jam, every color of the rainbow represented in the undulating mass.

"This is it," Whitman said, sweeping his left hand grandly to take in the huge valley, its green trampled to mush at its center, where the Green River coursed its lazy way through the valley floor lined with trees, and the whole rendezvous bordered with tall grasses and summer flowers as perfect as needlepoint on a picture frame. "This is where it really begins."

Narcissa Whitman, somewhat less romantic than her husband, said, "And where does it end, Marcus?"

The minister shrugged. "God knows," he said.

Narcissa was overwhelmed by the spectacle. "My God!" she said. "Look at that, Marcus. It's . . . I don't know what to say."

Her husband stood in the wagon, leaning forward, the reins clenched in one fist. "There must be thousands of people down there," he said. "I couldn't begin to guess how many. And the Indians, look at them all."

A moment later, a figure on horseback loomed up on Narcissa's side of the wagon. Whitman knew, without even turning to look at the newcomer, that it was Joe Meek, one of the trappers who had ridden out to meet the caravan once Fitzpatrick had sent word on ahead that he was getting close. The trappers were anxious for their supplies, and when they learned that white women were among the caravan members, their curiosity was too much to resist.

"Bet you never expected nothin' like that, Mrs. Whitman," Meek shouted, leaning toward the wagon.

Narcissa smiled at him. "No, Mr. Meek, I certainly didn't. I especially didn't expect to see so many Indians."

"Oh, we got Injuns to spare, Mrs. Whitman. We got Cayuses and Shoshones, Utes and Flatheads, Bannocks and Nez Percés. I expect you'll be seeing plenty of them, though."

"What do you mean?"

"The way I hear it, you come all the way out here to bring 'em religion. Ain't that so?"

"It is, indeed, Mr. Meek."

"You need any help with that, you let me know. I reckon I know as much as any man about the red-skins in this part of the country."

"Pride goeth before a fall, Mr. Meek," Marcus Whitman said. The minister was obviously irritated by the attention paid to his wife. This was, after all, their honeymoon trip, and the last thing he wanted was to have a bunch of fur-clad barbarians mooning over his young bride. She was a handsome woman, he knew, and took pride in her full figure and attractive face, but the flesh was not something he was comfortable with, and when the flesh in question was that of his wife, he would prefer that it pass unnoticed among the uncouth hordes waiting in the valley below him.

"Then I reckon I'll fall soon, Dr. Whitman," Meek said, grinning broadly enough to show all of his teeth, white and yellow alike, "because I been proud of myself for quite a while. Good reason, too, I figure."

"We'll see about that, Mr. Meek."

"Oh, I'm sure you will, Reverend." Then, to Narcissa, Meek said, "If you like, I can take you on ahead, ma'am, introduce you around."

"Thank you, no, Mr. Meek. My place is with my husband."

"Well, I just thought I'd ask." He gave a cavalier bow, nearly toppling himself from the saddle, and both Whitmans caught a hint of alcohol in the air as he galloped off.

"Drunken buffoon," Whitman mumbled.

"Now, Marcus, don't be so hard on him. He was just being polite in his own way."

"Polite, was he? Fawning over you like a drunken schoolboy? I don't suppose you enjoyed it, too. Or did you?"

"Of course not. It's nice to be noticed, of course, but he meant no harm. And did none."

"If you encourage them, they'll be all over us, like bees in a hive. Is that what you want, Narcissa?"

"I think I'll go in back and lie down. I'm a little tired, and this dust is just horrible."

Whitman wasn't anxious to argue, knowing that it would just serve as some sort of backhanded encouragement for the likes of Joe Meek, so he let the subject drop.

After Narcissa crawled into the back of the wagon, he concentrated on handling the horses. Behind him, additional wagons carried supplies and the Reverend Henry Spalding and his wife, Eliza. The other members of his party were on horseback: the two young Nez Percés he had brought east the previous year, and several workers assigned by the Mission Board: William Gray, who was already getting on his nerves, Miles Goodyear, and the boy Dulin, whose first name he kept forgetting. James was it, or Billy? He wasn't sure. He had doubts about them all, but then he had genuine confidence only in himself.

The more uncertain the future, the more he stiffened his spine, and the less he listened to advice, no matter the source. He wanted to do things his own way or not at all. Hardly a romantic, he still looked forward to settling in the Columbia Basin, envisioning himself as the savior of hordes of unfortunate savages, drawing them into the church and civilizing them. He had learned a bit about the region the previous summer, but knew next to nothing about the people who lived there. And despite his store of conventional wisdom, he ignored the warning about the dangers posed by a little knowledge.

His reverie was interrupted by an Indian on horseback, who leaned over and thrust a crumpled envelope into his surprised hand, then galloped off. Tending the reins with one hand, he ripped open the envelope to find a letter from Samuel Parker, the missionary with whom he had come west the previous year. The letter was dated May 14, and Whitman was disappointed to learn that Parker was not going to meet him, as they had planned, but was instead heading to Fort Vancouver. The letter was brief and told the minister nothing about conditions on the Columbia, contained no advice as to where to set up his mission, and generally left him baffled and angry. He stuffed it into his pocket and snapped the reins harder than necessary.

Chapter 11

As THE WAGONS STARTED down into the broad, sweeping valley, switching back and forth as they tried to keep from toppling over and rolling bed over wheels all the way to the bottom, Whitman had the opportunity to study the colorful panorama spread out before him. He was impressed, and more than a little frightened, but didn't want to let it show. He felt that Narcissa was looking to him for support, as was fitting for a new bride, and ignorance was hardly likely to inspire confidence. Terror would help no more. He trusted his instincts and hoped that his quick wits would enable him to cover the gaps in his experience. But the sheer numbers of men below were enough to curl the edges of his veneer of supreme confidence.

And they were not ordinary men. He knew enough about the trappers and mountain men to know that it took a peculiar kind of human being to endure the hardships, the long silences, and the incessant threats to life and limb in the American west. He had seen them in action the previous year, seen firsthand the nearly uncontrollable release of the unbearable tensions. Liquor flowed nonstop at the annual rendezvous; gambling, fistfights, sometimes even murder were certainties; and the commerce in women was appalling. Half the trappers seemed to have Indian wives, taken without benefit of matrimony, sometimes purchased for a handful of geegaws. And as often as not, the women were abandoned before the year was out. These were not the sort of men to worry about the sanctity of a sacrament.

The closer he came to the bottom of the valley, the more Whitman found his revulsion difficult to check. He wondered whether it was because he was now married and that having Narcissa along was, as Bacon said, giving a hostage to fortune. But he tried to suppress his distaste, knowing that the trappers would sense it, and the Indians would react to it with mistrust.

The caravan was so long that on each leg of the switchback, Whitman could look up the slope and see the tail of the pack train still negotiating the previous leg. By the time the wagon reached the valley floor, he had managed to regain his composure. But his physical discomfort was harder to control. His back was still stiff, and he could smell the stench of the encampment, so strong that it made his nostrils twitch.

A contingent of impatient trappers flooded across the campsite toward the lead animals, where Whitman saw Tom Fitzpatrick waving his hat over his head and shouting like a savage. The trappers were on foot, and they looked like children surrounding a pied piper as Fitzpatrick kicked his mount repeatedly to keep the head of the caravan moving.

The flood of mountain men swept along both sides of the train, and gunshots punctuated the wild yips and hollers as more and more of the men raced forward to greet Fitzpatrick. When the wagon master finally called a halt, Whitman breathed a sigh of relief. But his trials were just beginning. Starved for the sight of a white woman, the men swarmed along the now motionless pack train, going from wagon to wagon until they discovered Narcissa.

It was a tide of shaggy hair and unwashed clothing, the sun-darkened faces upturned, slashed by smiles full of broken teeth. Narcissa waved and started passing out Bible pamphlets, which the men took only to look up at her in confusion. This wasn't what they had in mind. But one look at the handsome woman kneeling on the wagon seat and the smiles returned. Tucking the pamphlets under their arms, the men milled around, shouting hellos that were all but unintelligible.

Whitman breathed a sigh of relief when he saw Fitzpatrick kneeing his mount back through the throng. Edging in toward the wagon, the wagon master shouted, "You best pull out of the train, Dr. Whitman, and we'll see can we find you a little privacy."

Whitman nodded, jerked the reins, and started the team with a lurch. The wagon creaked and groaned as it turned, the men parting only reluctantly as the minister cracked his whip twice to get the animals into the traces. It was not easy going for the big wagon, and the flood of excited trappers boiled around its flanks like muddy water carrying it away on a rising tide.

"Whiskey, boys," someone shouted, and the men snapped their heads around. Here was something else they could get excited about. "Whiskey, whiskey," the chant began, slow at first, just a few of the men picking it up, but slowly growing in volume. The men started to fall away now and the wagon continued to lurch toward a stand of tall cottonwoods halfway across the valley floor.

The chant died away behind the wagon as Whitman used the whip again and then once more. When he reached the cottonwoods, he was sweating, the dust on his forehead lined with small gullies where the trickling perspiration had washed it clean. He reached up with one hand and rubbed the paste until it flaked away in tiny brown balls.

Narcissa was still kneeling on the wagon seat, staring back at the motley array of whites and Indians.

Whitman shook his head. "You better sit down, Narcissa. You'll fall."

"I'm all right," she said.

"I'm hard put to tell the savages from the civilized," the minister said.

His wife laughed. "You have to relax a little, Marcus. There's no point in making them resentful. You'll get used to it."

"It doesn't bother you?"

"No, of course not. I didn't know quite what to expect, but I knew we wouldn't find a choir in black robes and starched collars out here."

Whitman let his breath out in a long, slow sigh. "Certainly not. Why don't you nap in the wagon while I get the others settled?"

"I'm too excited to sleep," she said. "I'll just—"

"You'd better just stay here. These men are half-mad with drink. There's no telling what they're capable of."

"Oh, Marcus, don't be so priggish. It's a hard life they lead. You can't expect drawing-room manners. Not out here."

The Spaldings arrived shortly thereafter, along

with Dulin, Goodyear, and Gray, who had their hands full driving a small herd of cattle through a cloud of wondering Indians, who had never seen such animals. They pressed in all around the small knot of beeves, poking and prodding, and provoking such a din from the frightened stock that Gray was forced to shoo them away. But the Indians wouldn't leave, settling for falling back a few paces and moving ahead with the steers at the center of a tight circle.

As the men began to set up their camp, more and more Indians, including some Flatheads and Nez Percé Whitman had met the previous year, pressed in around the small campsite, making it almost impossible to get any work done. The two Nez Percé boys who had accompanied him eastward spotted their families in the crowd and pushed through to greet them. The emotional reunion took some of the attention away from the members of the missionary party and allowed them to finish making their camp habitable, if not comfortable.

Henry Spalding was in a foul mood, and when Whitman told him about Parker's letter, he exploded. "You mean to say we don't know where we're going from here? Is that what you're telling me? No preparations have been made for our arrival?"

"Apparently not."

Whitman dragged Spalding into the trees, to try to discuss the problem in private. He had sense enough to know that bickering in front of their prospective converts was unwise. But Spalding had a short fuse and kept raising his voice. "I would have thought you could have made better arrangements than this, Marcus."

"Dr. Parker was supposed to handle it."

"Well, he didn't. And neither did you."

"We'll just have to make the best of it. We'll be all right."

"Easy for you to say. We're in the middle of nowhere, surrounded by half-naked savages and white men who live on whiskey, and you think it's all right."

"We came to convert them, Henry. If they were already civilized, they wouldn't need us, would they?"

"Don't try to make excuses."

But Whitman could see that his argument was beginning to sink in. Spalding's voice dropped to a conversational level again. There was still an edge to his words, but at least he was talking instead of screaming.

"I don't know how Eliza will take this news," Spalding said.

"She'll be fine. We don't give our wives enough credit, sometimes. They're a lot stronger than we want to believe. Stronger than we are, in some ways."

Spalding nodded. "Perhaps you're right," he said.

"Of course I am. I'm sorry for the confusion, but it couldn't be helped."

Spalding spat some trail dust onto the grass, then shook his head. "You're right," he said. "We'll make out."

As they stepped back out of the trees William Gray nodded to them. He had just finished knotting a rope around the trunks of several widely spaced cottonwoods to fashion a makeshift pen for the still frightened livestock.

Whitman started toward the wagon to get Narcissa when a volley of gunfire exploded far up the slope. He jumped involuntarily, then looked toward the point where the sound originated. He was astonished to see a broad column of Indians marching down the center of the rendezvous, ignoring campfires and tents and making straight toward the Whitman wagon.

Joe Meek came galloping toward the wagon, scattering the Indian women who were still babbling about the livestock. He skidded to a halt and leaped from the saddle, letting the reins drag. He raced toward Narcissa, who was talking to Mrs. Spalding, and took her by one hand, snatching at Eliza Spalding's arm with the other. "Come on, ladies," he shouted. "This is in your honor."

He started to drag the two women toward the advancing column. Eliza struggled, but Narcissa seemed excited, and broke free of Meek's grip and darted around to take Eliza's other arm. "Come on, Eliza, it'll be fun," she said.

Whitman and Spalding saw what was happening and raced after Meek and the women. Whitman was hollering for Narcissa to come back, but she ignored him, tugging still harder on Eliza Spalding's right arm.

Bursts of gunfire spewed smoke into the air as the trappers fired volley after volley. The din of drums and wooden flutes was almost deafening, even at that range, and the closer the parade came, the louder it got. Whitman caught up to Narcissa and tried to tear her grip loose, but she refused to let go. "Marcus, don't be so stuffy. This is for our benefit. You don't want to offend our hosts, do you?"

Whitman fumed. "They're stark naked, for Lord's sake. Narcissa, it isn't right."

"It's the custom, Marcus. We have to respect that." The first contingent of warriors was just a hundred yards away now, and Whitman glanced up at the oncoming horde, shaking his head as if to signify that he didn't know what to do. The drumming grew more insistent, and the lead brigade of warriors began to chant.

"They're Bannock," Meek explained. "The buggers right behind them are Shoshone. You folks ought to be mighty pleased. It ain't every day a newcomer gets a reception like this."

The Bannock warriors left off their chanting, and a horrible howling broke out from the Shoshones. The welter of color in daubs and stripes of war paint was almost enough to keep attention away from the oiled and glistening flesh beneath it.

"It's immoral," Whitman said. He felt someone tug at his sleeve and whirled impatiently, shouting, "What is it? What do you . . . ?" He saw Henry Spalding then, still tugging on his sleeve.

"Dr. Whitman," the young minister said, "I don't think it's appropriate for the women to see this sort of thing. Eliza! Come away."

Eliza Spalding turned to look at her husband, but Narcissa refused to let go and jerked Eliza's arm to get her to turn back to the festivities.

Behind the Shoshones came a mounted war party of Nez Percé. Most of the horses had distinctive brown splotches on their lighter haunches. The Indians carried lances and elaborately feathered shields. As they passed the missionary party they gave vent to an ear-shattering yell that startled even Narcissa.

"I've never seen anything like it in my life," she said. "It's so . . . so . . ."

"It's revolting, is what it is," Spalding suggested.

"Grown man walking around like that in front of women. They should be ashamed."

"They don't think about such things, least not the way we do, anyhow," Meek explained. "Like I said, it's a way of thanking you for coming."

"I'm almost sorry I did," Spalding shot back.

"Now, Mr. Spalding, that's no way for a man of the cloth to be talkin'. What about your responsibility to these poor heathens?"

Meek was mocking him, but Spalding didn't know how to respond. Instead, he just spluttered something unintelligible and stalked back to the campsite. Meek laughed, then started toward the still-advancing column. The Utes were passing now, their faces garishly painted with stripes in wild colors. They saluted Narcissa with their bows as another wave of gunfire rippled and crackled in the distance.

Meek stood with hands on hips until the parade was over. Narcissa was enthralled, Eliza horrified but unable to turn away. When the last contingent of warriors had passed in review, Meek said, "Welcome to the west, ladies." He laughed heartily.

"There's nothing to laugh about," Eliza Spalding scolded.

"Laughs are hard to come by out here, Mrs. Spalding. You best learn to take them where you find them."

Marcus Whitman was already nearly back at the campsite by the time Narcissa said good-bye to Meek. With Eliza tagging along behind her, she started back down the slope. She could see a throng of Indians gathered around the campsite, including many of the warriors who had just paraded past.

They hadn't bothered to dress after their march, and Eliza Spalding closed her eyes, groping ahead of her, trying to keep one hand on Narcissa's shoulder.

An argument was in progress, not between the missionaries and the Indians but between two groups of Indians. Narcissa worked her way through the crowd until she reached her husband's side. He was watching the debaters and kept leaning toward Samuel Temoni, an English-speaking Nez Percé, for translations of both sides of the discussion.

"What's going on, Marcus?" Narcissa asked. She watched Eliza Spalding disappear into the wagon and Henry climb in after her. Whitman hadn't responded to her question, so she repeated it.

The minister tried to hush her up, but she persisted, and finally he whispered, "They're arguing about which tribe we should go to. The Nez Percé want us to come to them, and the Cayuse want us with them."

"Why can't we do both?"

"How do you mean?"

"It might be best if Henry and Eliza had their own mission, don't you think?"

"Henry getting on your nerves, is he?"

"Isn't he getting on yours?" she asked pointedly.

"I find it difficult having him around, knowing he had proposed to you before I met you."

"Don't worry about that. Just be glad I turned him down. I know I am."

"I am, too. But I wonder whether that's sufficient reason for us to split up. It might weaken us, blunt the impact we could have. Imagine if we all work together, what kind of progress we could make."

"I can imagine. But I can also imagine it all going

up in smoke if we're unable to iron out our disagreements. Henry can be difficult. And Eliza is so . . . priggish."

"Just because the woman was offended by naked savages doesn't make her a prig. You should be more tolerant. In fact, it's more than a little unbecoming the way you stood there gawking at them all."

Narcissa started to respond, but realized she was about to commit the same transgression she had just accused Henry Spalding of committing, and held her tongue.

Whitman turned back to the dispute, and Narcissa listened, imagining she could understand the argument, but in reality simply reading the tone and the language of the debaters' bodies. It seemed as if the disagreement would never be settled.

Someone started calling Whitman's name, and he looked up. Narcissa, too, looked to see what caused the disturbance and saw a white man working his way through the outer fringes of the onlooking throng. Marcus told Temoni to advise the Indians that he would need some time to consider all the angles. He would advise them when he had made up his mind. Then he excused himself, even as the Nez Percé tried to explain to the disputants what Whitman had told him.

The white man on the edge of the crowd barked something in an Indian language, Whitman wasn't sure which, but all the combatants seemed to understand, and they parted to let him through. Sticking out a hamlike hand, he said, "I'm John McLeod, Mr. Whitman. I got a letter for you from Dr. Parker." He fished an envelope from inside his shirt and handed it over.

"Where is Dr. Parker?" Whitman asked as he tore the envelope open.

"Last I knew he was in Fort Vancouver. Don't know if he's still there or not. The way I understand it, he wants me to take you folks with me to the Columbia when I leave here."

Whitman nodded, then said, "Excuse me a moment, Mr. McLeod," and paused to read the letter. Humming to himself, he perused the three pages, which were as empty of real information as the previous one. When he was finished, he looked up at McLeod. "I guess I don't really have any choice, Mr. McLeod. If it's no imposition, I'd be glad to go with you."

"No imposition, Dr. Whitman. I'm going that way anyhow."

"When do you leave?"

"About a week, I guess."

"A week! But—"

"Got work to do first, Dr. Whitman. I lugged hundreds of pounds of trade goods over them mountains. I ain't leaving here with 'em, and I ain't leaving them behind. Got to sell 'em."

"But a week . . ."

McLeod thumped his chest. "Great outdoors, Doctor. Do you some good to see a bit of the country. Get to know some of the Indians. We'll talk in a couple days, soon as I get a better idea of my plans. All right?"

"There's no chance you could leave sooner, I suppose?"

"Not a one, Dr. Whitman. Not a one."

Chapter 12 ═══════════

Columbia River Basin—1836

THE TRIP OVER THE MOUNTAINS had been grueling. It took nearly six weeks, which saw the women begin to lose their composure and the Spaldings refine their bickering to a high art. William Gray, too, found little contentment, and well before the party reached Fort Vancouver, it was agreed that Gray would spend a year with the Flatheads, in hopes of convincing them to accept a mission of their own. Marcus Whitman, tired of the Spaldings' sniping and the constant tension caused by Narcissa's ill humor, agreed that Henry and Eliza would open a separate mission. All that remained to be decided was where, and for that he was hoping to receive some guidance from Samuel Parker.

Miles Goodyear, lured by the romance of the trappers, went off with a party of mountain men to trap beaver in the Bannock country. It seemed to Whitman that his group was slowly being worn away, like a new saw held to grindstone. McLeod and his Hudson's Bay men were understanding, to a point, and tried to be helpful, but Whitman was stubborn. Eventually, even the wagon, which McLeod had tried to convince the minister to leave behind, quit on Whitman. It broke an axle, and it was cut down to a two-wheeled cart, but the rougher reaches of the mountains were too much, even for this modified vehicle, and it was finally abandoned, one more casualty of the exhausting terrain.

By the time they had reached Fort Vancouver, they learned that Parker was long gone, but he had left behind a suggestion or two concerning possible locations for the mission settlement. In October of 1835, Whitman and Spalding left the women in the care of Pierre Pambrun, a Hudson's Bay man, at Fort Walla Walla, and traveled up the Walla Walla River, in the company of several Nez Percé and Cayuse.

The bickering between the two tribes had still been unresolved, and it seemed to both Whitman and Spalding that their decision to go their separate ways might have been a blessing in disguise. Whitman was looking for an ideal site, one that would be central, to enable as many Indians as possible to have easy access, and one that offered good water and fertile ground for the crops he planned to introduce. He was convinced that the only hope for the Indians was to learn the ways of the white man. He knew that hordes of whites were gathering back east and that it would not be long before the dam broke and the white tide poured into the Columbia Basin. Chasing buffalo and gathering camas roots for sustenance was a way of life the days of which were numbered.

Twenty-two miles up the Walla Walla, at a place the Cayuse called Waiilatpu, Whitman had found what he was looking for. The Nez Percé were not happy that the "Bostons," as they called the minis-

ter and by extension all whites, had chosen to settle among the Cayuse people, but Whitman could
not be swayed, and he drove a stake into the
ground with all the zest and finality of a Roman
soldier driving a nail into the cross. All the way
back to Walla Walla, the Nez Percé complained bitterly. The Cayuse were not to be trusted, they said.
They tried every argument they could imagine to
persuade Whitman to change his mind, but the
minister would not listen. He told them that the
Spaldings would come to them, that they would
have their own mission, and that this way God's
work could be done for two peoples instead of one.

Now all that remained was to find a place for the
Spaldings and their own mission. Dr. Parker had suggested a location on the Clearwater River, and after
ordering supplies to be sent to Waiilatpu, the two
ministers, accompanied by a handful of Nez Percé,
pushed on into the mountains, angling back the way
they had come. In the meantime, William Gray
would oversee the shipment and begin construction
of a house at the site of the Whitman mission.

Tackensuatis, a Nez Percé chief whom Whitman
had met the previous summer and who spoke some
English, led the expedition up the Clearwater. He
had a site in mind, a place where a smaller stream
fed into the Clearwater, one the Indians called
Lapwai—which meant the place of the butterflies—
but when the small party reached it, Whitman and
Spalding found that the high canyon walls and the
relatively poor soil made it unacceptable.
Undaunted, Tackensuatis led them farther up
Lapwai Creek. Two miles above the junction with
the Clearwater, they found a broad meadow with

deep, rich soil and open to the sun, ideal for farming. Spalding opted for this location, and Whitman, anxious to have things settled, agreed.

The land was claimed by a Nez Percé chief named Thunder Strikes, who was also a shaman, and he was not pleased to have the white men take it for their own purposes. Thunder Strikes was even more annoyed when he learned that he was not to be paid for surrendering his claim to the site. All the tribes in the Columbia Basin thought of the Bostons as generous, more so than the rather niggardly Hudson's Bay Company traders, and called the Americans the "big hearts of the east." Thunder Strikes learned that big hearts did not necessarily have deep pockets, and his bitterness was something that Whitman should have sensed.

With the second mission site selected, the two ministers returned for their wives, made some last-minute arrangements for additional supplies, particularly for the Lapwai mission, and in late November they went their separate ways.

The Nez Percé were delighted to have their mission at last, something they had desired for thirty years, ever since William Clark had shown Twisted Hair his Heavenly Book. At Lapwai, Henry Spalding directed the willing Indians in constructing a house for himself and his wife, one that would serve not only as living quarters for the missionary couple but also as a schoolroom, where Bible studies and the English language would begin to bridge the gap between the two cultures.

It was a large house, nearly fifty feet long and eighteen feet wide. The plan was for logs to be used, but since there was little timber at the site,

trees had to be cut down on the banks of the
Clearwater and lugged the two miles overland.
Even Tackensuatis threw himself into the labor.
Unused to this kind of work, since lodging was
usually constructed by Nez Percé women, the chief
made a valiant attempt at using an ax to fell trees
and shape the logs, but after several hours of nearly
futile effort, he allowed his wife to take the ax from
his hand and contented himself with hauling the
shaped logs upstream to the building site.

Already, though, the gap between the cultures,
and the blindness of Henry Spalding to its size, was
beginning to make itself felt. Many of the warriors
grumbled at having to perform such demeaning
work, and others refused to participate at all. But
Spalding was oblivious to the discontent. Once the
walls were up, a roof was made of woven grasses
and clay plaster. When it was finished two days
before Christmas, Spalding stood back proudly, his
hands on his hips, wiped the sweat from his brow,
and pronounced himself delighted. Eliza wasn't so
sure, but she threw herself into planning for the
education of the Nez Percé.

Already, she had begun to work on mastering
the language, but it was slow going. Even the presence of some English-speaking Nez Percé was of
only modest help.

Food was going to be a problem. They had
arrived too late to plant, and the winter could be
long and harsh. Tackensuatis, though, promised his
help. Fish and game, while not plentiful, were
some help, and Spalding had arranged to purchase
supplies from the Hudson's Bay Company trading
post at Fort Colville. Tackensuatis took charge of

the provision runs, and a small but steady supply of food flowed into the mission.

The more serious business of conversion could now get under way. The morning after the house was completed, Spalding held his first indoor service. John Ais, one of the two Nez Percé boys Whitman had brought east with him for education the year before, served as interpreter. It made for a laborious and even convoluted liturgy.

As Spalding stood there, the Nez Percé a sea of expectant faces all but motionless before him, bodies canted forward as if to speed their acquaintance with the Word of the white man's God, he wondered whether he was up to the challenge. But he had come three thousand miles, and there was no point in waiting any longer.

"I want to talk to you about the importance of doing good," he began, then waited for Ais to translate before continuing, "and the avoidance of evil, which is just as important. There is much for me to tell you, much for you to learn. It will not be easy, and it will not be quick. But if we work together, we can do it."

He watched the eager listeners, who were hanging on every word, and wondered how much of what he wanted to tell them they were capable of understanding. There were times, usually late at night when he couldn't sleep, when he doubted his own understanding. How much more difficult it must be, then, for these poor, ignorant savages.

"You have your own gods, but they are nothing alongside the one, true God," he continued. "And it is very important for you to realize that He knows everything, even those secrets locked deep in your hearts, the most private thoughts you have. And God holds us accountable not only for what we do, but for what we think about doing, even for what we think."

He listened to the translation and saw the faces continue to stare expectantly up at him, as if he had left something out. He tried to remember what he had meant to say, and felt it out there just on the edge of his consciousness, slipping away like a minnow through his fingers.

He tried again. "Everything we say and do is . . ." He stopped, realizing he could not find the right words. But he had to end the sentence, somehow. "Everything we say and do is judged by God. If we do evil, He knows it, and He will punish us for that evil."

Once more he felt a current ripple through the packed room, as if he had offended the worshipers somehow, but they were too polite to show it.

Stumbling over his own uncertainties, he managed to limp his way through a paraphrase of the sermon that, on paper, had seemed so precise, so finely crafted. It felt like so much mush in his mouth now, and he wanted to run away and hide.

When it was over, Eliza joined him and tried to get the Nez Percé to sing along with her. She had worked hard at getting them to absorb the English words of several hymns. She hoped soon to have them translated, but there was so much to do and so little time. Even books were in short supply, and she spent more time than she would have liked, most of it really, in transcribing lessons by hand.

Now, a pitch pipe clutched in one hand, she tried to beat tune in the air. Her voice sounded scratchy to her, off-key and out of tune, as she started "Shall We Gather at the River?" But she pushed on, as her husband had done, and gradually the voices of the women in the group began to swell. The children seemed more certain of the words, even though they understood none of them, and dragged the adults along with them.

"Abide with Me" was a little better, as if confidence were slowly building. The performance made up in volume what it lacked in polish, and Eliza felt for a moment as if she were actually accomplishing something.

When the service was over, many of the Indians joined Henry in his makeshift workshed, where he was trying to fashion a supply of cultivating tools. He had already secured seed for the spring planting, but there was no plow, and the earth would have to be prepared by hand. The work was proceeding slowly, because the Indians who were willing to help with the work were uncertain what the tools were for. He had tried explaining but, as so often happened, lost his temper. "Do what I do," he told them, slamming his tools down on the plank table in disgust. "Just do what I do."

And so it went, from day to day, each one dragging into the next. The hours were long, even in the darkness of winter, and it sometimes seemed that spring would never come. Spalding was counting on an early thaw, because he wanted the first planting to succeed. He knew that if the crops were meager, or failed altogether, he would have a difficult time persuading the reluctant farmers to try again the following year.

Chapter 13 ===

MARCUS WHITMAN WAS HAVING no better luck at Waiilatpu. Like Spalding, he was made uncomfortable by the alien customs of the Nez Percé. But like Spalding, he meant well, and he was not one to surrender without a fight, even if he was fighting the wrong battle, with the wrong adversary.

After a promising beginning, attendance at services had fallen off badly. By late winter, new converts were confined almost exclusively to children singing hymns and an occasional woman or old man who had nothing to lose and maybe just some slight advantage to gain by accepting the God of the Bostons. Spokan Garry was well-known to the Cayuse. He was among the first of the Columbia Basin Indians to embrace Christianity, and certainly the most influential. His teachings, although considerably diluted and more than a little modified to suit the cultural biases of the Spokan, had had a modest ripple effect that had reached as far as the Flatheads to the east and the Coeur d'Alène to the north. The Cayuse, too, had been tempted, and the residual effect of that temptation led some to cling to Whitman's coattails.

The missionaries' only hope was the obvious dedication to their teachings of some of the chiefs, including Tu-eka-kas, and another Nez Percé chief named Tamootsin, whom they called Joseph and Timothy, respectively.

As spring came and the mountain passes began to clear, Whitman began to think of expanding the small herd of livestock. The Cayuse had gotten over their initial fascination with the cattle, but the small herd had done well over the winter, making the minister think of introducing hogs and sheep, as well as additional beeves.

The only way to get more stock, though, was by bringing it in from the east. The Mission Board had given him only a modest budget, which was now almost depleted, so if the stock were to be purchased, he was going to have to find some way to pay for it on his own. William Gray had convinced the Flatheads to trade some horses in order to establish a herd of cattle, and he approached Whitman about convincing the Cayuse to do the same.

Umtippe, the chief who controlled the area around Waiilatpu, was angry with Whitman and disinclined to cooperate. It almost seemed as if the Cayuse had gotten over their desire to have white men among them, as if they no longer believed in the big medicine of the Bostons. They had already seen that a white man from the east did not necessarily have a big heart. If he couldn't deliver on his promises, there was then no reason at all to tolerate his presence among them.

But Umtippe was an old man, and when he died in early March, he was succeeded by Tilokaikt, whom Whitman had befriended the year before. And it was Tilokaikt Whitman turned to when Gray suggested the cooperative effort.

The young chief, more affable than most of the younger warriors, and eager to keep Whitman among his people, always came running when the minister sent for him. Now Gray and Whitman were sitting at a table in the Whitman mission, Tilokaikt taking a seat on the opposite side.

"Mr. Gray has an interesting proposal for me, Tilokaikt," Whitman began.

"Proposal?"

"Umm, how to say . . . a suggestion, an idea."

"And what is this idea?"

"The Flatheads have agreed to trade some of their horses in order to get some cattle."

"How does this concern me?"

"I thought perhaps you might wish to do the same."

"We already have cattle."

"But not enough. If the herd were larger, there would be more milk, which would be better for the children. And if it were larger, there would soon be even more cattle, enough to feed your people meat all year long."

"There is the buffalo for meat. There is the deer, the bighorn. What do we need with more animals for meat when we have those?"

"Those animals may not be around much longer. The buffalo are far away, and there is much danger in hunting them. The Blackfeet are always attacking your people when they cross the Bitterroots to hunt."

"We are not afraid of Blackfeet. So we are not afraid to hunt the buffalo."

"But every summer your men are away for months at a time, leaving their families alone."

"It is as it has always been."

"But a husband should be with his wife, a father with his children."

"Wives have their duties and husbands have other duties. Why do you want to change our ways?"

Whitman was not adept at arguing with the Cayuse. Their logic was as precise as his own, but their concerns and his were very different. He drummed his fingers on the table, trying to find some way to convince the reluctant Tilokaikt to go along. Before he found it, Gray said, "Tilokaikt, if the Flatheads raise their own cattle, they will have more meat, and they will not have to trade with you for food. Wouldn't it be better if you had another thing to trade with some of the other tribes? If you have cattle and the Spokans do not, then you can trade cattle as well as horses. You can trade meat for fish, or for the beads that you travel all the way to the Dalles to get. Wouldn't that be better?"

The chief thought about it. It was obvious he wasn't completely convinced, but he was beginning to waver. "I will have to think about this and ask the others. For myself, I am not against this idea, but it will take many horses, will it not?"

"You have plenty of horses. More than you need. Why not trade them for something you don't have?"

"A good thing, if this something I don't have is something I want or need."

"You have to trust me, Tilokaikt," Whitman said. "It will make your lives better than they are now, and it will cost you nothing much."

"This is hard to understand for me. If I give little, how can I expect to get much?"

Gray laughed out loud. "Chief, you drive a hard bargain, you know that?"

Tilokaikt looked at Whitman. "Is this a good thing?"

"In business," Whitman said, "yes, it is a good thing."

"For white men only? Or for my people, too?"

This time Whitman laughed. "Yes, for you and your people, too."

"Then I will talk to the council about this idea. I will tell you tomorrow or the next day."

"That's all I ask, Tilokaikt. In the meantime, I'm going to talk to Dr. Spalding, to see if the Nez Percé wish to join us. They have even more horses than your people."

"They have very good horses. Almost as good as mine." The young chief smiled and stood up. "Thank you for telling me about this idea."

Whitman walked him to the door. The chief mounted his horse and quickly rode off. Only when he was out of sight did Whitman turn to Gray, who was hovering at his elbow. "What do you think, Marcus?" Gray asked. "Will he do it?"

"I don't know. I suppose it will depend partly on what the Nez Percé do. They won't want to be outdone by their cousins."

"When will you know?"

"Henry is due here later this afternoon. We may know as early as that."

"I'm anxious to get going," Gray said. "It's a long trip, and I want to get back before the winter. I don't relish the thought of spending six months in Montana watching a bunch of cows."

"We'll go as fast as we can, Will. We can't make

these people do anything they don't want to do. And one thing they don't seem to want to do is to make up their minds very quickly. About anything."

"I know. It's so aggravating. It's not like we're trying to trick them into doing something foolish."

"I wish it was as simple as that."

"Isn't it?"

Two hours later, Henry Spalding arrived on horseback. He greeted Whitman coolly, almost as if he expected that he had been summoned for a reprimand of some kind. "I have a lot of work to do, Marcus. I hope this is important."

"I'm not in the habit of wasting anyone's time, Henry. You know that."

"Well, what is it?"

Gray, who stood to one side in front of the Whitman house, said, "We're going to take some horses back east, trade them for livestock."

"Where are you going to get the horses?" Spalding asked.

"The Flatheads and the Cayuse are providing them." This wasn't quite true, and Gray glanced at Whitman to see whether the minister would correct him, but Whitman remained silent.

"I don't understand. How will it be done?"

"I'll take some of the Indians from each tribe, a handful should be enough, and drive the horses over the Bitterroots. We'll stop at the rendezvous on Green River, then head east, make the trade, and drive the cattle back."

"That's an awfully long trip, William. Are you up to it?"

"You saying I'm not?"

Spalding shook his head. "No, just wondering if

you've considered all the dangers."

"We'll be armed. The Indians can take care of themselves. If everything goes well, I should be back by early September. It'll make it easier to convince the Indians that farming is the best thing for them. All I can do right now is talk about it. They know about the cattle here, and they're a little envious. Marcus has talked to Tilokaikt and he's in favor of the idea. If your people want to join us, they're welcome. Many hands make light work, and all that."

"I don't know. I'll have to talk to the chiefs. The Nez Percé are so proud of their horses, you know. They don't part with them lightly."

"But this will be a good opportunity for them to expand their farming. The meat, the milk, all those things, you know . . ." Gray shrugged.

"I'm aware of the value of cattle, William. I just don't know whether the Nez Percé care what I think. Especially if it means giving up prized possessions to achieve it."

"Well, find out, damn it," Gray snapped. "That's what you're here for."

"Don't tell me my job, Mr. Gray. I know it far better than you."

"Gentlemen," Whitman interrupted, "there's no point in squabbling among ourselves. We understand how difficult it might be, Henry, but William and I thought you should give your people the opportunity to participate. If they choose not to, that's their right. But we didn't want to go ahead without letting you know. That might breed resentment."

Spalding grunted. "There's enough of that to go around as it is," he said. "It seems like everything I do is wrong. And from the rumors I hear, you two aren't faring much better than I am."

"What have you heard?" Whitman seemed concerned. He leaned across the table toward Spalding, who just shrugged his shoulders.

"Nothing specific. Just grumbling. I think they think we're taking too much control of their lives, that's all."

Whitman relaxed a bit. "Of course we are," he said. "But it's for their own good. They should understand that."

"I'll have to let you know," Spalding said. He sipped his coffee noisily, looked embarrassed for a moment, then wiped his lips with his sleeve. "Hot," he said.

"Don't sit on it, Henry," Gray said. "I'll have to leave in ten days to two weeks."

"I can't promise anything. As long as you understand that, I'll do what I can."

"Understood."

Chapter 14 ═══════

Bitterroot Mountains—June 1837

IT WAS A SMALL PARTY. In addition to William Gray,
Henry Spalding had convinced several Nez Percé to
accompany the herd. It had been difficult persuading the Indians to part with horses, but once they
realized that the trip was going to take place and
the Flatheads were going to participate in the ven-
ture, the Nez Percé had reluctantly agreed. Ellis,
the son of a prominent chief, had volunteered to go
along. Two chiefs had also agreed to accompany
the herd, the Hat, named for the dapper top hat
bestowed on him by a trapper at the previous rendezvous, and Blue Cloak. But Tilokaikt had
changed his mind and, following his lead, the rest
of the Cayuse had chosen not to participate.

Gray had left the Spokan country in early April,
traveling with McLeod and his Hudson's Bay men.
Two months later, they reached the Big Hole Basin
on the far side of the mountains. He had made
arrangements to meet the Nez Percé, with their
horses, at the annual Green River rendezvous.
Whitman, feeling insecure, had decided not to
press the Cayuse to participate. Gray had not been
happy when Whitman backed out, but used the dis-

appointment to his advantage by getting permission from the missionary to solicit more mission workers while he was back east.

After stopping with the Flatheads for several days, during which time he tried once more to persuade them to accept him as head of their own mission station, he continued on to the rendezvous. Twice, bands of Blackfeet attacked the small party, but each time the Indians had been driven off with no casualties on either side.

Unused to the terrors of an Indian attack, Gray was beginning to wonder whether he had made the right decision. He resented Whitman's authority and found the minister's rigidity a constant source of irritation. As a subordinate, he had only one avenue of redress open to him, and he took considerable advantage of it. Almost monthly, he had been writing to the Mission Board, complaining about both Whitman and Spalding. He took great pains to sound objective, as if he were concerned solely with the welfare of the two clergymen's Indian charges, but his letters left no doubt that he believed things would be vastly improved were he in charge.

Gray did not get along with the British trappers either, but was unwilling to travel on his own. The previous year, when he had been taken ill, John McLeod, concerned with the rapid approach of winter, had refused to stop his caravan long enough for Gray to recover. Instead he had left Gray behind with one man to tend to him. McLeod had responsibilities far broader than the health of William Gray, but Gray had not forgotten, or forgiven, the slight. But he was not above taking advantage of McLeod's hospitality during the long trek.

At the rendezvous, things were as hectic as they had been the previous year. The trading was fierce, the gambling raucous, and the fistfights frequent. Already, silk had been making inroads into the hatters' trade, and beaver prices were falling. The feverish activity at the rendezvous was perhaps an attempt to forget about the bleak economic future the trappers faced, but whatever its genesis, it did not sit well with the straitlaced Gray. He objected particularly to the heavy drinking and the trade in Indian women, in which wives of convenience were often purchased for a season or two at the cost of a handful of baubles.

Gray arrived two days ahead of the scheduled arrival of the Nez Percé, and made a general nuisance of himself trying to throw cold water on the more objectionable behavior of the drunken mountain men. He made no progress, and succeeded only in arousing contempt for his prissy ways. By the time the Nez Percé arrived, he was more than ready to push on.

The herd was small, no more than a hundred horses, but he had several Flatheads as well as the Nez Percé to help him. There was even a transplanted Iroquois named Big Ignace. But Gray was in a foul mood, and the Nez Percé were getting annoyed with him. He was impatient to be off, and finally convinced the Hat to accompany him with some of the Flatheads. Ellis and Blue Cloak decided not to go with him, choosing instead to stay at the rendezvous awhile longer, then to return home.

McLeod tried to convince him not to be so impetuous. "You don't know anything about the plains Indians," he said. "The herd will slow you

down, and you'll be fair game for Sioux or
Cheyenne war parties. If they find you, the best you
can hope for is losing the herd. At the worst . . ."
McLeod paused for effect, then lifted a forelock of
his bushy hair and drew a finger across his forehead. "You understand what I mean, lad?"

"Nothing will happen," Gray insisted. "White
Owl and Two Snakes tell me they're not afraid of
the Sioux."

"You don't want to pay any attention to that. I
never yet met an Indian who would admit he was
afraid of some other tribe. Wait until Drips and the
others are ready to leave. They'll stay with you all
the way to St. Louis."

"I don't want to wait, Mr. McLeod. I have a long
trip, and I have to get the cattle back before winter.
Every day I wait is a day wasted." He looked
around at the sound of a gunshot, then fixed his
eye on one of the gambling tents from which a
dozen men spilled in a tangled knot of arms and
legs. Another gun went off as one of the onlooking
trappers gave a whoop of celebration, egging the
combatants on.

"You think I like seeing men act like that?" Gray
asked, waving at the brawl in disgust.

"You don't have to like it to put up with it. If it
means keeping your hair in place, you might even
appreciate it a little."

"No. I'm leaving in the morning, at first light."

"Whatever you say," McLeod told him. "It's your
decision, but I think you're making a mistake."

"I appreciate your concern, Mr. McLeod, but I'm
not afraid of responsibility." McLeod shook his head
at Gray's words, but made no further argument.

Instead, he walked uphill to watch the rest of the brawl. Gray watched the big trapper push his way in among the growing crowd, then went back to his tent.

The following morning was bright and sunny, almost perfect weather, with the sky a deep, unclouded blue and a bit of a breeze to ward off the worst of the heat and keep the bugs in motion. As they drove the herd upslope and away from the Green River, Gray refused even to look back. He wanted to pretend that the seething iniquity on the meadows below did not exist.

The first few days went by without incident, allowing Gray the luxury of stewing in his own resentments. He said little to the Indians, despite the fact that Big Ignace, the Hat, and White Owl all spoke some English. For their part, the rest of the Flatheads were content to keep to themselves. The prickly ways of the white missionaries were becoming all too familiar, and it was easier to avoid them than try to guess which of their own actions would be found particularly objectionable that day.

Despite his persistent arguments, Gray had succeeded only in convincing three French Canadian trappers to accompany his little band. But the trappers, too, were none too fond of William Gray. He felt alone, more like a spurned lover than anything else, and as the days wore on he became more and more introverted, often going hours without speaking a word to anyone.

A week out from the rendezvous, Big Ignace called Gray's attention to a cloud of dust to the northeast. It was still quite some distance away, but the Iroquois seemed worried. "Could be Cheyenne," he said. "Or Sioux."

"I doubt it," Gray said. "Besides, it doesn't matter who they are. We're going as fast as we can. If they catch up to us, we'll deal with them if we have to."

Big Ignace shook his head uncertainly. "Could be a big war party, Mr. Gray."

"Could be just a caravan heading to the rendezvous, too."

"Not from that direction, I don't think."

Gray said nothing more and spurred his horse out toward the front of the herd. He could hear Big Ignace shouting to the other Indians. One of the French Canadians moved around the point of the herd and settled in alongside him. "Looks like trouble, Mr. Gray."

"I don't think so. Probably nothing to worry about."

The trapper looked dubious, but shook his head and rejoined his two compatriots.

For more than an hour, the cloud drew closer. With the bright glare of the late-morning sun, it was all but impossible to see anything but a blur of swirling dust at its bottom. Big Ignace twice had tried to convince Gray to leave the horses and make a run for it, but both times the missionary dismissed the Iroquois's concern.

After another twenty minutes, the figures of mounted men swam out of the cloud one by one, then were swept away again before anyone could form a firm impression of who or what they were. But Gray was growing edgy. Able finally to put his own sense of superiority aside and credit the sixth sense of the Iroquois as something more than superstition, he began to think the approaching riders might indeed pose a threat.

As he watched over his left shoulder the cloud began to segment, each of its halves gradually pulling away from the other. It now appeared as if the riders meant to surround them. The dust was thinner now, and Big Ignace came rushing back to Gray once more. "Sioux," he shouted. "Many Sioux."

"They won't bother us," Gray told him, but the Iroquois was not so easily persuaded.

"They want the horses, I think," Ignace said.

"They won't get them," Gray said "I'll be damned if they do."

By now there was no doubt. Each band was composed of better than twenty warriors, possibly twice that many. The swirling clouds of dust still made it difficult to determine much with precision. One band of the Sioux picked up its pace and angled to a point ahead of the herd while the other swung around behind White Owl, the drag rider of the moment.

A volley of gunshots exploded from the Sioux war party to the front of the herd, plumes of whitish-gray gunsmoke spurting into the beige dust and gradually mingling with the darker haze. "We'd better stop," one of the Canadians yelled.

"Run for it," Gray shouted back. "Leave the horses!"

They broke away then, swinging to the south in an effort to get ahead of the foremost of the two Sioux bands. There was little cover close at hand, but a couple of miles to the southwest, a shallow ravine studded with outcroppings of rock offered some shelter, maybe enough to hold off the Sioux, if they could manage to make it that far.

Gray was terrified now. He knew that no matter

what happened from here on out, he had lost the horses. He would return home empty-handed, if he lived to return at all. The Flatheads rode well, better than Gray and the trappers, and they were soon out in front. They reached the edge of the shallow ravine a good two hundred yards ahead of the whites.

So far, the only gunfire had been intended as a warning, but as Gray neared the ravine gouts of dirt started spouting up all around him, and he realized the Sioux were now shooting in earnest.

The Flatheads, under the direction of White Owl, had drawn their rifles and were sniping at the charging Sioux. The sporadic fire slowed the charge long enough for Gray and the others to reach cover, but did not stop it. The two groups of Sioux now merged into a single mass, staying just outside of rifle range and spreading out in a long, single line, as if to impress on the small party of hostlers just how severely the odds were stacked against them.

A solitary figure dismounted and started toward them, still wreathed in the dust kicked up by the Sioux ponies. The man took his time and appeared to be unarmed. He drifted toward them, his feet wrapped in the settling dust cloud, making it appear as if he were gliding along on the cloud itself rather than walking. When he was close enough to be heard clearly, he shouted, "Hello, Americans."

"What do you want?" Gray shouted back.

The man had a thick French accent, but he could still be understood. "Why don't you surrender to the Indians. They mean you no harm."

"What do they want?"

The Frenchman waved for Gray to come out and talk to him. Gray hesitated, but one of the trappers gave him a shove. "Talk to him, Mr. Gray. It's our best chance."

"Come with me," Gray said, scrambling up over the lip of the ravine.

The trappers shrugged and started out of the ravine after him. The four men approached the Frenchman, their weapons held at the ready.

"What do you want?" Gray asked for the third time.

"Not me, monsieur. The Sioux. They do not mean to harm you."

"Then what?"

The Frenchman cocked his head. "They want your friends, monsieur."

"What do you mean?"

"They have no quarrel with white men. Look at me. They have not harmed me, have they?"

"But I can't. . . ."

"You must, monsieur. Just walk past me and keep on walking. Nothing will happen to you. I promise."

Gray was trembling now. The thought of abandoning the Indians appalled him. "I . . ."

The Frenchman pressed him. "Monsieur, do you want to live or would you prefer to die with your friends? That would be quite noble but useless, no?"

Gray put his head down. He raised his eyes slowly, stared for a long moment into the Frenchman's eyes, then nodded. "All right," he said, his voice breaking despite its hoarse whisper.

The Frenchman turned, waved a hand, and the air was shredded by a bloodcurdling howl. The Sioux ponies broke into a full gallop, thundering past Gray and the French Canadians on both sides.

Gunfire erupted from the ravine, but the Sioux thundered on. Volley after volley of rifle fire crackled, and the Sioux screeched and howled, their war cries blurring into one monstrous shriek.

William Gray sank to his knees, looked bleakly at the Frenchman for a moment, hoping for sympathy. But all he saw was contempt. Gray leaned over then, and threw up. The Frenchman spat, turned on his heel, and walked away.

Chapter 15 ═══════

Lapwai—Summer 1837

HENRY SPALDING WAS UP EARLY. Outside, he could already hear the sound of hammers as the work crew continued laying the floor of the mill. He was working harder than he'd ever worked in his life, harder, in fact, than he ever thought he would have to. His shoulders ached, his calves felt as if they had turned to stone, and his back seemed to have been set on fire. But he couldn't stop, not now. He had come so far, and the Nez Percé were starting to come around. It was slow, even painful progress, but it was progress all the same.

He poured fresh water into a pan, picked up the brown soap in his cramped fingers, and scrubbed his face and neck, then soaped his arms and hands. He had his eyes closed and was groping for the pitcher of water to rinse off when someone rapped on the door. Eliza was still asleep, and he felt around for a towel, wiped the soap from his eyes, and still blinking away the fire, clomped to the door.

When it swung open, William Craig stood there, a cigarette clamped in the corner of his mouth, as usual. Unlike the other whites in the area, especially those who worked for Spalding, Craig didn't feel the need to take off his hat when addressing the minister. There was a certain contempt in his treatment of the Spaldings, one that got Henry's back up, but he was a valuable asset at Lapwai because the Indians trusted him and because he spoke their language, so after several attempts to improve his manners, the minister had decided to let Craig be himself, warts and all.

"Mr. Craig," Spalding said. "Good morning. What can I do for you?"

"Someone here wants to talk to you, Mr. Spalding." Craig moved to one side and a handsome Nez Percé warrior, somewhere in his late thirties or thereabouts, stepped sideways into view. "His name's Tu-eka-kas, Mr. Spalding. He has pretty good English and he has a few questions. I told him you were busy, but he made me bring him over at least for an introduction."

Spalding pushed the screen door open and stepped outside, still holding the soap-smeared towel in his left hand. The Nez Percé nodded his head then reached out to shake Spalding's hand. The minister started to respond, realized his hands were still soapy, and wiped the palm of his right hand on his trousers before taking the Indian's hand in his own.

"Tu-eka-kas, I'm pleased to meet you," Spalding said. "What can I do for you?"

"I have many things to talk to you about. I was a boy when the Bostons first came to my people."

"He means Lewis and Clark, Henry," Craig said.

The Indian nodded agreement. "Yes. Mr. Clark was a good man. Mr. Lewis was a good man, too. I knew them both. They stayed in my village when I was a boy, maybe eight or nine years old."

"I see."

"Yes, and Mr. Clark had a book. He showed it to Twisted Hair, who was in charge of the village because Broken Arm was away in the south. I saw the book myself. I have learned many things from the book, and I have heard the one you call Spokan Garry preach many times. I, too, would like to be a preacher, but there is much I have to learn."

Spalding nodded, as if to encourage the man, but it was the manner of a man humoring a child. The very idea that this near savage could learn to preach from the Bible struck him as a pipe dream. He had heard a great deal about Spokan Garry, and he and Marcus Whitman had made a special trip to the Spokan country to hear him preach at a week-long gathering. Garry was eloquent, there was no denying it, but his grasp of the fundamentals of Christianity was shaky at best. That he had considerable influence, and a great many followers, was beyond doubt. Whether they were learning the essence of Christianity was far less certain.

And here, apparently, came another who would follow in Spokan Garry's footsteps. Probably wanted influence among his people, Spalding thought. That, after all, is what they all want, it seemed.

Tu-eka-kas waited patiently on the porch and Spalding had to shake himself before responding. "Well, yes, I think that would be a good idea, Tu-eka-kas. But you have to understand that there is a great deal of study that must be done before one can preach."

"I understand. I have already started to study, but I know there is much more that I have to learn.

But I want to learn, and I think that is the most important thing, is it not?"

"Oh, absolutely," Spalding said. "Have you been to any of our prayer services? We have them daily, and special services on Sundays."

"Yes, I have been many times. But the teaching is going slowly. I will be an old man before you get to the end of the Heavenly Book. I wanted to ask if there was some way I could study more quickly."

"Of course, of course, there is. I just, I . . . well, your request has come as a bit of a surprise. I'll have to think about it, and see what I can devise."

"Very good. Then I would like to come here to the mission with my family. I will work on the mill, or help in any other way I can."

"And in exchange you would like special lessons, is that it?"

The Nez Percé nodded. "Is that acceptable?"

Spalding shook his head affirmatively. "Yes, of course. Can you come see me this evening, after we stop work on the mill? We can talk about it more then."

"Yes, I can. I have already brought my family, since I have heard many good things about the mission and I knew that you would not turn me away. I will work with William today, and we will talk tonight."

Before Spalding could reply, Tu-eka-kas turned and left the porch, heading across the clearing to where several Indians were already hard at work on the mill. Spalding watched him go, then turned his attention to the mill itself. In two or three days, they would be ready to begin framing the walls. Work was progressing even more splendidly than he had thought, and he had to admit that William Craig deserved much of the credit for the speedy construction.

"You treat that man well, Mr. Spalding. He's not just any Indian. He's a chief."

"Oh really?"

"Yes, sir, and not just any chief, neither. He's one of the most respected men, not just in his own village, but all over the basin. The Cayuse know him, too. He's related to them by marriage. One of his wives is a Cayuse."

"I don't need to be told my business, Mr. Craig."

"I wish I could believe that, Henry. Fact is, you don't know half about these Indians you think you do, and what you think you know ain't half what you ought to know."

"And I suppose you know all of that and more."

"I do indeed," Craig said, smiling. "I spent years up here trappin', and I've lived with 'em for years. My wife's a Nez Percé, as I suppose you know."

"Yes, I do, although as I understand it, that marriage has never been sanctioned by the church."

"Me and my wife don't need nobody to tell us we're married. We already know it. That's what counts."

"Well, I suppose if that's what you believe, then we have nothing to discuss on the matter. I'll see you later, then, Mr. Craig. I'll be out as soon as I finish cleaning up."

"Better move your butt, Henry. It's gonna be a hot day. We got a lot to do before—"

But Spalding, irritated by the profanity, mild as it might have been, turned and went back inside while Craig was still speaking. He closed the door, peered through the glass at the exasperated man, who backed down the steps shaking his head, then shuffled across the clearing toward the foundation of the mill. Spalding went back to his toilet, wondering about the man who'd come to see him. There was a certain confidence, even power the man exuded. It came, Spalding supposed, from being a chief. If people respected you, it just naturally seemed that you felt better about yourself. He wished he was capable of that sort of confidence. It would come someday, he was sure. But he wished it could be sooner rather than later.

Back at the makeshift washstand, he poured water on the now sticky film of half-dried lather, wiped his arms free of the soap, then poured a full pitcher over his head and shoulders to rinse the rest off.

Drying his hands on the towel, he looked at them, at the calluses on his palms and fingers. They seemed to him like scars from a battle that only he knew he was fighting. He tried to imagine shaking hands with a member of the Mission Board, and what it would be like to squeeze a hand as soft and vulnerable as his own hand used to be. For a moment he allowed himself to take pleasure in the thought, then pushed it away, knowing it was unbecoming, but still relishing it even as it faded into the background.

Outside, he walked quickly, snapping his suspenders in place over his shoulders. He thought for a moment of Eliza, still sleeping, and how she would get up soon and start to make her paintings of scenes from the Bible. He used these illustrations in his prayer services, a way to make the elusive concepts of the Bible more real to the childlike congregation, make them see things they couldn't quite understand.

At the mill, nearly a dozen Indians were working on laying the thick planks of the floor. Some of the Nez Percé refused to help, claiming that building structures was woman's work. But the timbers of the mill were too heavy for all but the strongest of the women, and a few of the men had overcome their initial resistance to pitch in. He knew it was a sacrifice for them, one they made reluctantly, but it was a difficult thing for him to appreciate.

Craig was directing several more Nez Percé sawing additional planks. Craig had the respect of the men who worked with him and seemed to get along with them much better than the minister himself could manage. It was easy, though, Spalding thought, to get along with people when you took their side, as Craig almost always did.

The labor went smoothly, if a little more slowly than the impatient cleric would have liked. He wanted everything done by the time of the grain harvest in September. They would probably make it, but it would be a close call. Not that there was all that much grain this year. But the reality of the mission was sinking in only slowly, and Spalding wanted to work miracles. He had started to identify with the mission in a way that his wife said was unhealthy. Eliza thought he was seeing himself too much in the progress of the constructions. A failure to finish on time was something he would not permit himself to accept. But he pushed the Nez Percé too hard, she thought, and told him so. Spalding thought it was the foolishness of a woman who didn't understand that discipline was paramount.

Let them do things their own way, he said, and they will walk all over you. Once that happens, the mission would be doomed. They might as well pack up and go back to New York.

Spalding worked as hard as anyone and was not afraid to get his hands dirty. The Indians recognized this, and respected it, although they found the cleric too stiff and unyielding, too humorless for their taste. They liked Eliza much better, because she seemed to take more trouble understanding their ways. Just as Craig did.

It was nearly two o'clock before Spalding quit for lunch. He had been working for nearly five hours by that point, and the midday sun was relentless. Driving one final nail in the last available floorboard, he laid his hammer down. It was time for lunch, and afterward more boards would be ready, because the crews on the saws were already back from their meal and starting to hack at several more boards, shaping them to Spalding's specifications, under Craig's watchful eye.

Dropping off the floor to the ground at one end of the building, he saw several horses being driven down through the meadow behind his house, and squinted against the bright sun to identify the riders behind them.

The wranglers were Indians, he could see that much, but not who they were. One of them detached himself from the herd and rode slowly across the bottom of the meadow toward the mission. Several of the work crew shouted and started to gather in the clearing, chattering among themselves.

"It's Ellis," one of them said. "He's come back."

Spalding knew that couldn't be. Ellis was well on

the way to St. Louis with William Gray. And those were horses, not cattle. He wiped his brow with a dirty rag and pushed his way through the gathering crowd. People were coming down from several of the outlying villages as word spread quickly.

And by the time he reached the front of the assembly, Spalding realized the man had been correct. It *was* Ellis. As the young chief's son dropped from horseback, Spalding rushed at him. "What are you *doing* here?" he demanded.

Ellis, taken aback by the assault, stepped back a pace or two. "I live here," he said.

"But where are the cattle? Why have you brought the horses back?"

"I changed my mind. I didn't want to go with Mr. Gray, so I came home."

"But you can't. You have to. . . ."

"No, Dr. Spalding, I don't have to do anything. These horses belong to my people. If I don't wish to trade them for your cows, I don't have to do it."

Spalding was nearly apoplectic. Another of the herders rode up and dismounted hurriedly. Spalding recognized Blue Cloak, and spluttered, "You too? Why I ought to . . ." He stepped forward and grabbed Ellis by the arm.

The young chief pulled free. "Don't do that," he said. His voice was restrained, the veneer of politeness barely concealing the anger beneath it. "Don't touch me," he said again. "You don't tell me what to do."

"The hell I don't," Spalding shouted. "I run this mission. I tell you what to do. You don't tell me. I tell you, do you understand?"

Ellis shook his head. "No, I don't understand,

Dr. Spalding. I don't understand at all. What right do you have to tell another man what to do with his property? Where is this written in your holy book? Show me the words."

Spalding turned on his heel and charged toward his house. The Indians talked excitedly among themselves, the stay-at-homes crowding around Ellis and Blue Cloak, besieging them with a hundred questions, each shouted louder than the last. The noise was such that none of them noticed Spalding rushing back. William Craig, sensing that something out of the ordinary was about to occur, shoved his way through the throng and reached Ellis just as Spalding burst through the last ring around the chiefs.

Spalding held a whip in his left hand, his knuckles clenched whitely around its handle. He moved toward Ellis, and Craig intercepted him. "I wouldn't do that, Mr. Spalding."

"Mind your own business, Craig," Spalding snarled. "Get out of my way." He tried to pull free, but Craig refused to let go of his arm.

"Let him go, William," Ellis said.

Craig nodded. "All right." He shoved Spalding away from him, and the smaller man stumbled and fell to one knee. Ellis stepped close to him, reached down, and helped him up.

"Are you going to whip me?" Ellis asked.

"No, not me. I don't whip people. I command others to whip those who need whipping." The minister turned to the crowd, now beginning to back away from its center, leaving Ellis and Blue Cloak with Craig and Spalding, the knot of them like Saturn surrounded by its rings. Spalding rushed toward the onlookers, thrust the whip at one of the taller men, and said, "Here, you whip him. Whip them both. Fifty lashes."

The warrior, repelled by the thought, backed away. Spalding turned to another. "Here," he commanded, "you do it. Whip them! Do as I say!"

Ellis stepped toward the minister. "Is this the way your God does things, Mr. Spalding? You want me whipped, then do it yourself. Don't ask others to do your work for you." He stripped off his shirt and turned his back to Spalding. "Go on, do it!"

Spalding held the whip. He trembled like a frightened child, but it was rage, not fear, that made him shiver.

"Mr. Spalding," Craig started, "I don't think—"

"I told you to mind your own business, Craig."

One of the warriors in the crowd stepped forward. In his hand was one of Eliza's watercolors. It showed an angry God pointing to a captive and, between them, a young man with a rod in his fist. "This is how it is with your God," Ellis said, snatching the painting and shoving it under Spalding's nose. "Your God does not whip, and you say you are in the place of your God. But I think your God is behind you and so *you* should do the whipping. Or you are a liar, and your pictures lie and your book lies."

"I don't . . ."

"Then whip me yourself," Ellis taunted. "Do it! Do it!" Once more, the young chief turned his back to the minister. Spalding, still beside himself with anger and realizing that the logic Ellis had used was inescapable, snarled as he backed up. He brought the whip high overhead then brought it down hard on the chief's naked shoulders. The whip rose and again it came down. In the silence, everyone heard the whistle of the lash as it descended. Again and again. Ellis grunted, but refused to cry out.

Again and again, Spalding raised and lowered the whip. Instead of backing away from his rage, he seemed to wallow in it, trying harder with each stroke, as if he was determined to make the chief succumb.

The Indians slowly backed away as the whipping continued. And at the end, only Craig was still there. Spalding dropped to one knee, his cheeks red with the exertion, tears of frustration streaking the dust on his face. Craig stepped forward to take the lash from the clenched fist. Spalding's fingers were cramped around the handle, the knuckles still bone white, and Craig had to pry them away from the grip.

Spalding looked up at Craig, his face blank, his eyes bulging. His lower lip trembled and his nose was running. He wiped the back of his right hand, its crabbed fingers stiff and crooked as the claw of a dead chicken, and when he brought it down, a string of glistening snot trailed through the sweat-darkened dust like the track of an invisible snail.

Ellis turned to look at the minister. His jaw was clenched so tightly that knots of muscle bulged at the hinge on either side, almost as white as Spalding's knuckles. But he said nothing, and walked off dragging his shirt in the dust.

One of the onlookers detached himself from the crowd and knelt beside the minister. Spalding looked at him but didn't seem to recognize him.

"This is not the right thing," he said, and Spalding nodded dumbly. "This is something that your book does not talk about. This is not something you can do with us. We do not tell each other what to do. We are free men, Dr. Spalding. Do you understand? We think for ourselves. We make our own decisions. This is a bad thing you have done."

Spalding nodded again, but his eyes were glazed, the eyes of a dead man who hadn't yet fallen over. The Indian helped the minister to his feet. "I will take you home," he said.

"Tu-eka-kas," Craig said, "maybe you should let me do that."

"No, I will do it, William. I have to explain to Dr. Spalding why this cannot be done. He must understand if his teachings are to take root among my people. This is a bad thing he has done."

"I know that, but I don't think there is any way you can make him see it. If he don't know it by now, he never will know it."

"No. He can learn this thing. I can teach him this, just as I hope he can teach me many things about his heavenly father."

"I got a feeling you'd be a damn sight better off, Tu-eka-kas, if you didn't know as much as you already do. You've just seen the Gospel according to Henry Spalding, and it wasn't a very pretty sight."

The Nez Percé nodded, but ignored Craig's advice. He straightened, then reached down to lift Spalding to his feet. Draping one of the minister's arms over his shoulder, he started toward the Spalding house.

Craig watched them until they disappeared, then went back to the mill. He sat on one edge of the fin-

ished floor and held a hammer in his lap, looking
at it as if he'd never seen one before. By the time
the sun went down, no one had returned to work
with him. He set the hammer down quietly, wondering if anyone ever would. And wondering, too,
if it might not be better to put the unfinished mill
to the torch. It would save Spalding a lot of grief in
the long run and, more important, it would save a
way of life for the Nez Percé. He just knew that it
wouldn't save it for very long.

Dropping to the ground, he walked along Lapwai
Creek, listening to the water lap against the stones.
Just before rounding a bend in the creek, he turned
to look at the Spalding house. Through a lighted
window, he saw the minister, his head in his
hands, sitting at a table. Across from him, Tu-eka-
kas was reading. The book in his hands appeared to
be Spalding's Bible.

Chapter 16 ═══════════

Waiilatpu—1839

THE FERTILE SOIL of the Clearwater Basin's sheltered valleys seemed to grow more than camas roots and wild berries. It proved to breed trouble for the stiff-necked Henry Spalding and Marcus Whitman, and men of the cloth seemed almost as rampant as bunchgrass in the meadows and salmon in the rivers.

Cushing Eells and his wife, Lucinda, as well as Elkanah and Susan Walker, had come west at Whitman's urging, sent like Whitman himself by the Mission Board. They had started with the Whitmans at Waiilatpu, then moved on to Tshimakain when the Spokan Indians requested they have white missionaries of their own. Neither couple got on well with the Whitmans or the Spaldings, and it was beginning to look to some of the more skeptical Nez Percé as if all of the white man's talk about loving one's neighbor was little more than that, and talk not to be taken any too seriously, either.

But Spalding had drawn the worst hand in Asa Smith and his wife, Sarah. Like Gray, Smith was an inveterate letter writer, and most were directed to the Mission Board, an endless stream of complaints about Spalding's handling of the Nez Percé, his inability to understand the customs of the people he was meant to serve, and the profound lack of respect with which both Spalding and Whitman were regarded by their charges. Much of the character assassination in the letters was reasonably accurate. But Reverend Smith neglected one small matter in his complaints, namely, that he had even less understanding of the Nez Percé and their customs, and was even more ill-suited to be their salvation than was the rigid Dr. Spalding.

At a gathering in March of 1839, Spalding pleaded the case of Tu-eka-kas and Tamootsin. The chiefs had continued to study Christianity with Spalding, often spending weeks at a time at Lapwai for intensive instruction. They were earnest and sincere, and to Spalding they seemed ripe for conversion and formal acceptance into the faith.

But Eells was opposed, as were Walker and, most vehemently, Asa Smith.

"Look, Asa," Spalding argued. "Do you know how many Nez Percé have been baptized in the last two years?" Smith remained silent, and Spalding pressed his assault. "Do you, or not?"

Smith shook his head. "No, I don't."

"I didn't think so, but I'll be happy to tell you—precisely two. And both of them were young girls. Both of them were dying at the time. They have since died, of course. That represents a net gain of Christian souls of exactly zero. None, Asa, not a single one. That's not acceptable."

"These people aren't ready. They're still savages, Henry. They don't understand the simplest tenets of the faith, let alone everything they ought to know before they can dream of being baptized. You don't just throw water on someone and make them a Christian. It's more complicated than that. I've studied for years, both at seminary and on my own, and I'm still amazed by how much more there is to learn after all that work and all those years. And you want to make these savages Christians by waving a magic wand. But it won't do. And I can't sanction it."

"What about Tu-eka-kas and Tamootsin? You've met them both. You've talked with them. You've seen how earnest they are in their studies, their attendance at services. Surely they're ready."

"No, they're not. They are devoted, I don't doubt that. But devotion is not enough."

Spalding's temper was beginning to fray at the edges. He slammed his fist on the table, and the Bible at the center of the rude table leaped into the air. "What in heaven's name must these people do before you'll be willing to accept them?"

Smith smiled, raising one eyebrow before answering. "It's very simple, Henry. They must demonstrate an acceptable degree of understanding. These men haven't done that; they've done nothing close to it. Why, they still walk around half-naked, dripping beads and feathers. That's just not enough evidence for me, I'm afraid."

Spalding turned to Whitman. "Marcus, help me convince him, please. I know you can't agree with Asa. And you know Tu-eka-kas better than he does, and longer, too."

Whitman shrugged. "It's not something I can just force Asa to accept. You know that, Henry."

"Then maybe we should vote on it," Spalding suggested.

"No, that's ridiculous," Smith said. "It's not a question of majority rule, Henry. You know it isn't."

"I have no objection if we vote," Eells said.

"Nor do I," Whitman added.

"Very well, then," Smith said. "But you already know what my vote is."

Spalding stared at Eells. "Cushing, how do you vote?" he demanded. "Yes or no?"

"I'm afraid I agree with Asa, Henry. I vote no."

"Marcus?" Spalding asked.

"I say yes."

"Very good, Marcus. And I vote yes as well. That makes it two for and two against."

Elkanah Walker hadn't said a word since the discussion began. A quiet man, almost meditative by disposition, he seldom said much, except for his prayer services. Politics, church or otherwise, held no interest for him, and small talk seemed like the devil's work.

"How do you vote, Elkanah?" Spalding asked. "It's up to you."

"No."

Spalding couldn't believe his ears. "But why? We've had more than two thousand Indians through these missions long before you ever left the east. How can you come out here and obstruct our work like this? You're like misers with your approval. But this is not your money. It's God's, and you refuse to spend it. You have no right."

Smith leaned back in his chair, folded his hands, and licked his lips. "Henry, you wanted a vote.

You got what you wanted. It simply didn't turn out the way you wanted it to. You'll have to learn to live with it."

"We are going to lose these Indians, I'm warning you. Already, the Catholics are gaining converts among the Pend Oreille and the Coeur d'Alène. The Nez Percé will be next, unless you stop being so difficult." Spalding pushed back his chair and stomped toward the door, stopping for just a moment to splutter, "This will come to no good end. I'm warning you. All of you."

A moment later, he was gone. Whitman sighed. "Henry's disappointed, but he'll cool off. When he calms down, he'll realize he overreacted."

"I don't care whether he cools off or not," Smith said. "I wish he would surrender the mission. The man's an idiot. He ought to be removed."

"That's uncharitable, Asa. You have no corner on wisdom out here. Henry's made some mistakes, but no more than any of the rest of us. And he's learned a great deal the last few years."

"He doesn't even know the language, Marcus."

"That's not his fault."

"He's not morally culpable, of course, but it certainly demonstrates his lack of fitness for his position. I've a good mind to write the board about it, I don't mind telling you."

"I wish you wouldn't, Asa," Whitman pleaded. "We have troubles enough keeping their support. And, frankly, Henry's got a point. If we can't start demonstrating some progress here, the board might close the missions altogether."

"Then let Spalding do the necessary work. Let him have some genuine progress to show the board." Smith stared at each of the others in turn, his chin jutting out pugnaciously, daring any of them to disagree with him. When no one did, he got to his feet. "This has been a waste of time, and I've a great deal to do at Kamiah. I've got to be getting back."

Later that spring, Spalding tried again, and again was rebuffed. Tu-eka-kas let him know that he was getting disillusioned. It galled the minister to have to tell his most promising potential convert that he wasn't yet fit to be accepted formally into the church.

Marcus Whitman was sympathetic, but sympathy wasn't enough. Spalding wanted Whitman to be more forceful, take the lead and encourage not only Tamootsin and Tu-eka-kas, but others among the Nez Percé who had been zealous and industrious in their pursuit of Christianity.

"We'll lose these people, Marcus. I know we will. It's not like I haven't made mistakes. I have, and I admit it, but this is more than a mistake, it's a misjudgment of colossal dimensions. We are telling these people they are not good enough for us. And I can't explain why, because I don't know why. They are losing respect for me, and for the church. That can't be a good thing."

"Henry, I understand what you're saying, but all I can do is tell you to wait. Asa will come around. He's just being difficult because Tu-eka-kas would be your convert, not his."

"This isn't a competition, Marcus."

"Oh, but you're wrong, Henry. It is a competition. We are in competition with the Catholics, and among ourselves as well."

"Then why are we letting our competitors make the rules?"

Whitman had no answer, but he was not willing to force the issue, and it dragged on for several more months. In late summer Spalding tried once more, riding to Kamiah, where Asa Smith had his mission, but Smith remained uncooperative.

The ride home was long, and Spalding had a good deal of time to think. He dreaded telling Tu-eka-kas yet again that he and his family weren't ready. He turned the problem over and over in his mind, and the last night of the return journey, he stayed up well into the early morning before making up his mind. He had one way out, and he meant to take it. Smith, Eells, and Walker were Congregationalists. They required that a consensus be obtained on any convert before admitting him to the church. But as a Presbyterian, Spalding was not bound by that requirement. The call was his to make, and he determined to make it. He could baptize Tu-eka-kas if he chose, and once he had done so, it was irrevocable. Smith could complain until he was blue in the face, but complain is all he *could* do. He wouldn't be able to undo what Spalding had done.

And in November he got his chance. Tu-eka-kas and his family came to pay one last visit to Lapwai before the winter. After sending word to Whitman, advising him what he proposed to do, Spalding made preparations for the baptism.

On the morning of the seventeenth, a bright, clear, and chilly day, he walked to the edge of Lapwai Creek. Behind him came Tu-eka-kas and his wife, Khapkhaponimi, and Tamootsin and his wife, Tamar.

Wading into the creek up to his waist, he ignored the chilly water. Tu-eka-kas waded out to meet him, and Spalding dipped a pewter cup into the swift current, held it aloft as if to catch the brilliant sunlight, and pouring the water slowly over Tu-eka-kas's head, said, "I baptize thee, Joseph, in the name of the Father and the Son and the Holy Spirit." The chief seemed stunned to have his dream realized at long last, and stood there waist-deep in the creek while Khapkhaponimi was received, Spalding changing her name to Asenoth. Then it was time for Tamootsin, and Tamar. The former he renamed Timothy. Wading out of the creek, his trousers still dripping wet, the minister next performed a double wedding, sanctifying marriages that had already produced two children for Timothy and Tamar and four for Joseph and Asenoth.

A week later, he baptized the six children, giving each of them a Christian name, to the delight of the proud parents. Word eventually reached Asa Smith at Kamiah, but it was long past time for him to do anything about it. For Henry Spalding, it was a great victory, and the first of many. In each of the next two years, Joseph and Asenoth added a son to their family, and Spalding baptized both, this time with no opposition from Asa Smith. The first was christened Ephraim, but everyone insisted on calling him Young Joseph, and the second was Ollakot.

Chapter 17 ═══════════

TENSIONS AMONG THE MISSIONARIES rose and fell like
the tides. Asa Smith continued to agitate for the
removal of Henry Spalding and, when he tired of
the backbiting, implored the Mission Board to send
him to Siam or China. Whitman and Spalding
maintained an uneasy truce, but it was easily and
often broken, more often than not by Spalding's fits
of temper. As much as he believed he was doing
the right thing for the Nez Percé, he was unable to
appreciate the difference between his view of the
world, one steeped in fire and leavened with brim-
stone, and that of the Nez Percé, which placed a
premium on individual integrity.

The friction was not lost on the Cayuse at
Waiilatpu or the Nez Percé at Lapwai. Rumors had
begun to circulate·that the Bostons were no more
than shills for a tide of white immigrants that
would break over the Columbia and Snake river
basins, sweeping all the red men out to sea.
Already, wagon trains were coiling through the
Snake country with increasing frequency, tens and
hundreds each year, and always more the next year
and the year after that.

159

The settlers kept on coming. And the missionaries welcomed the visitors, even those passing through. Every wagonload of whites, no matter how fleeting its passage, relieved the sense of isolation and tempered for a time the siege mentality that kept them on edge. But most of the settlers stopped just long enough to buy supplies from the missionaries and their charges, grain at a dollar a bushel, potatoes at half that price. Ragged cattle and hard-driven horses were exchanged with the Nez Percé and Cayuse herd owners, and the settlers pushed on, leaving the missionaries forlorn once more, and adding more fuel to the fire under the caldron of rumors and resentments that continued to simmer month in and month out.

Some of the rumors were being spread by the mountain men, who had gravitated to the missions to settle and even sometimes to find work. Once the demand for beaver hats petered out entirely, the need being filled now by silk, which was cheaper and more durable, the fur trade was all but dead.

Most of the former trappers had Indian wives, and what ties of family they felt were to the Indians. If anything, they were even more skeptical of the missionaries, and all too familiar with white ways. They had seen what had happened in the east as tribe after tribe had been pushed off its land, shoved westward and southward. And they knew that promises from the government weren't worth the paper they had been written on, if anyone even bothered to record them.

Dislocated Indians, too, brought their own distaste to the mix. Mostly Delawares and Iroquois, they had lived through one upheaval after another as they were uprooted from their original home along the Delaware River and in New York and Pennsylvania, then pushed to Ohio, and when that wasn't far enough west, all the way to Missouri. Tales of the Cherokee, Choctaw, and Creek, too, were common knowledge, as was the barren wasteland they had been given in exchange for the mountain forests of the East Coast.

The discontent had already led to clashes between whites and Indians in the fertile valleys west of the Cascades. Word filtered back, sometimes distorted, about the military suppression of the Indians, and the people at Waiilatpu and Lapwai were getting restless. Even Joseph and Timothy were not immune to the suspicions.

To make matters worse, the whites could not agree among themselves to whom the Columbia River Basin belonged, but the British were increasingly inclined to cede much of it to the Americans. All that remained was to agree on the northern boundary of the territory. Dr. Elijah White, an erstwhile minister who would have preferred to be governor of the new territory, when and if it were formally defined, had managed after nearly three years of petitions, manipulation, and incessant string pulling, to get himself appointed Indian subagent for the entire basin.

Concerned about the rumors of unrest, he knew he had to do something to put a lid on the pressure cooker. Convinced that the Nez Percé was the most tractable tribe in his territory, he gathered a small band of armed men and set out for Lapwai from the Willamette Valley, a land already full of whites from the east who had started to build towns and establish commercial ties to the states.

He reached Lapwai on December 9, just in time to find an ominous gathering of Nez Percé already beginning to surround the Spalding mission. Marcus Whitman had gone back to Boston to try to persuade the Mission Board to send him more help and to arrange for more settlers, who, he hoped, would settle around Waiilatpu and Lapwai to provide incontrovertible proof to the Nez Percé and the Cayuse that their resentments were pointless. He felt that the presence of more whites would be an incentive for the Indians to pursue their agricultural endeavors with more zeal than they had so far demonstrated.

Narcissa had been frightened half to death one night in late November when she awoke to find a painted warrior in her bedroom. Her screams had chased the intruder, but she had run for Fort Vancouver and agreed to accompany Elijah White on his trip to Lapwai.

White was industrious in his efforts and managed to get representatives of most of the Nez Percé bands, as well as from the Cayuse, Umatilla, and other tribes in the area. He knew what was troubling the Indians, and thought he had the solution. What they needed was a code of laws they could live by, laws that reflected the white man's view of law and order. If the red men were to be civilized, they might as well begin to get used to the strictures of white law.

Unfortunately for White and, ultimately, for the Nez Percé, he knew next to nothing about the people for whom he proposed to play Hammurabi. But he didn't let that stop him.

When he arrived at Lapwai, most of the chiefs were still en route, and it would be two or three days before the impromptu council could begin. But Henry Spalding was delighted to see him.

"I'm glad you've come, Elijah," Spalding said the morning after White's arrival. "I hope you'll be able to do something to lighten our burden."

"That's why I'm here, Henry," White said. "I stopped by Waiilatpu on the way. I was appalled. I don't know how long it's been since Marcus left for Boston, but it might as well have been a century. The place is falling apart."

Spalding shook his head. "The Indians just can't seem to take their responsibilities seriously. No matter how we try to explain things to them, they just don't seem to understand. It's as if they think buildings repair themselves and grain crawls into the mill to lie down between the stones."

"You have to be patient, Henry. They're savages, after all. But we'll make white men out of them yet . . . well, civilized men anyway, just you wait and see. Is there anything particular I ought to know?"

Spalding shook his head. "Not really. If you've seen the mission at Waiilatpu, then . . . I mean, I've tried my best to instill some sort of discipline in them. They've felt the lash, and it seems to work in the short term, but . . ." He shrugged.

"Well, Henry, the thing we have to do is to get them to police themselves. I think we can make that work, if we give it a little time."

"I certainly hope so."

The chiefs started to filter in later that day, sometimes coming alone, sometimes bringing a handful of people from their respective villages.

Two days later, they were all on hand, twenty-two chiefs and several other important men. Two hundred Indians had accompanied their leaders and gathered around the council listening intently as White began to speak.

"I want you all to understand that I have been sent here by the government in Washington," he began. The audience nodded gravely. Washington meant serious business, that much they knew. And if this man before them had come from there, then he was a man to be listened to.

"I know that you have been having your share of problems with white men. And I'll be the first one to admit that there are some rascals in white skins. Make no mistake about it, I don't intend to let any man, red or white, take what belongs to you, to come among you selling whiskey, to harm any single one of you. If any white man causes trouble, I will deal with him, and I promise you that he will trouble you no more. I know it's tempting, when someone does you wrong, to take the law into your own hands and pay him back in kind, but that's not the best way to ensure law and order. There's a better way, and that's the way I want to explain to you all."

The chiefs seemed interested, if not enthusiastic, although some of the skeptics among them sat back silently, determined to be shown actions rather than to accept words alone.

"But at the same time," White continued, "Indians sometimes cause trouble, too. Sometimes they steal from other Indians, sometimes they steal from white men. But that's got to stop. Now! Who's your head chief?"

The sea of blank faces staring at him should have made it clear to White that the question had no meaning for the Indians arrayed before him, but it didn't seem to make an impression on him, and he repeated the question. "Who speaks for all of you? Who is the head chief? Is he here?"

Joseph shook his head. "There is no head chief," he explained. "Each of us is chief in his own village. There is no one above me in my village. And I am above no one who is not in my village."

"You mean to tell me," White asked, unable to conceal his astonishment, "that no one is in charge of you all? There is no final authority?"

Joseph shook his head.

"Well, that's part of your problem right there. We'll have to fix that, and the sooner the better. Joseph, who would you like to see as head chief?"

"No one. Our ways have always worked well in the past. There is no reason to change."

"But you have to."

"Why?"

"Because that's the way it's got to work. If an Indian does wrong, who punishes him?"

"No one punishes him. He has to live with himself, and he is shunned by his family and friends. That is enough. He usually learns."

"What about murder? What about when an Indian kills someone? Do you think that is enough punishment even then?"

"We have never taken a life without reason. We wage war against the Bannock and the Snakes and the Blackfeet, but only when we are forced to. We have never killed a white man. Not since the great captains Lewis and Clark first came to our country.

Even when white men have killed our people, we have not killed whites in revenge."

White seemed confused, as if he didn't quite understand what Joseph was trying to tell him. "I still say you need laws. And to make them work, you need a head chief."

Red Grizzly Bear responded. "I was here when the Great Captains were here. I was a chief then. They gave me a flag of truce, which I have used. They gave me an American flag, which I flew with pride over my village. It seems to me that you are like them. They were good men and I believe that you are also a good man. But this is something new for us, something strange for us to try and understand. We will need to think about it, talk about it among ourselves. Do you mean that there should be a chief over all other chiefs?"

"Yes, that's exactly what I mean."

"Then we will have to discuss this very carefully. I don't know if this is something we can do, even if the Great Father in Washington has sent you to tell us to do this thing. We will talk and we will see."

"You'll have to make up your mind quickly. We should talk tomorrow again."

Red Grizzly Bear nodded. White sighed and thanked the chiefs for their attention, then sat glumly while they went back to their temporary camps.

To Spalding he said, "What do you think, Henry?"

"I think you have to make them understand. It's absolutely essential that they come under discipline. It makes our work here almost impossible the way it is now."

"I'll do what I can, Henry, but . . ." White held his hands out, palms up, to indicate his helplessness.

The chiefs talked half the night, trying to clarify the concept in their own minds. Some even thought that it was an idea that might work. They seemed to think that the Great Father in Washington expected this of them, and that it must be a good thing for them to learn. Some even thought that the head chief might be above the Nez Percé and the Cayuse the same way the Great Father was over the white men.

But by morning, they still had not reached a consensus. Part of the trouble was trying to decide which chief among them was best suited to the position. Some of the Nez Percé had argued for walking out of the council, others for trying to meet White halfway. But few thought the agent's plan was workable.

"Have you decided who should be the head chief?" White asked, when the preliminaries were out of the way and the last wisps of smoke from the peace pipe still lingered in the air.

"No," Joseph said. "This is a very difficult thing you ask of us."

"I know it. I know that, I do. But it has to be done. Unless the white man, unless *I* know who is responsible, how can I help you?"

"We are all responsible," Joseph insisted. "But we know the Great Father means well, and we will try."

"So, who shall it be?"

Joseph shrugged.

White had already made up his own mind. Timothy was too much a creature of the white man.

There was no doubt in his mind that Joseph or
Looking Glass, one of the most accomplished war
chiefs, would be the best selections, but they were
too independent, too likely to make his job harder,
so he pushed for his own choice, the young chief
they called Ellis. Ellis had the respect of the others,
enough at least that they might follow his lead, but
his youth meant that he would be pliable, which,
above all else, was what Elijah White wanted.

"I explained to you yesterday about voting. I
think we should do that now. Until you have elected a head chief, there is nothing else we can
accomplish at this council."

The chiefs were reluctantly agreeable, although
more than a little skeptical. And the first vote
failed to yield a clear majority for any of the likely
candidates. When the votes were tallied, White was
pleased to see that Ellis had received a few,
although he was not the leading candidate. Seeing
his chance, he pushed. "How about Ellis? He seems
a strong and responsible young man. You all know
him. You all respect him. I think he would be a
good choice."

The older chiefs were not so certain, but White
continued to push, and after three more votes, Ellis
was "elected."

"Now that that's done, I think it's important that
you have a code of laws. The white man has one,
and you should have your own. Dr. Spalding and I
have thought long and hard about this matter, and
we have a code that we think will do nicely.
Simple, clear, and comprehensive. Just ten, and
some of you know the commandments, so the number should be comfortable. I'll read them to you."

He began slowly, intoning each of the regulations in a solemn voice. But as he moved through the code the Indians grew uneasy. The first rule was a harsh one, prescribing hanging for "willfully taking a life." Rule number two also prescribed hanging. As White worked his way down the list the assembled chiefs realized that he had also institutionalized the lash, which in the past had just been a product of Spalding's hot temper. But the agent continued to drone on, pausing only for the translation of each law on his list.

When the last of the ten had been translated, he said, "There is one other thing. If an Indian breaks these laws, then it is Indians who will punish him. If a white man breaks the white man's laws, then he shall be reported to me, and shall be punished by me."

His business done, White asked for comment, and when there was none forthcoming, he closed the council, leaving the chiefs to wonder what had just happened. Most expected that things would not change very much and a small number even expressed the belief that things would be better. But the wisest among them, Joseph, Twisted Hair's son Lawyer and the ancient Red Grizzly Bear, knew better. They were left to hope that things would not get as bad as they feared.

Chapter 18 ═══════

ELIJAH WHITE'S CODE OF LAWS proved to be little more than a piece of paper. The individual bands of Nez Percé and Cayuse were too used to their own kind of democracy. A man's behavior was governed as much by the subtle sanctions of tribal living as by fear of punishment. And since the code did not govern the conduct of the white settlers at all, it did nothing to preserve peace in the high country.

Rumors of white abuses, of the coastal and lowland basin tribes being driven from their land and forced to steal to feed themselves, were as constant a flow upland as the current of the Snake was toward the sea.

Ellis was not having much influence as head chief because he was too young for the position and allowed himself to lord it over the other chiefs. His haughtiness offended most of them, and when he tried to use his imagined influence, he simply succeeded in alienating them. But White was safe in the Willamette Valley, and seemed neither to know nor care how effective his innovation was. And his ten commandments yellowed with the paper they had been written on.

Henry Spalding, of course, continued to use the whip, and the discontent of the Indians continued to simmer. Even staunch Christians like Joseph and Timothy and Lawyer, paid little attention to the new ways. They were alien and seemed to be more trouble than they were worth without a strong and wise leader to see to it that they were enforced.

And when Elijah, the son of the Cayuse chief Peopeo Moxmox, was killed by whites in California, the system broke down altogether. The Indians knew the name of the murderer, and they knew where he was. White was informed of the murder, and of the killer's name and whereabouts. The Indians expected that the killer, Grove Cook, would be tried and hanged. That, after all, was the punishment for willfully taking the life of another. But White had no intention of observing the letter of the law, let alone its spirit. Instead, he wrote letters to the American consul in California, the governor of the Oregon Territory, and nearly anyone else he could think of, trying to postpone the day of judgment in hopes that the Cayuse chief's outrage would subside. It was not, after all, *his* son who had been murdered in cold blood, so there was no harm in waiting. Or so Elijah White seemed to think.

But when all else failed him, White simply let the matter die. Peopeo Moxmox was not so compliant as White had hoped. He called a council and considered raising an army of two thousand Indians, enough, he thought, to kill all the white settlers in the Willamette, and in California. He told the Hudson's Bay Company representative at Fort Vancouver, John McLoughlin, of his plans, and McLoughlin convinced the angry and frustrated chief that such a war would be futile, and might just lead to a war of extermination, not only against

the Cayuse, but against all the upland Indians, and
the chief reluctantly abandoned his plans. But the
fuse was lit, and it was burning slowly down to an
uncertain explosive.

Henry Spalding felt the wrath of the angry
Indians, who surrounded his mission in the middle
of the night. Hearing a noise, he went outside to see
what had caused it and found a small band of
Cayuse stripping the fence rails and uprooting the
posts around his mission. A fire was already burning in the gristmill, and a second was started to
accommodate the fence timbers.

When Spalding protested, he was hurled into the
flames himself. His heavy buffalo robe saved him
from harm, but he was frightened almost out of his
wits. For days, his nostrils were full of the stench
of singed buffalo hair, and he took to carrying a gun
wherever he went on the mission lands.

Spalding sensed that the Indians were slipping
away from him, and didn't know what to do. Even
Joseph and Timothy seemed to feel a sudden
reserve. They still attended services, still sang
hymns, and still attended Bible study classes. But
their enthusiasm was almost gone.

Marcus Whitman, back from Boston, was finding
the same sort of erosion at Waiilatpu. It seemed to
him that the Cáyuse were sullen most of the time,
and he was at a loss how to stop the bleeding. And
the steady rumble of wagon wheels was like an
ominous, muttering thunder filling the valleys.

Most of the Nez Percé were still friendly, but
there was a certain reticence about them. They still
traded with the immigrants, and there had been no
bloodshed, but more and more of the Nez Percé were

coming to believe that they would be better off if the whites would stop coming and better off still if those who had already come would simply go away.

· But not only wouldn't they go away, they kept coming in ever greater numbers, fifteen hundred one year, two thousand the next, and three thousand the year after that. It seemed to the Nez Percé as if there was an endless supply of white men, few of whom reminded them of William Clark. Unlike the Captain, the newcomers were greedy and intolerant, and instead of gifts, they brought bad habits and disease.

In 1847, a particularly virulent epidemic of measles broke out among the Cayuse, and before it was over, it had killed nearly a third of the tribe. There was no treatment for the illness, and even the Heavenly Book of Joseph and Timothy was useless to stem the tide of pestilence. Nor was it lost on the Indians that the missionaries were powerless to help them.

The list of grievances was almost endless: whippings from Spalding, measles, stolen horses, murder, expropriated land, whiskey, and insults added to the unending skein of injuries. The frustration and impotence finally boiled over in November 1847.

The Cayuse chief Tilokaikt, weary of dealing with the intolerance of the Whitmans and the Spaldings, enraged by the loss of family members to the epidemic, and frustrated that there still had been no punishment for the man who murdered Elijah, paid a visit to Marcus Whitman.

He entered the Whitman house at Waiilatpu with a friend, Tomahas, and asked the missionary for some medicine for the measles. Frightened and uneasy, Whitman turned away for a moment to buy some time, and Tomahas seized the instant to attack. He struck Whitman in the head with a tomahawk.

Stunned, the missionary turned. "Why did you do that? What's wrong with you?" Tomahas raised the tomahawk and hit the missionary again, this time catching him on the arm as he tried to ward off the blow. The blade opened an ugly gash in Whitman's hand, and Tomahas, frightened by the blood, hit him again and again, landing two sharp blows on Whitman's face, laying open his cheek until the white bone showed through.

Together, the two Cayuse dragged Whitman outside. Other Indians, suddenly galvanized by what had happened, attacked the mission buildings with guns, knives, and bows and arrows. Marcus Whitman was shot, and when Narcissa ran to help him, she was shot as well.

The mission exploded then. Narcissa was dragged through the mud, shot several more times, and stabbed repeatedly by enraged Cayuse warriors. The other whites spilled out of the buildings, terrified by the uproar and unaware of what was happening. Some tried to fight and others ran for their lives. But neither group was spared.

When their fury had been spent, the attackers rounded up all the surviving whites, nearly fifty of them, and imprisoned them in the main building. Bodies, fifteen in all, were strewn around the grounds, hacked and bloodied by the enraged Cayuses and left in the mud.

Messengers were sent to the Cayuse villages, telling the people what had happened, and hoping to stir up a general uprising against all whites in the Clearwater and Snake valleys. The Nez Percé, too, were invited to join the war.

When word reached Lapwai, Henry Spalding was not there. But Joseph and Timothy—knowing that it would not be long before the vengeful Cayuse embarked on a course that would not end until they had slaughtered all the whites they could find, or until the government in the Willamette got word and sent soldiers in to quell the uprising—gathered Eliza Spalding, her children, and the white employees of the Lapwai mission and took them to William Craig's for protection.

When Tilokaikt arrived at Lapwai, he was furious, and confronted Joseph. "Give the white people to me," he said. "I will put an end to the misery they have brought among us."

"You have no idea of the misery you yourself have just brought down upon us," Joseph told him.

"You are an old woman," Tilokaikt shouted. "Give them to me. I will kill them. You can sit here in your lodge and pretend that you are a white man, but I will not harm you. Sooner or later, you will see that what I have done is what had to be done."

"No," Joseph insisted, pointedly testing the string of his bow. "You have done a terrible thing. And it is the Indians who will pay. Not just the Cayuses, but all Indians."

"Your Christian God will help you, if He can." Tilokaikt sneered. "But I don't think I have to fear Him." The young chief thumped his chest. "See, I am still strong. My heart is sound. No thunder comes to shake the earth. No lightning strikes me like an old tree."

"You will be sorry for what you have done,"

Joseph said. "Dr. Whitman was not perfect, but he meant no harm."

"I don't care what he meant. He *did* harm. That is all the whites know how to do is harm. They bring their sickness to us, they take our land, they steal our horses. They even shoot our children. Tu-eka-kas," he said, using Joseph's Indian name, "you have children. Would you want your own sons to die like the son of Peopeo Moxmox? Would you want a white man to take their lives for no reason? And would you then sit on your hands and wait for the white man's law to avenge you?"

"The law is not for vengeance. The law is to make it so vengeance is not necessary."

"But Elijah is still dead, law or no law. What will you do? Will you hold me here?"

Joseph shook his head. "No. You have done a wrong thing, a terrible thing, but it is not my place to judge you. You should look into your own heart and decide what to do."

"What would you have me do?"

"The right thing."

"And what is that?"

"That is for you to decide, Tilokaikt."

The young chief seemed almost embarrassed by Joseph's refusal to berate him. It was as if Tilokaikt wanted to be punished, but could only provoke a fight in order to bring the punishment down on him.

Joseph watched him for a long moment, then said, "You should go. The whites will be safe with me, and if you bring more warriors, I will fight you to keep them safe. It is the only thing I can do."

"I wish I was as sure of myself as you are."

"Just go, Tilokaikt. Better you never come back.

But you should free the prisoners at Waiilatpu. The whites will hold you responsible if anything happens to them. It is too late to undo what you have already done, but you can see that it gets no worse."

Tilokaikt said nothing. He slipped out of the lodge and into the night. Joseph sat there for a long time, staring into the fire. His sons, sensing that something was wrong, sat beside him without speaking.

Absently, Joseph reached out to embrace them, sweeping both boys toward him with his strong arms. Tears rolled down his cheeks, and when one landed on Young Joseph's shoulder, he looked up at his father, started to ask a question, but stopped when the man shook his head.

THE END
1855–1871

Chapter 19 ═══════════

Columbia River Basin—1855

ISAAC STEVENS WAS A MAN in a hurry. Pulling every string he could lay his hands on, he had managed to get himself appointed governor of the newly created Washington Territory. His head was large enough to accommodate more than one hat, so he was also the Indian agent for the territory and an agent, as well, for the railroad, seeking a route through the northwest to the Puget Sound.

Settlers had been flooding the plains and pouring over the mountains and into the rich Columbia River Basin. So far, only isolated pockets of whites had intruded on the Nez Percé country, but that wouldn't last and Stevens knew it. And to make matters worse, the only feasible route for the railroad ran right through the heart of the Nez Percé lands.

After the murders of Marcus and Narcissa Whitman, there had been a war against the Cayuse Indians, fitfully fought, but fought nonetheless, for nearly two years. There had also been trouble between whites and Indians in the valley of the Willamette and in the rich bottomlands west of the Cascade Mountains, where the bulk of the white settlers had chosen to stake their claims. And

Congress was doing its best to encourage additional settlement, by guaranteeing every man the right to three hundred and twenty acres of his own. If he was married, his wife would be entitled to an additional parcel of the same size.

The mountain valleys of the Nez Percé were better suited to raising horses than to farming, but the tide of whites was growing year by year, and sooner or later, Stevens knew, the whites would start to stake their claims east of the Blue Mountains. If his railroad route were to be adopted, he would have to guarantee freedom from Indian attack. The route would have the same difficulty on the plains east of the Bitterroots, and he knew that peace would have to be negotiated hard, and enforced even harder. The Sioux had been pushed westward, and the Crows, Blackfeet, Cheyenne, and Shoshone would have to be dealt with, but it was the Nez Percé that concerned him most.

Traveling with his assistant, Joel Palmer, Stevens made the rounds of the mountain tribes, inviting them to a peace council to take place in late spring. The Umatilla, Cayuse, and Walla Walla were less than enthusiastic about his proposal. The Cayuse in particular were suspicious. They had already fought one war after the Whitman mission had been destroyed, and had been frustrated in their efforts to bring to justice the murderer of Elijah, the son of Peopeo Moxmox, one of the most influential Cayuse chiefs. Although Elijah White had formulated a code of laws, the Indians had seen it enforced in only one direction. The leaders of the Whitman massacre had been hanged, but no one seemed willing to lift a finger to find the man who'd killed the chief's son.

Of all the tribes in the area, it was the Nez Percé who were crucial. Stevens knew they were the largest and most powerful tribe. They had blood ties to most of the other tribes in the area and the most extensive land holdings. If he could get them to sign a treaty, he was certain the other tribes would go along.

In the middle of May, he set out for the designated location, a meadow on Mill Creek in the Walla Walla Valley, no more than six miles from the ruins of the Whitman mission at Waiilatpu. With him was a detachment of riflemen under Major Gabriel Rains, Joel Palmer, now the superintendant of Indian affairs for the territory, and several whites to serve as interpreters, including Marcus Whitman's son, Perrin. Two Catholic priests from the Jesuit mission to the Yakimas also went along.

When Stevens arrived at the council site, it was deserted. He knew that it might take a few days for the Indians to straggle in, and spent the time supervising the construction of two arbors, one of which would serve for the council meeting hall and one as a banquet hall.

On the morning of the fourth day, Charlie Dalton, a sergeant in Rains's command, came galloping across the meadow. He dismounted before his horse had come to a halt and shouted for Rains. "Major, Major, Injuns comin', hundreds of 'em."

Rains ran out of his tent, strapping on his sidearm. "Where are they, Sergeant?"

Dalton pointed up toward the ridge. So far, there was nothing to be seen. But Rains called for Stevens to join him and started walking up the long, gentle slope toward the top of the meadow.

The two men were followed by several soldiers, all nervously clutching their rifles. The small party was almost to the center of the meadow, knee-deep in new grass, when the first Indian broke over the hilltop. The distance was too great for the white men to recognize the mounted warrior, whose horse reared up as he looked back over his shoulder and raised his right arm. Then, as if released from a slingshot, the warrior plunged over the ridge and downhill toward the waiting whites.

Behind him, two abreast, all mounted, came a column of Nez Percé. Their horses thundered down through the grass, hooves pounding, while the riders yipped and howled. As they drew closer it was apparent that horses and men alike had all been painted with streaks of red, white, and yellow.

"War paint, Major," one of the riflemen said.

"Hold steady, boys," Rains barked. He glanced over his shoulder at the men, who were fidgeting restlessly, some on their knees with their rifles almost to their shoulders. "Put up your weapons," Rains snapped. "Now!"

The lead Indian headed straight for Stevens at a full gallop. When he had closed to within a hundred yards, Stevens recognized him. "That's Lawyer," he said. "The head chief."

Lawyer charged on downhill, the column behind him still snaking its way over the ridge. It looked for a moment as if the chief meant to run Stevens down, but he reined in at the last second, clods of dirt and clumps of grass scattering around the feet of the governor and the major. Lawyer then broke into a gallop and led the Nez Percé in a great circle. Around and around they rode, Lawyer closing on the tail rider, the circle turning and turning like a carousel while the warriors raised their bows and lances, rattled their shields, and howled nonstop.

At a signal from Lawyer, they dismounted, and a thunder of drums began as the Indians chanted and some began to dance. Soon all but the drummers were dancing in half a dozen circles as the drums pounded and thundered, and the chanting turned to a dull roar in Stevens's ears.

The demonstration continued for nearly an hour while Stevens, Rains, and the rifle company stood rooted to the spot, as motionless as Lot's wife. The governor had to remind himself to breathe every so often, as he stood transfixed, wondering whether the Indians meant to turn on them and slaughter them all.

Suddenly the drumming stopped. Stevens saw Lawyer in the center of the throng, one hand raised. The chief started to walk toward him, followed by several others. As they drew close their features were distinguishable under the garish smears of paint. He recognized Timothy and Joseph, as well as two other old chiefs, Red Wolf and Big Thunder. Lawyer planted himself directly in front of Stevens. He introduced the others, including several chiefs Stevens had never met.

"We will talk tomorrow," Lawyer said. Then, without another word, the chief turned and walked back to his horse, mounted up, and signaled for the others to do the same. There was another roll of thunder as the horses galloped up and over the ridge, and then were gone.

"What in the hell was that all about?" Rains wondered aloud.

"They want us to know they are not afraid of us," Stevens said. "I only wish I wasn't afraid of them, either."

"That was touch and go," Rains said. "Sergeant Dalton, I want sentries posted tonight."

"Yes, sir."

"You think they're really here to talk?" Rains asked, turning to Stevens.

The governor took a deep breath. "We'll see tomorrow."

"Those were all Nez Percé. Where the hell are the rest of them?"

"Something tells me they're not far away, Major," Stevens said, turning to head back to his tent. "Not far away at all."

The white men spent a restless night. They could hear the sound of drums and chanting all through the night, and when the sun came up, Rains sent a small patrol under Dalton out to scout the surrounding area. The men were back in an hour, their faces masks of apprehension.

"There's thousands of Indians out there," Dalton told his commander. "Not just Nez Percé, neither. Must be five thousand, at least. Warriors, women, children. It looks like every damn Indian from here to Canada showed up."

"And it looks like they're ready to palaver," Rains said, pointing toward the hilltop.

A party of some fifty Indians stood looking down at them, and as if they realized they had been spotted, they started downhill. The original band was followed at some distance by a crowd of several hundred. They swept over the ridge like a human tide, women and children among them, and when the lead party came close enough for its individual members to be recognized, Stevens saw that it consisted of all the chiefs he had met the previous day and twice as many more. Some of them were men he knew, chiefs of the other tribes he had invited to the council. It was time for serious business, and he felt a lump in his throat.

"Sergeant Dalton, would you get Mr. Palmer and the interpreters for me, please? Tell them we're about ready to begin."

The sergeant sprinted toward Palmer's tent, and Stevens turned back to watch the chiefs continue down the hill. He welcomed them with a raised hand, then led them to a rude bench he had set up under one of the arbors. Palmer came running, a portfolio tucked under one arm, and was nearly breathless when he arrived.

"You have everything we need, Joel?" Stevens asked.

Palmer shook his head. "I think so."

"Good, then you sit on the bench with me." He looked at Perrin Whitman then, and asked him to have the chiefs array themselves around the bench.

The chiefs arranged themselves in a huge semicircle with the bench at its focus. The hundreds of other Indians formed a half circle of tiers, rank upon rank. There were a thousand or more, and Stevens sat on the bench watching nervously until the last Indian had taken a seat. He was about to begin, when Lawyer produced a peace pipe, lit it, and passed it around the circle. By the time all the chiefs had smoked and passed the pipe to Stevens and Palmer, nearly an hour had passed. And Stevens couldn't stop the nervous tapping of his foot.

He glanced at it as if it belonged to someone else, then pressed his knee with the flat of one hand. He saw several of the chiefs watching him, and when they realized he saw them, they leaned together to whisper among themselves.

When Palmer had drawn the thick tobacco smoke into his lungs, he handed the pipe back to Lawyer, and Stevens stood up.

"This is a great day," he began, then waited for his words to be translated. The translation was then spread through the crowd by several criers who hastened back and forth after each sentence, making sure that the entire assembly knew everything that was said. It was a tedious process, and one with benefits as well as drawbacks. It allowed Stevens to frame each statement carefully, but it also gave him time to be nervous as he watched his words spread through the crowd and the ripple of reaction after each line was translated.

"I am pleased to see you all here," he said. "It has been a long time since I have seen many of you. But I consider you all my friends, and the Great Father in Washington considers you all his children."

Stevens saw the skeptical looks on several faces, but pushed on. "I am pleased that you have had success in learning some of the ways of the white man. Many of you have learned to farm, some of you are raising cattle as well as the beautiful horses you used to raise, and many of you have been trading with the settlers passing through on their way to the far ocean. But there is much more for you to learn, many skills that you need to master if you are to continue to prosper.

"There are many white people to the east, more

than the grasshoppers that cover the meadows in summer, more than the salmon that fill the rivers, and one day some of these people will come here to live. It is the hope of the Great Father that you and they will be friends. But these things that I said you needed to learn will make it easier for you to be friends. You will have the same skills, speak the same language, worship the same God, and in time to come, even read the same books.

"But it is not always easy for the red man and the white man to get along as friends. In years past, there was trouble between red people and white, and the Great Father, who was Andrew Jackson at that time, helped the red people. He moved them to new lands, where their lives would be easier, lands that were their own, and that to this day are their own."

There was a discontented murmur spreading through the crowd, and Stevens rushed on, trying to explain what he meant without upsetting the Indians any further. "I don't mean that you will all have to move. But you will have to make room for the hundreds and thousands of white people who one day will come to live among you. That means that we must make sure now that you have your land that no one can take from you. The Great Father has given me instructions to make arrangements with you to see that your lands are yours forever, and that there will be room for the white men when they come. But the Great Father does not want just to take your land, he wants to pay you for it. In exchange he will give you schools and gristmills, sawmills, and forges. You will be taught new skills, skills you will need when things change. You will learn to make plows and build houses, learn to read and write, and the Great Father will send money every year, money you can use to acquire other things you will need."

Stevens could hear how strident his voice had become. He was shouting to be heard by those at the very back of the throng, knowing even as he did that they could not understand English. But he was desperate for them to accept what he was saying, and it seemed that if he said it long enough and loud enough, the Indians would have no choice but to accept it.

"You will each have your own land, a place to have your homes and to raise your families. And that land will be yours, and some of the land will be given by the Great Father to his white children. But I am tired of speaking now. I think it would be best if you went to your lodges and thought about the things I have said. Tomorrow we will meet again, and we can talk more and I will get your thoughts."

Chapter 20

Isaac Stevens spoke again the following day, trying somehow to restate his arguments, to make them sound more convincing at least to his own ears. He knew he was not telling the complete truth, and he knew, too, that the Great Father had a rather spotty history of fulfilling his promises, especially to red men.

The Indians were getting restless, and it was apparent that some among them were far from convinced that the treaty was a good thing for them. Kamiakin, a Yakima chief who had relatives in virtually every tribe represented at the council, was the most adamantly opposed. The other chiefs were pressuring him, arguing that they should take the offer before it was withdrawn, but Kamiakin was disturbed by the notion of having tribes thrown together on one reservation, tribes who had their own histories, their own customs, and no matter how friendly their relations with their neighbors, their own sense of how things should be done. If such people were forced to move onto the land of another tribe, how would these differences be reconciled? Would the host nation have to surrender its autonomy to keep the peace? Would the guest nations have to submerge themselves in the customs of their hosts?

The chiefs spent every night arguing among themselves. At one particularly heated conference, Kamiakin lost his temper and threatened to pull out of the council altogether.

"It would be better," he said, "if the Yakima people went to war and fought to keep their lands. Better to die on your own land than to live like a prisoner of the white man."

Skloom, Kamiakin's brother-in-law, was more receptive to the treaty. "These things that Governor Stevens promises are good things. These are things that our people need to live beside the white man. You heard what he said. The whites are thick as grasshoppers. They will swarm over our lands and there will be nothing left for us. But if we sign the treaty, the white man's laws will say, 'This is Indian land. Only Indians may live here. That is white man's land, and only white men may live there.' If a white man comes on our land without our permission, he will be punished by the white man's laws."

"The white man's laws are worth nothing," Kamiakin shouted. "Elijah White came to us and said, 'These will be the laws for the red man and the white man. If a white man harms a red man, the white man's law will punish him. If a red man harms a white man, the red man's law will punish him.' That is what Elijah White said, and we believed him. But when the Cayuse people killed the Whitman missionaries, it was a white man's rope around Tilokaikt's neck. Red Grizzly Bear remembers."

"That was different," Red Grizzly Bear argued. "That was not the kind of thing that Dr. White meant."

Kamiakin snorted. "That is always the way it is.

It is always different when a white man hurts one of us. There is always some reason that the law cannot work to punish him. But there is always rope to hang the red man."

"You have to be patient, Kamiakin," Joseph said. "We have to give the laws time to work. They are not perfect."

Kamiakin stood up and waved his arms. "They are not perfect and they will never be perfect. So long as it is the white man who is in charge, they will not work."

Peopeo Moxmox asked for the floor. "When my son was murdered, the laws were not perfect, and that is many years now, and always when I ask, they tell me no, nothing has been done. I told Elijah White who the murderer is, and White did nothing. They cannot find the man. But they know where he is." He thumped his chest with both fists and said, "*I* know where he is. But if I go to this man and say, 'You have committed a crime, you must be punished,' and I take his life, it is *my* neck that will wear the white man's rope."

Lawyer said, "Peopeo Moxmox is right."

"What would you have us do?" Timothy asked. "Should we all go on the warpath and kill all the whites? You saw what happened when the Cayuse did that. Soldiers came, and there was much killing. Women and children died, not just warriors. And now there are thousands more of the whites. They have more and better guns. They have thousands upon thousands of people. We know this because every year we see the wagon trains. You have been to the Dalles and seen the fort and the soldiers. You have seen soldiers at Fort

Vancouver and Fort Owen and Fort Colville. Soldiers at every one. They have the big cannons that can kill a dozen men at one time."

"Is Timothy afraid?" Kamiakin sneered. "Is Timothy a white man on the inside and red only to the depth of his skin?"

"The Heavenly Book teaches that it is not right to take lives," Joseph said.

"That is the white man's God talking. But when a white man wants to take a life, does he ask permission of his God? Does his God punish him? Is there thunder and lightning and the man who has committed the crime made to vanish? Or does his life go on as always?"

"It goes on as always," Red Grizzly Bear said. It sounded as if he was beginning to be swayed by Kamiakin, either convinced by the chief's logic or bowled over by the fury of its presentation.

"And that is what I want for our people," Kamiakin shouted. "I want life to go on as always. I want to catch fish in the spring and summer. I want to hunt deer in the mountains and raise horses on the high meadows. I want to go where I have always gone and do what I have always done. I don't want to push a plow and raise corn. I want to live in a lodge, not a white man's house. And so do the rest of you, but you're afraid to admit it to yourselves. But I am not afraid."

And so it went, night after night. Stevens talked for two more days, and on the fourth day Joel Palmer made his own argument. Maps were set up showing the lands that would be set aside for the reservations. Joseph was concerned that he not have to give up the Wallowa Valley, where his people had lived as long as he could remember, and once he saw that the Wallowa would be part of the Nez Percé reservation, most of his fears were quelled, though not easily. Many of the Nez Percé chiefs were favorably disposed. Some of the other chiefs thought this was because the Nez Percé were to keep their own land, and more of it than any other tribe. They accused Joseph and Timothy and Lawyer of caring only about their own people at the expense of the others.

Lawyer was the most eager to sign. He had seen what happened to the Cayuse, and he knew that white soldiers had also been skirmishing with the Bannock. He finally stirred himself to say, "Stevens has told us how the Great Father wishes to take care of us. He told us about the tribes in the east, and how they were moved in order to help them. We are more fortunate. We don't have to move."

A Delaware Indian who was attending with the Nez Percé, called Delaware Jim, took issue with Lawyer's optimism. "I know about the tribes being moved. My own people once lived on the Delaware River, almost on the shores of the great eastern ocean. But the whites wanted our land. So they moved us. Then the whites wanted the land they moved us to, so they moved us again. The Cherokee, that Stevens told you about, were treated the same. They gave up rich forests and good hunting and cool mountains for hot, dry wasteland, little better than a desert. And they call it Indian Territory. Their treaties are worthless. If they sign them at all, you will all be old men before you see the money they promise. I know how they honor their treaties."

"You are an outsider," Lawyer snapped. "It is

not for you to tell us how to live our lives."

"Maybe not, but I can tell you that your lives will be worth nothing if you listen to their lies. You will have a reservation only until some white man finds gold, or wants to farm it, or finds some other reason to take it for himself. Stevens tells you that no white men will be allowed on your reservation without your permission, but that is a lie. If someone finds gold, the miners will come like flies on a carcass, and you will not have enough bullets to keep them away. And the law will not help you."

"I say again," Lawyer shouted, getting to his feet, "this is not your business."

"Have it your way," Jim said.

"It is getting late. I think we should sleep, and we will talk to Stevens again in the morning," Lawyer suggested. "Think about what Kamiakin has said. Think about what Joseph has said. Think about what Red Grizzly Bear has said."

"And remember what Delaware Jim has said," the Delaware shouted. "Most of all, think about that."

They returned to their lodges, more to put an end to the talking than to get any genuine sleep, which was all but impossible under the circumstances. Just after sunrise, the criers passed among the lodges and tipis, calling the chiefs to the council once more.

Stevens again brought out the maps and made a summary presentation of his arguments. Then, looking at Palmer for support, he said, "Now it is time for you to tell me what you think."

Lawyer went first. "I think the treaty is a good one. I think there are problems that we must resolve. I am afraid that we are going too fast. There is much to think about and there are many tribes that are not here, even though they will have to move from their lands. It is not right that we speak for them. We should meet again next year."

"There's no time to waste," Stevens argued. "If we don't act now, then everything will change."

Kamiakin exploded. "You want us to sell our lands and we have not had time to consider what it means. People will live on Yakima land who are not Yakima people. That is not right. You should ask them. You should not tell them."

"They were invited," Palmer said. "If they chose not to come, it cannot be helped. You must decide quickly."

Joseph shook his head. "I do not know if this treaty is a good thing. I do not know if I wish to sign this treaty. But I do know that you ask us to sell the land, but the land is not ours to sell. We are the land's, the land is not ours. I was a small boy when Lewis and Clark came from the Great Father. They were good men. Since then, my people have always been friendly to the whites. But now the whites tell me that I cannot live where I want to, and that people who are not my people can live on my people's land. I am troubled by this, very much troubled. I know that the Great Father means no harm. But the Great Father is not here. He will not live with us. I am worried about the white people who will come to live among us. I don't think we know enough yet whether to sign this treaty or not. There are many questions."

"There is no time for questions, Joseph," Stevens said. "I have tried to get the best arrangement for your people that I could get. If you do not sign this treaty, maybe the next treaty will not be so generous."

"I don't want to be threatened," Joseph said. "I am not a small child any longer. I am a man and I know what a man knows. And I know that the earth is our mother and we cannot sell our mother."

A stir went through the crowd gathered behind the council circle, and Stevens looked up to see what had caused it. He spotted a band of warriors on horseback galloping down through the meadow.

"Looking Glass," Kamiakin said. "We should hear what he has to say."

The war chief charged his mount through the crowd heading straight for the arbor. He leaped from the animal and bulled his way to the front of the council circle. "What is this?" Looking Glass shouted. "I go to hunt buffalo and you sell our land behind my back? There is no place for me to build my lodge?"

Joseph tried to calm him. "We will talk," he said. Then, to Stevens: "We need to listen to Looking Glass and tell him our minds. We cannot make a decision now."

Stevens shook his head in frustration. "All right, all right, but you must hurry. We will meet again this afternoon. By then, you must decide. Those who sign will find the treaty honored, those who don't will have to fend for themselves."

The council broke up almost as quickly as a cloud ripped apart by the wind. Looking Glass accompanied Lawyer and Joseph to the Nez Percé lodges, where he listened impatiently as they explained the terms of the treaty.

The old chief was not happy. Nearly seventy, he

had lived long enough to see many changes, but this was one change he was not about to accept without a fight. Lawyer tried to explain why the treaty should be signed, but Looking Glass refused to listen. "I know what I want," he said. "And I will tell Stevens what I want."

When the chiefs returned that afternoon, Stevens was a nervous wreck. He sensed the treaty slipping away, and with it the peace necessary for the railroad and for continuing the flow of white settlers. He offered to read the terms of the treaty, if it would help. He looked to Looking Glass, who nodded that he should go ahead.

Term by term, he read, waiting, as before, for each line to be translated and spread by the criers. When he was finished, Looking Glass asked to see the map. When Stevens spread it on the bench for the old chief to examine, Looking Glass stabbed at the paper with his finger. "This is the land that should be the reservation," he said, proceeding to trace the full extent of the current Nez Percé lands.

"And this should be the Yakima land," Kamiakin said, tracing Yakima country without surrendering an acre. Several other chiefs did the same, showing the governor where they wanted their reservation to be located, and by the time they were finished, the entire territory was earmarked as Indian land.

"No, no, you can't do that," Stevens said. "You can't do that."

"I don't tell white people where to go," Looking Glass snapped. "And if anyone will tell my people where to go, it will be me, not a white man. We should wait and have another council. There is much that has to be discussed."

One of Lawyer's followers said, "We have already discussed everything. It is time to sign the treaty."

But one of the other doubters, Tauitau, said, "Looking Glass is talking. He talks for us."

"I thought we appointed Lawyer head chief," Stevens said.

"We need to discuss this again," Tauitau said.

With that, Looking Glass stalked back to his camp, followed by most of the Nez Percé headmen. They argued among themselves all that night, but Lawyer finally managed to assemble enough support, and the following morning they reconvened at the arbor.

"Are you ready to sign?" Stevens asked.

When no one argued, the governor said, "I now call upon Lawyer to sign. After Lawyer has signed, each of you should sign next to your name. Lawyer?"

Lawyer stepped forward and made his mark. Looking Glass and Joseph were called next. Both chiefs, despite their misgivings, signed. One by one they were called, and not knowing what else to do, one by one they signed away their land . . . and freedom.

Chapter 21 ═══════════════

JOSEPH LEFT THE COUNCIL GROUNDS in the morning, riding ahead of the others with Young Joseph by his side. As Mill Creek fell away behind him the old chief turned to look over his shoulder. At the top of the first ridge, he reined in and pointed down at the arbors and the tents. "Look, Joseph," he said.

His fifteen-year-old son shook his head.

"What do you see?" his father asked.

"Tents, the lodges without walls." The boy shrugged.

"Remember what you see, son. Don't ever forget it. What happened here is something I do not like. And we have not heard the last of it. I did not wish to sign away our lands, so I argued until they were made part of the reservation. But I think it will not be long before the white men come back to us and say, 'We need more land. You did not give us enough. We want you to give us more.' That is what I think will happen. But I will not do it. I will never again sign the white man's paper."

"Why, Father?"

"Because the paper burns, and when it burns, the words are just ashes. But they do not write the words here." And he tapped his chest with the flat of one hand. "They do not write the words on their hearts. We have seen it before, how they tell us something and we listen and we believe and we do what we are asked to do, and they tell us what they will do. But even though we do what we agree to do, they do not. So I think there will be trouble, sooner or later."

"Why do they need the land?" Young Joseph asked.

"They do not need it. They want it. And they don't want our people to live on it even though it is what we have always done. I am getting old and it is important that you learn these things. One day you will take my place in the council, and then you will have to speak for all the Wil-lam-wat-kin people and the words you speak will rattle around among the trees like spirits. They will come back to haunt you the way the ghosts of the dead come back to haunt the living."

The old chief urged his horse into a gallop, and the son was hard-pressed to keep up with him. They made good time, but by nightfall they still had two days' travel ahead of them. Young Joseph made a small fire as they camped for the night. His father said little during the meal, but when they had finished eating, he said, "Now we should talk."

"Talk about what, Father?"

Old Joseph shrugged. "Many things. It is hard to know where to begin, but I have to begin. I remember a long time ago, when the first white men came to our country. I was a small boy, and the first of our people to see them, the captains Clark and Lewis. I ran to get Twisted Hair to tell him what I had seen. I was frightened. Twisted Hair was uncertain about what to do, just as I am uncertain now. Most of the warriors were away, some fighting against the Bannock and some in the buffalo country. I think he was frightened, too, not of the captains, who were good men, but of what would happen in years to come. I understand now why he was frightened."

"You did not have to sign the white man's paper."

"Yes, I did. They threatened us. They said that if we did not sign, they would change things, maybe take the land and give us nothing, maybe take the Wallowa Valley. This way, by signing the paper, at least that land is still ours. But we will have to fight to keep it. Delaware Jim told us at the council how the white man makes treaties then doesn't honor them. We gave them land and they promised to give us things in exchange—churches, schools, mills like the one Dr. Spalding built at Lapwai. These things are good things, and if the white men give them to us . . . we will see." He pressed one hand against his eyes, massaging them with his fingertips. "I am very tired. It is time to sleep, son."

In the morning Old Joseph was anxious to get on the trail. They ate little and spoke not at all. Young Joseph could see that his father was pushing himself, as if he felt some sense of urgency that he could not, or would not, explain. By the time they reached the Wallowa Valley, the sturdy Appaloosa stallions were near exhaustion.

As they rode up over the last ridge above the village, Joseph looked around, then swept an arm across the vista. "This has always been the home of the Wil-lam-wat-kin, Joseph. My father and mother are buried here. Their fathers and mothers are

buried here. We have always lived here, and if I
have anything to say about it, we always will. You
must look at this valley with sharp eyes, see it as it
is now and, when I am gone, keep it this way, as it
always was, and as it always should be."

"I think you are worrying too much, Father. The
treaty will be kept."

"We will see." The old man pushed his mount
onto the downward slope, letting it walk at its own
pace. He kept his eyes on the horizon as if trying to
commit the entire sweeping view to memory. In the
center of the huge valley, the deep blue of Wallowa
Lake reflected the clouds drifting high above.
Along its edges, the water looked green, where
inverted trees and rocks mirrored the shoreline.

When they reached the village two hours later,
the dogs began a furious barking, and people
spilled out of the lodges as word spread that the
chief had returned. They gathered around him as
he dismounted, asking where the others were, why
just the two of them had returned.

"I will tell you about it tonight. Now we have
much work to do," Joseph said. "Get me four or
five axes. Joseph, pick three men and come with
me." Young Joseph looked at the crowd, picking
three men at random. Others pushed to the front
with axes and thrust them at the chief.

Joseph sat on the ground and accepted the axes,
then checked the blades one by one. "This one is
good," he said. "Sharpen this one. And this one."

The warriors selected by the chief's son took the
dull-bladed axes, scurried to find a whetstone, and
returned ten minutes later. The rest of the people
stood by silently, wondering what the chief had in

mind. After several attempts to question him, they realized that he was as good as his word. He would tell them when he was ready, and no amount of pressure would pry anything out of him until then.

Old Joseph stood and handed out the axes, one to his son and to each of the three warriors, keeping the fifth one for himself. He took a whetstone and tucked it into his shirt. "Follow me," he said, starting out of the village. He still explained nothing, even when the village fell away behind him, but walked swiftly, almost mechanically, holding the short-handled ax by its head and thumping his leg with the wooden handle.

Several times he turned to look down on the village, as if trying to find something, the perfect spot.

"What are you doing, Father? What are you looking for?" Young Joseph asked.

"You will see soon enough," the chief told him. He continued up the hill until he reached the crest. Striding toward a stand of small pines, he started to hack away at the limbs. Grunting as he wielded the ax, he instructed Young Joseph and the three warriors to strip more saplings.

They all looked at him for a long moment, but soon set to work, hacking the short limbs off at the trunks until the entire stand of ten trees had been reduced to bare, ruined spires. When the last limb had fallen to the ax, Old Joseph said, "Cut them down," and immediately began to hack through the trunk nearest him just above ground level. One by one the naked trunks were leveled. Grabbing one, the chief hacked the spindly top off then stood the shortened trunk upright and chipped away at one end until it had been sharpened to a point.

This time, without needing instructions, the four men with him followed suit. When they were done, nearly three dozen stakes had been fashioned.

"What are they for?" Gray Fox asked. He scrutinized the chief's face almost as if he expected the answer to be in facial expression rather than words. But he got none at all. Instead, the chief took one of the stakes and drove it into the ground with two dozen fierce blows. Wrapping his fingers around the stake, he tried to move it, but found it solidly planted, and nodded his approval.

Hoisting three or four of the stakes, he propped them on his shoulder and started walking. "Bring as many as you can," he shouted without turning around or breaking stride.

One by one the stakes were driven, and when they were all gone, more were fashioned. These, too, were driven into the ground. By now, the men were working at a rhythm, some fashioning stakes while others sharpened them and the chief drove them into the ground, stake after stake.

It was nearing sundown when Old Joseph finally called a halt. "We will have to come back tomorrow and the next day and the next, until it is all done."

"Until *what* is done? What are we doing?" Young Joseph asked.

The chief sat down on a rock, cradling the ax across his lap, his thumb idly testing the blade's edge. Taking the whetstone from his shirt, he started to restore the edge with swift strokes of the rough stone. The rasp of stone on metal continued for several minutes. When he was satisfied, Old Joseph lowered the ax to the ground. "We are marking the boundaries of our land. You saw the map. You know that this is all included in the reservation. But white men read maps only when they want to. This way we will know and *they* will know that this land belongs to the Wil-lam-wat-kin people. That is what the treaty says, and that is how it will be."

"But that will take a long time," Yellow Bear said. "There is so much land. The boundary is so long."

"I am not so old that I cannot finish. And if we do not do it, the boundary will soon be not so long as it is now. One day it will shrink away to nothing, and squeeze the Wil-lam-wat-kin people out altogether. Do you want to be the last one, Yellow Bear? Do you want to stand and feel the boundary tighten around your ankles until you have no choice but to move off the land or let it cut you off and leave nothing but bloody moccasins behind to show that you have ever been here? Is that what you want?"

"No, I . . ."

"But that is what could happen unless we are vigilant. The white man's paper says this is our land. And *I* say that this is our land. But one day I will be gone. And the paper will be put away in Washington and no one will ever look at it. I have learned to speak the white man's language. I have seen the words on the paper, and I have heard tales of what happens to such words. They put the papers away not because they are valuable, but because they don't want to remember what the words say."

He took Young Joseph's ax then and started to sharpen its blade.

"Shouldn't we go down to the village, Father?" Young Joseph asked.

"No, there is much that I have to tell you. We

will spend the night here. The others will go down to the village and tell them. They will come back tomorrow at sunrise, and we will continue."

"Shall we bring others when we return?" Yellow Bear asked.

"No. We will do it ourselves. I am one man, and I can only drive so many stakes in a day."

"But others can—"

"No!" the chief snapped. "I signed the white man's paper. And I will drive the stakes."

He turned back to the second ax. The three warriors started down the hill as the last blades of sunlight speared out from behind the clouds massed on the western horizon. To the northwest, the Blue Mountains turned black as the edges of the clouds above them caught fire, glowing orange like the edge of a burning paper.

And then it was dark.

Chapter 22 ═══════

Wallowa Valley—1860

JOSEPH ROSE EARLY and woke his sons just at day-break.

"What's wrong?" Young Joseph asked.

"Nothing," the chief said. "I want you two to come with me. Hurry and get ready."

Ollakot, the younger boy, looked at his brother with a quizzical expression as their father stepped out of the lodge and into the gray-streaked dawn. It took the boys just five minutes to join their father outdoors.

Without speaking, the chief, who was now more than sixty years old, started out of the village, knowing that his sons would follow him. He was still vigorous, and his stride was that of a much younger man. As they climbed through a meadow away from the village, Young Joseph looked over his shoulder at the deep blue of Wallowa Lake, its surface rippled by a stiff early-autumn breeze. The water of the lake looked dark, almost gray, the way it did on a rainy day when it reflected the sky and seemed to hide its color, blending in with the dreariness of the weather. But on clear, sunny days, the blue was almost green in spots, deep and clear.

Ollakot kept tugging on Young Joseph's arm and nodding his head toward their father, who stayed several steps ahead of them. He formed words on his lips, but didn't vocalize them. "What's wrong?" he asked.

Young Joseph shrugged, then held his empty palms upward before shrugging again. They had taken many walks with Joseph in the past, and always they had had a point. Young Joseph knew this time would be no different, but hadn't a clue what might be on his father's mind.

They were near the top of a long, low hill now, and the lake spread out behind them, beginning to brighten as the sun peeked over the horizon. It looked like a huge flower just about to open, almost pulsing as it swelled. Suddenly Joseph stopped and stabbed a finger at the rising sun, then turned to his sons.

"Do you see that?" he asked.

"It's the sun," Ollakot said. "It comes up every day."

Joseph smiled. "I thought I had taught you better than that."

"I don't understand. . . ." Ollakot said.

"Wait."

Ollakot shrugged again as Joseph turned to face uphill once more. Young Joseph held a finger to his lips and nodded. Ollakot frowned, but said nothing. When the chief started moving, the boys matched him stride for stride. The grass was tall in the meadow and studded with late flowers. Two months before, the meadow would have been alive with bees, but now most of the insects were gone. The only sounds were the wind whispering through the grass and the sharp hiss of deerskin leggings on the stiff blades.

Ollakot was still impatient, and Young Joseph kept an eye on him. He knew their father had a purpose, but at twenty he was wise enough to understand that that purpose would be revealed when the chief was ready and not before.

When they started down a gentle slope, where the meadow bellied into a shallow bowl, then started uphill more steeply, Joseph picked up his pace, as if he were growing anxious to reach the very top of the hill. His fingers trailed idly in the tall grass, almost fondling the tips of the taller blades, tugging at them but not breaking them or uprooting the plants. It looked to Young Joseph as if his father were trying to sift through the meadow for something he knew was there, but that he didn't quite know how to find.

The last fifty yards were very steep, but Joseph never slowed down. Only when he reached the crest of the hill did he stop and turn to look out at the broad expanse of Wallowa Lake, now a deep blue green. The sun was over the eastern horizon, and the early-autumn light looked cold, despite the sun's heat.

Joseph sat in the grass, folding his legs easily as he lowered himself to the ground. He patted the grass to his right and nodded for his sons to join him.

The chief stared at the lake, as if trying to fix it in his memory. His face was profoundly sad, and Young Joseph thought there might be a tear in the corner of one eye, but he wasn't sure and knew better than to ask.

It was nearly a half hour before he spoke. "I was very young when the first white men came to our country," he said. "I did not even have my *wyakin*. I remember the captains, Lewis and Clark. We called them the 'big hearts of the east' because they were so kind to our people, so generous. They made us many promises, some of which they kept and some of which they did not. I think, though, that the ones they did not keep were beyond their power."

Ollakot started to ask a question, but Young Joseph squeezed his brother's knee, then placed a finger to his lips again. Ollakot squinted, but shook his head.

"Our chiefs were mostly away, some hunting and some warring against the Bannock. But Twisted Hair was there, and he met the captains. I think he was afraid, not that anything would happen right then, but someday. I think he believed that things had changed in a way that could never be changed back. Now his son, the one we call Lawyer, is head chief and does what the white man wants him to do. But these white men are not like the captains, as Lawyer is not like Twisted Hair."

He stopped speaking and looked at his sons for the first time since sitting down. "Do you understand?"

"I'm not sure I do," Young Joseph said.

"These white men want what we have, and they don't care how they get it. They make marks on a piece of paper and say, 'This means that you give us this land, and this and this, and in exchange we will give you schools and houses and money and mills.' But it is five years, and they just now are signing the paper in Washington. For five years they have had our land and we have had nothing in exchange. And now I hear things—they want more land, they want to put all the Indians together. They will try to take the Wallowa Valley from us. I am sure of it."

"We can fight them," Ollakot suggested.

Joseph shook his head. "No, we can't. They are too many. We have pitiful little rifles, and very few, while they have great guns so big the horses have to pull them from place to place. Bows and bullets are like flies to such guns, and to such men. You have seen the soldiers come into our lands whenever they want, even though the treaty says no white men can come to our land without our permission. It used to be that each man did what he wanted to do. The land did not belong to any-one, it was just there, and we lived on it where we wanted to live. No one could buy it from us because it was not ours to sell. But now they say that we have sold it. . . ."

"We have our villages here," Young Joseph said. "We still have our place to live."

"But for how long? They say that Lawyer speaks for all the Nez Percé people, even though he doesn't ask us what we think. In council, we talk about what we want, but Lawyer does what the white men want him to do. Soon they will want the Wallowa, and I don't know how we can stop them from taking it."

The chief took a deep breath and held it for a long time. When he let it go with a great sigh, it was as if not just his breath but the very essence of the man were leaving in a single exhalation. "When the Yakima tried to fight, you saw what happened to them. The soldiers came and took everything. The white man's diseases spread like a fire in dry grass. Some villages are empty now, the lodges falling to pieces, the people gone. And the soldiers did not care who was a good man and who was not. They took everything—horses, food, cattle. If it belonged to an Indian, it was theirs to take. That is what they thought, and that is what they did. And guns cannot change that thinking."

"Why are you telling us all this again?" Ollakot asked. "You have told us such things before. Nothing has changed."

Joseph looked at his older son then. "Do you think nothing has changed, Hin-mah-too-yah-lat-kekht?"

Young Joseph gnawed on his lower lip. He knew what his father was getting at, but was reluctant to speak.

The chief watched him for a moment, then prodded, "Your name means Thunder Traveling to a Loftier Height. Does this name not suit you, or is the thunder afraid to speak its mind?"

"I'm not afraid," Young Joseph said, looking his father straight in the eye.

"Then speak. If not like thunder, then at least like my son."

"I think things have changed . . . a little, but what Tu-eka-kas means is that they will change much more, and soon."

"How soon?"

Young Joseph shrugged. "Soon. Perhaps tonight. Perhaps when the sun rises again."

The chief nodded, then tilted his head to one side, almost as if Young Joseph were wearing a mask and he were trying to peer around the edge of it. "And what will this change be?"

Young Joseph shook his head. "I don't know. I think maybe we will have to fight the white man, like Ollakot says."

"Do you want to fight?"

"No."

"But will you?"

"If I have to, yes."

"Why?"

"Because this"—and he stopped to sweep his arms wide as if to embrace the entire Wallowa Valley—"is worth fighting for. It is where we have always lived. It is our home. We did not ask the white men to come here. They chose to come. But I know that if we ask them to leave, they will refuse, and then we will have to decide."

Joseph nodded. "I still have the Bible that Dr. Whitman gave me, but I don't read it as often as I used to. It seems that the Great Spirit in that book is not as powerful as the Bostons told us. But you should read this book, Hin-mah-too-yah-lat-kekht. You too, Ollakot."

"Why?" Ollakot demanded. "Why should we read the white man's holy book? He doesn't live by it. Should we?"

"There is much that is good in the Heavenly Book. Would you throw out the wheat with the chaff?"

"I would not raise wheat," Ollakot snapped. "Let the white man raise his grain. I am not made to stand behind a plow, or to wear white man's clothes. None of us are."

"But we may not be able to help it, Ollakot. That is why you should read the Heavenly Book. To learn how the white man thinks, and to learn what he expects of us. I am not saying we have to be what he wishes us to be, but if we wish to understand him, then it is a place to start."

"I know all I need to," Ollakot said.

"No one knows all he needs to. And the man who thinks he knows it all is the man who has the most to learn."

"Why did you bring us up here?" Young Joseph asked.

"To show you the land, and to tell you to love it as I do, and even more. If you don't love it, you will lose it."

"No," Young Joseph said, "never."

Chapter 23

Wallowa Valley—March 1863

JOSEPH LOOKED AT THE CHIEFS arrayed around the council fire. He thought how pitifully few they were now. So many of the great chiefs were gone— either, like Peopeo Moxmox, dead at the hands of the white man, or, like Timothy and Lawyer, so deeply in the white man's pocket they were unable to climb out. Some were old and feeble, like Looking Glass, who was more than seventy years old, or Big Thunder, who coughed frequently and sometimes spat blood.

Everything around them was changing. The old ways were dying, and in their place was an array of new things that could not take their places.

Eagle from the Light and White Bird and Looking Glass waited patiently for Joseph to speak his mind. It was he who had called them together, and it was up to him to begin. Young Joseph and Ollakot and Looking Glass's son Allalimya Takanin, who was also called Looking Glass, were there, too, more as observers than as participants, but Joseph knew that his generation was fading fast, and it would be up to the young men to defend the old ways, not like the impetuous young warriors of the Yakima, who had

217

started a war that ended in the destruction of their people, but by using the white man's logic against him, by holding him accountable for the words he scattered like seeds and that, landing on stone, bore no fruit.

Finally he nodded his head as if he had just made up his mind and began to speak. "Eight years ago, we signed the paper that guaranteed to us that we would always have our homes, we would have the land we hunted and the camas fields and the rivers where we gathered our food. I told you then that things were changing, and that we should be careful not to trust the white man too much. Some of you understood what I meant. But some of our people did not understand. They traded their freedom for empty promises."

"This is not news, Tu-eka-kas," Big Thunder said. He paused to cough into his fist, and when he resumed, his voice was hoarse, and his hands shook. "We have talked about these things many times, and always it is the same—talk."

"But things are different now," Joseph said. "Now the white man has found gold on our reservation. Every year they find their gold in new places, and every year more and more white men come into our land, even though the treaty says they cannot. Once, there were four thousand Nez Percé and no white men on our lands. Now there are still four thousand Nez Percé, but there are twenty thousand whites, and more coming every month. They build cities on our land, and there is nothing we can do to stop them."

"We can fight them," Looking Glass said.

Joseph looked at the old war chief. Looking

Glass stared back at him, his face grave, and his head shaking the least little bit with the strain of sitting and talking. He knew Looking Glass was serious, and he knew, too, that Looking Glass knew they could not win such a fight. He wondered if there was a reason to fight anyway, knowing they would lose, and that once they lost, they would be finished as an independent people.

"Does Looking Glass say we should send our sons to be slaughtered by the white soldiers, as the Walla Walla chiefs sent their sons? And the Yakima? And the Cayuse? Does Looking Glass care nothing for the life of Allalimya Takanin?"

Looking Glass smiled for a moment. He looked down at the small mirror he wore around his neck, the glass he had received from Lewis and Clark and that had given him his name. He fingered it idly, smudging it with his thumb then holding it close to his lips and misting it with his breath before wiping it clean on his leggings. "Does Tu-eka-kas not care for Hin-mah-too-yah-lat-kekht? Does he not care for Ollakot?"

"Of course I do," Joseph snapped.

"Then do not suggest that I do not care for the life of my son. Like Tu-eka-kas, I worry for my children. And for their children. That is why I think we might not have a choice. It sometimes seems to me that if we fight, we will lose our lives and our land, but if we do not fight, we will lose everything, even our dignity. And we have little dignity left to lose. I just wonder if we should not try to save what is left so that our children and their children will not think too badly of us when we are gone. They will know that we tried to save their land and their way of life. It is a shameful thing to lose, but it is more shameful still to lose without fighting."

"There are many ways to fight, and I think we must plan on how to fight without inviting disaster for our families and our people. Lawyer must be made to understand that he does not speak for us. We must stop him from telling the white man that he has the right to sell our lands."

"The white man will hear what he wants to hear. He will let Lawyer speak for us because Lawyer will tell him what he wants to hear." Looking Glass looked at the other chiefs as if daring them to disagree. When they didn't, he nodded in satisfaction, but the movement seemed to take control of him, and his body shook and his head seemed to wobble on his shoulders.

"Maybe we should see to it that Lawyer cannot speak for anyone," Eagle from the Light suggested. "If he says nothing, then the white man cannot misunderstand."

White Bird shook his head. "No, we cannot turn against our own people, even when they are wrong. That is what the white man wants us to do."

"But Lawyer is not just wrong," Eagle from the Light argued. "He is worse than any white man. He sells our land and our people so the white man will give him money. And then, when there is no money, he sells more and still more, and still there is no money. He is a fool and a traitor to his own people."

"Lawyer means no harm," White Bird said. "But he does harmful things. He harms himself along with the rest of us."

"But do I have to let him harm me, even if he does not mean to? If a rock falls on my head, it means no harm, so should I then stand there and let it break my skull? Or should I get out of the way?"

"How do we get out of the white man's way?" Joseph asked. "That is what the reservation was for. The treaty said that we would have our lands and the white man would have his. We would be free to live as we have always lived, where we have always lived. But now the miners come and we cannot get out of their way. They are like maggots on a dead horse. There are more and more and more maggots and less and less horse until one day the horse is just bones and there is nothing for the maggots to eat. Is that what we want, a land of bones?"

"This is all the fault of the missionaries," Looking Glass said. "They made our people Christians, and when that was not good enough, they tried to make us slaves, no better than dogs that have to creep around the white man's lodges waiting for scraps. Our young men sell goods to the whites and spend the money they get on whiskey. Then they do no work and have nothing to sell, so they beg. They lose their dignity. If the missionaries had never come, no other whites would have come. They should have left us alone."

"It is too late for that," Joseph said. "I was a Christian, too. I remember Lawyer's father, Twisted Hair, talking with the captains from Boston. Lewis and Clark gave him a copy of their Heavenly Book, and Twisted Hair cherished it, even though he could not read it. Then later, when we learned to read the Heavenly Book, we saw that there were good white men and bad white men, just as there are good Indians and bad Indians."

"But there are more bad white men than bad

Indians," Eagle from the Light said. "And the laws
in the Heavenly Book are hypocritical. They apply
to the Indian but not the white man. The Heavenly
Book says to turn the other cheek, but the white
man does not do that. Tu-eka-kas, you remember
how Spalding used the whip for no reason. That is
what we should do. We should use the whip ourselves, and drive the white men from our land."

"The law is not a bad thing," Joseph argued. "It
is the men who are supposed to see that the law is
kept who are bad. They keep changing agents. One
agent comes and sees that things here are bad, so
he writes a letter to Washington. Instead of correct-
ing what is wrong, they change the agent. We are
not strong enough to drive the white man away,
with whips or with guns. If we are to win, we must
use the law against the white man. We know that
the treaty signed eight years ago was never kept by
the white men. There are some among the whites
who know this. They have told me so, and they say
that once the treaty is broken by the white man, we
no longer have to honor it."

"But if Lawyer makes a new treaty, then the
white man will have time to break that one."

"That is why we must make Lawyer understand
that he does not speak for us. If we can do that, and
if the white man understands this, then he will
have to ask each of us to sign the new treaty. If we
do not sign, there is nothing he can do."

"They will not care," Looking Glass said. "They
will say that we signed when we did not, and who
will listen to us when we try to tell the truth?"

"They listen only to Lawyer," Joseph said. "That
is true, but if Lawyer tells them he cannot sell our

land, then where will they turn? They will have no choice but to come to each chief in turn. This is our best chance."

"How can we make Lawyer tell them anything? Lawyer's head is turned by the white man. He will say anything to keep being the white man's friend," Eagle from the Light said.

"We must draw up a list of broken promises. Even Lawyer has not gotten things he was promised. If we show him the list, and tell him that he must tell these things to the new agent when the council meets in two months, then we can convince him. I would fight if I thought it would be better for the people, but I know that it will not be better. You have seen what has happened to the tribes that fought the white soldiers. Some of them don't even exist. The Yakima are all but gone. The Walla Walla are gone. Peopeo Moxmox was a friend to the whites until they pushed him too far, and when he tried to fight back, they killed him. And the soldier chief, Wright, said that he would hang all Yakimas—men, women, and children— until nothing was left of the Yakimas but the river. I do not want the Wallowa Valley to be a land of trees that bear skeletons for fruit."

"No one wants that, Joseph, but if we ask the other tribes for help, we can gather thousands of warriors," White Bird said.

Joseph shook his head. "No, other tribes have tried that and it did not work. The white men are too many and they have new guns that are better than any guns we have. Even with the great war in the east, they have all the soldiers and guns they need to defeat all the Indians we could assemble. It is easy to die, but when you think about your families and what will happen to them, then it is not so easy."

"Joseph is right," Looking Glass said. "I have been a warrior all my life. You know that I am afraid of no one and nothing. But this is not the kind of fight we can win unless we fight in the only way the white man does not expect. If we go on the warpath, we will be making it easy for him. It is what he hopes we will do. It is what they have been trying to force us to do for as long as I can remember. We will have to find another way."

"We have two months' time," Joseph said. "Each of us will have to talk to as many chiefs as we can, even those like Timothy and Lawyer who are white men in red skins."

Eagle from the Light spat in the dirt. "I have nothing to say to Lawyer."

"It is our only chance," Joseph said. "We have to try."

Chapter 24

CALVIN HALE SAT IN HIS TENT, reading. Meticulous in his attention to detail, he knew that the following morning would require all his skills as a negotiator, and he wanted to be ready. The papers arrayed before him did not present a pretty picture. Piecing together the details of the federal government's relationship with the Nez Percé was a laborious process, but as each part of the puzzle clicked into place, it became increasingly apparent that he was on the shakiest of ground.

The Treaty of 1855 had clearly been abrogated by the failure of the government to hold up its end of the agreement. Promised money had not arrived, construction of mills and schools had been all but nonexistent, and the Congress had taken four years to ratify the agreement, then failed to live up to its terms, already well in arrears. Anyone with even a nodding acquaintance with the law could see that the Nez Percé were well within their rights to take back the ceded land.

The point was not lost on the military men who were charged with maintaining the rather fragile tranquillity of the Washington Territory. At least one, Major General John Wool, had said outright that the Indians had been deceived, and if there was trouble, it would not be the fault of the Indians. Men like Wool were going to make it even more difficult than it already was to keep the peace, Hale thought.

But Wool was overly sensitive to things like profiteering, and since Hale well knew that much of the inadequate payment rendered to the Nez Percé had found its way into white pockets, Wool's position was difficult to argue with. Wool had even issued orders prohibiting whites from entering the reservation, despite the discovery of gold on Nez Percé land. The order stayed in effect until Wool was replaced, much to the delight of those who were getting fat on generous contracts to supply the army. In their minds, a good Indian war was exactly what the territory, not to mention their bank accounts, needed.

The thrust of political opinion in the nation's capital, enlightened or not, was clearly against the Indians. When Congress established the Idaho Territory on March 3, it was after considerable manipulation on behalf of mining interests, and the power in the new territory was intent on getting further concessions from the Nez Percé, by whatever means necessary. This was Calvin Hale's mandate, and he knew it to the letter.

The Indians were not without ferment of their own, and there was considerable sentiment among them to take back their lands, by whatever means necessary. But that wasn't about to happen, and Calvin Hale knew it. In fact, it was his job to convince the Nez Percé to give up still more land. The pressure on the edges of the reservation was relentless. As it was, whites were trespassing regularly, by the thousands and with impunity. Some settlers had even appropriated reservation lands, and when apprised that they had no right to do so, rather than move themselves, they argued that the Indians should be moved.

There were several towns already rooted in the territory, three with populations in the thousands, and Hale knew that the tide was too strong to swim against, even if he were so inclined.

He wanted to be ready to counter every argument by the time the council opened, and if that meant bending the truth as if it were fashioned of Indian rubber, then so be it. He would lie, if necessary, but he was not good at it, and hoped it wouldn't come to that. He didn't really know the chiefs he would be dealing with, but knew only too well that they were divided among themselves, and that gave him an edge that he was counting on.

Packing the papers away, he went to bed, but lay there for a long time, trying to frame his opening argument. It was important to get in the first shot and try to take the initiative and keep it. If the Indians were on the defensive, forced to react to him instead of pressing their own positions, he just might be able to pull it off.

First thing in the morning, he conferred with Colonel Justus Steinberger, commander of the contingent of troops, a full six companies, on hand to make a show of strength in case there was any truth to the rumors circulating through the mountains that the Indians were planning a full-scale war. Later that morning, he met with Lawyer and learned that many of the disaffected Indians had stayed away because they feared the soldiers were there to drive them from their lands by force.

"That just isn't so, Lawyer," Hale said. "They are here to maintain order, and that is the only reason. We will have hundreds of people here, and it is important that things not get out of hand."

"I believe you, but they think the commissioners will not come. It might help if Henry Spalding could come. Many of the Christian Indians respect him, and they know that if he is here, then you are not planning to make war on us."

"I'll see if I can persuade him to come, but in the meantime, you should send word to all your people that the soldiers mean no harm. We cannot have a council until all your people who wish to attend have arrived here."

"I understand. But there is one other thing that you must do. It is important that the official interpreter be someone who understands our language. Perrin Whitman is the best choice, but he is on the lower Columbia River."

Hale shook his head. "That's an awful long trip. I don't know if he'd be willing to come."

"You must find out. Many Indians believe that all the troubles we have now are because the language was not clear at the treaty council in 1855. Many Indians did not understand what they were being asked to do, and the white men did not understand what the Indians were agreeing to do, and what they were not agreeing to do."

"I'll do what I can," Hale said.

And so Whitman was sent for, further delaying the beginning of the council. Many of the most significant opposition chiefs still had not arrived, and Hale was starting to worry that it was not just fear caused by the rumors that had kept them away. Joseph wasn't there. Looking Glass hadn't come in. Eagle from the Light and White Bird, too, were absent. Without these chiefs, especially Joseph, it would be difficult to do what he wanted to do, Hale knew, because it was Joseph's land that he most wanted to get from the Nez Percé.

Hale made a quick trip himself, traveling from village to village in order to dispel the Indians' fears and asking them please to come to the council.

By May 25, he was ready to begin, and Lawyer and his people agreed, despite their fears that the absent chiefs would be a problem. Hale started with a bald explanation of the council's purpose. "The reason we are here is that we wish to rearrange the boundaries of the reservation. We will make a new reservation, smaller than the one you now have." He explained the boundaries he proposed, and then said, "The new reservation will be divided into lots so that each of you will have his own land. You can each have a farm, with a paper showing that it is yours. This is what the whites do, and it is what you should do. That way the land will always be yours. We will buy the rest of the reservation, and the people who live on that land will be resettled within the boundaries of the new reservation. Any improvement you have made will be paid for—fences, buildings, and such."

Lawyer was worried, and so was Big Thunder. Their bands were already located on land within the proposed boundaries, but Joseph's land was to be taken, which would not make him happy. And his people would be forced to live with Big Thunder's people and with Lawyer's people. There had been continuing friction between these groups for a number of years, even at long range. The nontreaty Nez Percé, not just Joseph's people, but those of Eagle from the Light and White Bird and Looking Glass, would be forced to live among the treaty Indians as guests, and they would not like it at all.

And since Joseph and the other nontreaty chiefs were not here, they would never agree to any settlement Lawyer might negotiate with Hale. But that was only part of the problem. Even the treaty Nez Percé used the mountains and the valleys for hunting, roaming at will along the rivers to fish. Now they would not be permitted to do that. And the camas fields, too, were outside the boundaries of the new reservation. It looked to Lawyer like a cattle pen, and it made him uncomfortable. He knew there was no way he could get this bitter pill swallowed without a fight.

The day closed under a cloud, and Lawyer was convinced it was the harbinger of a great storm to come. In conference with Big Thunder and the young chief Utsinmalikin that night, he discovered that those chiefs, too, were disturbed. They agreed that Hale had to be pressed, and that some explanation of Hale's authority had to be gotten.

The following day Hale went over the same ground, but in much more detail. The Indians listened quietly, letting him display his maps of the new reservation, explain how deeds to the Indian property would work, and how each family would have a twenty-acre farm in its own name. When he was finished, he seemed to sense something, and hesitated before asking, "Is there anything that you don't understand?"

Utsinmalikin, as agreed, got to his feet. "We understand the proposal you are making," the old chief said, "but we want to know when this order came from Washington. We feel responsible to the Great Father, but want to know when the order came." It was a delicate question and a subtle one, as it was meant to be. Since Whitman had not yet arrived, the translation was critical.

Hale, offended by the perceived thrust, gave a long-winded history of the gold rush, a history with which the Indians present had all too familiar an acquaintance, and then explained how the government wanted to protect the Indians.

It was Lawyer's turn. "The treaty we made in 1855 was for twenty years. It is not yet twenty years, not even one half twenty years, and now you want to make another treaty with us. We kept that treaty, even though you have not. We wonder why it is necessary, before the twenty years have gone, to make a new treaty."

Hale was off balance. This was not what he had expected. Lawyer had put his finger on the most fatal of flaws in the treaty situation. He stumbled a bit, regained his composure, and said, "We will have the 1855 treaty read tomorrow. You will see that it is not as you think." Then, anxious to get off the hot seat, he adjourned the council for the day.

On the following morning, it was obvious to everyone present that he had read the 1855 Stevens Treaty overnight and understood just how feeble the government's argument was. Doing the only thing he could, he tried to explain the discrepancies away even before the treaty was read, but when he could no longer defer the reckoning, he took a seat while the entire document of 1855 was read to the assembly.

When the reading was finished, Lawyer stood up and took a small notebook from his pocket. In it, he said, were things that Governor Stevens had said at the treaty council. One by one he read the items on the list, and it was painfully obvious that it was a list of promises of which not one had been kept. Then, in summation, "Governor Stevens said," Lawyer read, "'The laws are forever and the Creator of those laws is looking down on us, and hearing what we say. And I speak the truth.'"

When Lawyer finished reading, there wasn't a sound. Even the wind seemed to have stopped.

And Calvin Hale had no choice but to adjourn for the day. And so it went for nearly two weeks, until large bands of antitreaty Nez Percé under Joseph and the other chiefs opposed to further cession of lands arrived at the council ground. The Indians had two days of discussion among themselves and devised a counterproposal, which Lawyer then presented to Hale. The Nez Percé proposed to cede only those lands on which gold had been discovered. Since such lands would not affect Joseph or Eagle from the Light or the other antitreaty chiefs, it was a proposal that was acceptable to all the chiefs present, pro- and antitreaty alike.

But Hale would not accept it. He was committed to the new boundaries and determined to have them. He lobbied intensively with the chiefs individually, getting most of the protreaty chiefs to agree and winning, as he expected, not a single concession from those, like Joseph, who were opposed.

The Indians had another council of their own as Hale was preparing to close the negotiations, and it was Joseph who took the lead.

"Lawyer," he said, "we cannot sign this new treaty. Our land is not for sale. The whites have not honored the last treaty, and as far as I am concerned, we are not obligated to surrender even more of our land to them."

"But there is no choice, Joseph. You know as well as I do that if we do not sign, they will take the land anyway. At least this way we get something for it."

"And what did we get for our last treaty? Did we get houses? Did we get schools? Did we get mills? Did we get money? Did even *you* get money? No. What we got was words, a bag of air. But the air is free to anyone who wants to breathe, Lawyer. And that is what my people want. They want to breathe free air, like free men have the right to do. Like our fathers and our grandfathers have done."

"I know that the whites have not done all they told us they would. I told them so, and Agent Hale acknowledges this. He says this will be different. We will get what we are promised. And we will get what we were promised by the last treaty," Lawyer said.

"You mean," Big Thunder interrupted, "the white men will get the money that was promised us, and then we will not see the agent again. That is why we have had so many agents. As soon as they get enough money, they go away and we don't see them again. What we get is nothing. Which is exactly what these new promises are worth."

"But—"

"Lawyer," Joseph said, "remember that Dr. White made us accept his code of laws, and when it came time to enforce those laws, it was always the Indians who were punished, but the whites were not. And he asked us to accept Ellis as head chief, and we did that because he told us it was necessary for the Indians to be able to protect themselves. But even though we did it, we are not protected. You have tried for many years to be the head chief and represent us to the white man, but you have achieved nothing for my people."

"As far as I am concerned," Big Thunder put in, "from this day on, there is no head chief. You are not my chief and you cannot speak for me."

"And you cannot speak for me," Joseph said, "or for my people."

"Each man," Big Thunder continued, "must speak for himself. And Hale should be told this so that he does not misunderstand. You can sign the new paper if you wish, but you cannot sign for me or my people."

It was nearly daybreak before the council broke up, and the chiefs got little sleep before Hale called them all together once more. When he presented the paper for signature, Lawyer signed first, and one by one fifty other chiefs stepped up to make their marks next to their names. But Joseph refused to sign and White Bird did not sign, nor did Big Thunder and Eagle from the Light. When the council adjourned, Joseph went to his lodge and shredded his copy of the treaty of 1855. As he was packing to leave for the Wallowa, he stayed on his knees for a long time.

Young Joseph noticed and asked, "Is anything wrong, Father?"

The old chief shook his head. As his son stepped closer he could see that Joseph held his copy of the New Testament in his hands, looking at it as if he had never seen it before. There were tears in his eyes as he opened the book. The chief held the first page in his fingers for a moment, then suddenly jerked it out of the binding. He let it drift to the ground then took a second page, pulled it free, and let it fall as well. One by one he tore the pages from the Heavenly Book. Young Joseph stood silently by until the last page had been torn from the Bible.

Then, with tears streaming down his face, the chief turned to his son. "These pages are like leaves in the wind," he said. "I am no longer a Christian from this day forward."

Chapter 25

Wallowa Valley—1871

THE DEER STOOD STILL, its head cocked to one side. The great animal's ears twitched, swiveled this way and that, listening. Young Joseph held his breath, knowing that the least sound now would spook the deer. It was a big buck, twelve-point antlers scarred and mossy with age. Young Joseph knew this was no ordinary deer.

Turning to look down through the massed pines, he could see Ollakot far below him, his head craned back until the long braids reached his waist, looking up like a man watching an eagle. Young Joseph raised one hand in a slight wave, cautious not to scrape the sleeve of his deerskin jacket on his side.

The deer was still poised, ready for flight at a moment's notice. The young chief reached back over his shoulder, groping for the arrows in his quiver. His fingers closed slowly over the notched haft of one, but he was reluctant to try to draw it free. If the other arrows in the quiver rattled, it would send the deer hightailing it through the pines before he could fit the arrow to his bowstring. A gun would have been easier, but the old way was better, made him feel somehow more in tune with his quarry.

Breathing through his mouth, holding each breath until his chest felt as if it would burst, he waited for some solution to the stalemate. In a way, he was even glad. The deer was so majestic, so huge and so obviously a survivor, it would be a shame to kill it. But then he felt that way about almost every deer. And every bighorn sheep.

The natural world seemed so precious to him, and each time he came close to a particularly impressive specimen, he thought about his father's love for the earth, for these mountains and valleys in particular, and how precariously balanced it all was. He thought of a child turning its first successful handspring, wavering on the frail support of one tiny wrist, the fingers too feeble to hold the tottering weight, and then, almost without warning, tumbling to the earth with a look of profound surprise on its face. All life in the Wallowa Valley seemed that precariously balanced.

But the earth couldn't stand still, any more than the Clearwater could stop flowing or the clouds stand still in the sky. Young Joseph started to draw the arrow, inch by inch, holding his breath again and listening for the first scrape of one arrow against another.

The deer lowered its head and started to munch on the leaves of a clump of brush, its ears still twitching but seemingly with less urgency. Then a rabbit darted out of the grass, zigzagged around the deer, and disappeared in the brush. The buck, satisfied that it had seen what had caught its attention, paid full attention now to its feeding and gave the young chief a chance to slide his arrow all the way out of the quiver.

Fitting the bowstring into the notch, Young Joseph twisted his head slightly to relieve the tension in his neck and shoulders, then drew the string taut, the great bow's graceful curves bending until they could bend no more.

Sighting on the deer's shoulder, he held the bow at full draw for a moment, then let the arrow fly. The string snapped with a musical thrum and the arrow sped toward the deer, now alerted by the noise. It lifted its head and started to turn in Young Joseph's direction just as the arrow hit home. The buck jumped as if startled, sprang once and landed on legs already rubbery, staggered two or three steps, and went down to its knees.

The young chief stepped into the clear and the buck watched him, its great, liquid brown eyes wide with what had to be surprise. It kept its gaze fixed on him as he approached. Twenty paces away, Young Joseph stopped in midstride as the buck shook its massive rack, snorted once, then fell over on its side.

The deer sighed once, then again, this time the death rattle echoing in its chest. Young Joseph took a step, then another and a third step, and the dark eyes opened once more, the buck's ears twitching, but spasmodically now. Leaning forward, one hand outstretched as if to comfort the wounded animal, the young chief could see himself reflected on the surface of the huge brown eye, and he turned away. It troubled him to think that the last thing the splendid animal would see was the figure of the creature that had taken its life.

Turning completely, he walked away, heading

down the side of the mountain again fifteen or twenty steps. He saw Ollakot, still tending the horses, and waved a hand to his brother, this time vigorously. Ollakot returned the wave, then Young Joseph summoned him, and watched while his brother started up the mountainside, tugging the three horses behind him.

The young chief couldn't bring himself to go back alone to the carcass of the deer. Instead, he watched his brother climbing toward him, alternately staring at the ground and up the side of the mountain. Ollakot kept vanishing among the trees and reappearing as he zigzagged upward, choosing the clearest path through the trees. When he was within hailing distance, Ollakot shouted, "Did you get him?"

Young Joseph didn't answer immediately, and when he did, it was with a simple nod of his head. When his brother was close enough to converse in normal tones, he said, "Yes, I got him."

"Where is he?" Ollakot asked, then before his brother could answer, he craned his neck and spotted the deer lying on its side. "Magnificent!" he said. "I've never seen a deer so large. And look at the antlers!"

He bounced past Joseph and knelt beside the buck, reaching out with one hand to stroke its flanks. Turning, he said, "Do you think we can carry him this way?"

Joseph shook his head. "It's far too heavy. We'll have to clean and dress it here, perhaps even leave some and come back for it later. Even with the three horses, it will be too much."

"We better get started then," Ollakot said,

pulling a knife from its sheath on his hip and getting to his feet. He sprinted back to the horses, cut a woven rope loose from the gear on the packhorse, then ran back to the carcass. Working quickly, he tied the rear legs together, then tossed one end of the rope high into the air, looping it over the nearest sturdy limb. "Help me," he said as he started to haul on the rope.

They hoisted the dead buck several feet off the ground, then Joseph took a knife from a sheath on his hip and slit the deer's throat. The blood gushed at first, then slowed to a steady stream and finally to a trickle. The backs of Joseph's hands were sticky with the first rush of blood, and he looked at them for a long moment and closed his eyes. He was not squeamish. He had hunted too long and too successfully for that, but this animal's blood disturbed him for some reason. Almost without thinking, he stepped away from the carcass and buried his hands in bunchgrass, then ripped fistfuls of the long smooth blades and scrubbed the mess from his hands and wrists.

It took more than an hour to dress the deer, and when they were finished, they realized it was still far too heavy for a single horse and were forced to section it. "I think we can get all the meat home in one trip," Ollakot said, then stopped to look at his brother. "You are very quiet today."

"I know."

"Anything wrong?"

Joseph shrugged. "I think so, but I don't know what. I just don't feel right. Let's hurry home." Then, without waiting for an answer, he started to load the cuts of venison onto the packhorse. "We'll have to load our own horses," he said, almost in a whisper.

Sensing that Joseph didn't feel like talking, Ollakot helped secure the venison, then nodded. "Let's go," he said, taking the bridle of the pack-horse and securing it to his own mount, then tying it to Joseph's stallion.

Ollakot led the way down the mountain. When they reached the lower edge of the pine forest, the sun was well down in the western sky. The Wallowa was flooded with pale orange light, and even the lake seemed to be changing color.

As they crested the last rise before the descent to their village, Young Joseph saw several warriors heading toward him on horseback. He tensed immediately, sensing that something was wrong. It couldn't be an attack, because the warriors would never have left the village undefended. And there would have been the sounds of battle. Instead, the valley was eerily quiet. As the warriors drew closer he recognized Looking Glass, the son of the great war chief of the same name and good friend to his father. White Bird was with him, and several other young men around his own age.

Looking Glass saw them as they broke over the top of the hill and charged toward them, waving one hand over his head. When he was within hailing range, he shouted, "Hin-mah-too-yah-lat-kekht, come quickly."

"What's wrong?" Joseph shouted.

Instead of answering, Looking Glass reined in and dismounted. White Bird, too, slipped from horseback. When the brothers were ten yards away, Looking Glass said, "Your father is very ill. Take my horse, and hurry."

Joseph sprang onto the borrowed animal, waited for Ollakot to mount White Bird's pony, then dug his heels into the animal's flanks. The brothers plunged headlong downhill, not bothering to switch back in their haste. When they reached the village, they saw a crowd around Joseph's lodge. Handing the bridles of their mounts to warriors on the edge of the crowd, they pushed through the throng and ducked into the lodge.

Tu-eka-kas lay on a buffalo robe. He had been feeble for some time, and his vision was all but gone. But he sensed the presence of his sons and reached out for Young Joseph's hand. He groped for it and, when he found it, closed his frail hands around it. "My son, I am returning to the body of my mother earth."

The son had to lean close to the father's lips to hear the whispered words. "You must think of your country when I am gone. Think of the people. You are their chief, and you must be certain to guide them well. They will look to you for guidance and you must look to them for wisdom. Remember that I never sold our country. Men will come and try to buy our country. They will say that it has been sold to them long ago. Cover your ears when you hear such talk, and never sign a treaty that requires you to give up the land. You must never give in to them. When I am gone, this land will hold the bones of your father and of your mother. It will hold the bones of your father's father, and of his father. Never sell the bones of your father and mother."

The old chief squeezed Joseph's hand, and coughed once, then squeezed it again. He reached out with his other hand for Ollakot, found his younger son's hand, and closed his own over it.

"Ollakot, you must look out for your brother. Help him. He will need you because it is no easy thing to be a chief."

"Don't worry, Father," Joseph said, patting his father's hand, "I will never let go of the land. I will not sell your bones or those of my mother."

A sad smile passed over the old chief's face, then seemed to vanish, and he lay still. Joseph looked up at the roof of the lodge, as if he'd heard something above him, then looked once more at his father's still features and closed his eyes.

He felt hands tugging at him and turned to see the two young wives of his father, their faces contorted with grief, their dresses tattered and smeared with grime. One of the young women led him to the door and the other tugged Ollakot, right behind him. They shoved the brothers out of the lodge. "We will take care of him now," they said.

The following morning Tu-eka-kas lay in state, dressed in fine new clothing that looked too large on his frail frame. His face was daubed with yellow, red, and white paint, as if for war. For two days the village mourned, and Indians came from all the nearby villages to pay their last respects.

On the third day Tu-eka-kas was wrapped in softened deerskin and carried on a stretcher made of poles to a grave that had already been dug. The body was lowered into the ground, the head to the rising sun. A shaman sang the praises of the venerated chief, then the grave was filled with stones and sharp wooden stakes to make sure scavengers would not uncover it.

As a final sign of respect, two of the old chief's

horses were killed, one laid near the grave and another speared with a post and propped upright over the grave. A single pole was driven into the ground at the head of the grave, a wooden arm attached to it from which was suspended a small red bell, as prescribed by the Dreamers cult to which Joseph had belonged.

The Dreamers, under Smohalla, a wise and ancient shaman, had been gaining influence. Their belief that the white man would disappear and the old ways return, had drawn old Joseph after he renounced his Christianity. Young Joseph and Ollakot, too, belonged to the cult.

With the women wailing in the background, Young Joseph looked at his brother, wiped a few tears away, then ignored those that followed. "It is up to us, now, Ollakot," he said.

THE WAR
1876–1877

Chapter 26 ═══════════

Wallowa Valley—June 1876

ALBERT "A.B." FINDLEY LEFT HIS NEW HOUSE early on a summer morning. Walking toward his corral, he noticed that several horses were missing from the open range beyond the corral fence, where they had been grazing. Rushing to the barn, he saddled his own mount and picked up a faint trail along the banks of Whiskey Creek, the quiet brook that marked one edge of his small homestead. The trail had been made by a handful of horses, anywhere from four to six or seven. He was missing five, and the odds were good the tracks had been left by his stock.

The trail led into the rolling hills behind his place, and he followed the horses for two or three miles without seeing them. The trail crossed and recrossed Whiskey Creek, and the thick pine forest was starting to spook him. Talk in town was of almost nothing but the Nez Percé and when they would finally go on the warpath.

Some folks even wanted to start the war themselves, arguing that it was going to happen sooner or later anyway, and if they got it over with, they could go on with their lives. Findley was not quite so militant, but the constant talk of marauding bands of

Indians, which no one had ever actually seen, and which had caused no damage that anyone could point to, made him as nervous as the next man.

Two Indians had already been killed that he knew of, and both times war had been narrowly avoided. At a small clearing on the bank of the creek, he got his best look at the tracks left by the horses. He still couldn't tell how many there were in the small herd, but he knew one thing—he wasn't going any further on his own. Wheeling his horse, he felt the hair rise on the back of his neck. He stopped to listen, his hand on the butt of his revolver, but the only sound was that of a solitary bird somewhere deeper in the forest.

Heading back to the town of Lostine, he kept glancing over his shoulder, certain that someone was following him, but he never saw a thing. By the time he reached town, his nerves had settled somewhat, but his anger had taken over. Stopping in the general store, he encountered a neighbor, Oren McNall, who was well known in the area, and not nearly as well liked.

McNall overheard him telling Dave Bracken, the storekeeper, about the missing horses. "What we ought to do," McNall suggested, "is get us a bunch of men and go on back out there. Most likely they been run off by Injuns. You done right comin' back, Findley. No sense gettin' your hair cut by anybody but a barber."

Findley shrugged. He didn't much care for McNall, but there was no way to shut him up without being rude. "I don't know whether there was Indians or not. Never saw one the whole time I followed the trail."

"Hell, Findley," McNall said, "horses don't up an' run off without no reason. Had to be Indians. What else could it be?"

While the two men chatted, Findley trying to find a way to change the subject, McNall's brother, Wells, came in with a man named Frank Miller. Oren started telling his brother about the missing horses and added a few embellishments of his own.

"Reckon we should go on back out there," Wells said. "You wait too long, Findley, and them horses will be long gone."

Miller was game, and all four men left the store and climbed into the saddle. Findley set a leisurely pace, but Wells McNall was jittery and kept prodding him to hurry. "We don't want to be out there after nightfall with them redskins runnin' loose. They took your horses, they'll be likely to be willin' to put up a fight to keep 'em."

"I already told you, Wells, I ain't sure it was Indians. Could be they just run off by theirselves. They was on open range. Maybe they got spooked and run away."

"Sure, and maybe they had some help."

"Why don't you just be quiet," Frank Miller snapped. "If there are Indians around here, they'll hear us comin' a mile away."

Wells glared at him, but said nothing. The trail was fading a bit after several hours, but Miller was a better tracker than Findley, and he gradually moved into the lead. When they reached the point where Findley had turned back a few hours earlier, Miller asked, "How many horses you say you're missing, Albert?"

"Five, why?"

"'Cause as near as I can figure, we're following half a dozen, at the most."

"Only takes one redskin to steal a horse," Wells interjected.

"Maybe so, but none of the horses we're following is carrying any load at all, let alone a full-grown man."

"That don't matter," McNall argued.

"Look, Wells, everybody in the territory knows you don't like Indians much. It's no secret. So it's likely you'd see moccasin prints under the bed every night, if you looked."

"Shut up, Frank. Don't matter what I think of redskins. If one of 'em stole Findley's horses, he ought to pay for it, that's all there is to it."

They were moving more slowly now. The trail faded in and out as the fleeing animals passed over patches of ground thickly carpeted with needles. But Miller kept them moving another mile before he reined in.

"What's wrong, Frank?" Findley asked. "You see somethin'?"

Miller pointed. Peering into the shadows of the forest, Findley saw several murky figures several feet off the ground. They seemed to undulate gently, as if they were bobbing in some invisible current. "What the hell are they?" he asked.

"Deer," Miller said. "Most likely there's a huntin' party around here somewheres. They hung the carcasses up to keep the scavengers away."

"Told you there was redskins," McNall said, gloating.

"Wells," Miller said, trying to hide his exasperation and failing miserably, "this is a big country.

It's Indian land, in fact, and it don't surprise me none that they might decide to hunt a few deer. That don't mean they stole the horses."

"It don't mean they didn't, neither," McNall rejoined.

"It's gettin' late. I think we best go on back to town. We can get an early start and come back tomorrow. Maybe we'll run into the hunters. They might have seen something."

"You don't think they'd tell us if they did, do you, Miller?"

"Wells, I'm gettin' damned tired of you. Why don't you just go on home and make your family miserable for a change. Or won't they let you in?"

Oren McNall eased his horse a little closer to Frank Miller. "No call to be talkin' to Wells like that, Miller."

"No call for Wells to be talkin' at all, Oren."

"Stop your damn bickerin'," Findley said. "They're my damn horses. I never should have said nothing about it."

"Too late for that," Miller said.

Findley sighed. "Let's go home." Without waiting for an answer, he swung his roan stallion around and started back for Lostine. Miller fell in behind him, and the McNalls, despite their fire-breathing rhetoric, were none too anxious to stay out alone, so they followed suit.

At Findley's home, Frank Miller said, "I'll come by in the morning, Albert. If you want to take another look, we'll go on back to them carcasses and pick up the trail right there."

"Good night, Frank, and thanks."

The three men rode on, leaving Findley to won-

der about his missing stock. He was worried, but
not so much about the possibility that Indians had
taken his horses. He just didn't know what had
happened, and it didn't much matter as long as he
could get them back. But if they *did* run into an
Indian hunting party, McNall's bad manners and
worse temper just might cause trouble.

He turned in early, but didn't sleep well. He'd
decided against telling his wife about the horses,
because there were already enough rumors circulating in the Wallowa Valley. The last thing in the
world he wanted to do was give her something else
to worry about.

At four o'clock, knowing he wasn't going to get
any more rest, he got out of bed and dressed. When
dawn came, he was still trying to decide what to
do. Going outside to have a cigarette, he sat on the
front step and leaned back against the door. He
rolled a smoke quickly, barely watching what he
was doing, and reached into his pocket for a match.
He scraped it aflame, and as he brought the tip of
the cigarette close, he heard the nicker of a horse. A
moment later, he saw Wells McNall round a clump
of cottonwoods.

Findley sucked the quivering flame into his
cigarette, filled his lungs with smoke, and shook
the match out, snapping it before tossing it aside.

McNall reined in fifteen yards from the front of
the house. "You ready, Albert?" he called.

"Where are the others?"

"Oren's in town with Miller and a couple more
men. They'll catch up to us."

Findley shook his head then walked to the corral, where he saddled his horse, fumbled in the

gloom of the barn for some extra ammunition for his carbine, dumped the shells into his shirt pocket, closed the flap, and went back outside. Swinging into the saddle, he said, "Wells, we run into any Indians, I want you to let me do the talkin', all right?"

"Whatever you say, Albert."

The two men followed Whiskey Creek back to the deer carcasses, which were still hanging from the trees. They dismounted and started toward the suspended venison. "Probably was only two or three Indians," Findley guessed. "Any more than that, they'd have taken the meat with them."

"Probably wanted to get your horses hid before they come back for the deer," McNall said.

"Wells, you don't know that."

"Don't need to know it, Albert. I—" He stopped and held a finger to his lips.

"What's wrong?" Findley asked.

"You hear something?"

Findley shook his head. "Nope. Nothin'."

A twig snapped, and Findley turned to see three Nez Percé warriors standing behind him. Keeping his eyes on the hunters, he said, "Wells, don't do nothing foolish now, I'm warning you. We got company."

McNall spun around. "What are you—" He stopped when he spotted the Indians.

All three carried rifles. "Hello," one of them, the oldest, said. He appeared to be about forty years old, and his English was heavily accented.

"Howdy," Findley said. He raised a hand, and the Indians set their rifles down against a tree. They walked toward the two white men, relaxed and smiling.

"Lost some horses," Findley said. "Followed their trail through here yesterday. Maybe you seen them?"

The Indian in the lead shook his head. "No horses," he said.

One of the men split off and moved toward the carcasses. He climbed up the tree from which the deer were suspended and started to untie the rope.

McNall started to fidget, and Findley was worried he might do something stupid. McNall didn't disappoint him. Pulling his revolver, he thumbed the hammer back and pointed it at the Indians, who froze in their tracks.

"Damn it all, Wells," Findley barked, "put up that damn gun!"

"The hell I will," McNall said. Then, to the Indians: "What'd you do with them horses you stole?"

"No horses," the Indian said again. He still seemed surprised to have the gun pointing at him. The hunter in the tree, apparently unaware of what was happening, finally loosed the rope, and as the carcass started to fall the rope hissed over the branch. McNall turned, and the Indian lunged for him, grabbing for the gun. Both men fell to the ground.

"Shoot him, Goddamn it, Albert," McNall shouted. "Shoot him!"

Findley stood as if turned to stone, watching the two men struggle over the weapon that was somewhere between them. "Stop it, Wells," he shouted. "Cut that out!"

The combatants struggled to their feet, each man refusing to let go of the gun still locked between them. The Indian backed away a step and twisted his body around, trying to flex McNall's gunhand over his hip.

The gun went off, and McNall fell to the ground. Findley, almost without thinking, fired his own gun as the warrior turned. The bullet caught him in the stomach, and he fell to one knee, then toppled over on his side.

McNall, uninjured, got to his feet. "Kill them other two, Albert," he said, scrambling to pick up his gun.

"No, sir, I won't do that, Wells."

In the moment of confusion, the man in the tree leaped to the ground and disappeared into the trees. The third Indian sprinted after him as McNall spun and fired. The shot missed, and a split second later the Indians were gone. All except the warrior who'd been shot. He lay on his back, bloody hands clenched over his stomach. His face still wore a look of surprise. Findley knelt beside him and leaned over to listen for a breath. The man was motionless. There was no heartbeat when Findley pressed an ear to the man's chest. He looked up at McNall and shook his head.

"Now you've done it, Wells," he said.

Chapter 27 ═══════

Wallowa Valley—May 1877

GENERAL OLIVER OTIS HOWARD stroked his beard with his one remaining arm. He'd lost the right at the battle of Fair Oaks during the Civil War. A man of determination bordering on iron will, he had gone back into action and seen combat at some of the worst scenes of carnage the war had to offer—Antietam, Chancellorsville, Gettysburg—and led two army corps on Sherman's march through Georgia. He was, first and foremost, a military man and fancied himself, not without reason, a good Christian. Whether he knew it or not, and it would not have mattered if he did, his troops called him the Christian General. And he was not without compassion.

He was fortunate in that his second in command was, if anything, even more moral than he was. Major Henry Clay Wood had been with him for several years. Like Howard, he had taken an interest in the Nez Percé question almost immediately upon his assignment to the Department of the Columbia, of which Howard had assumed command on September 1, 1874.

Wood sensed that his commander had something on his mind, but knew Howard well enough that he chose to bide his time rather than pry. For a long time, the only sound in the general's command tent was the rasp of five fingers on tangled whiskers. Howard was reading, hunched over his camp desk to see the papers more clearly in the dim light of a kerosene lamp. He grunted once, then shoved the papers away as he leaned back in his chair and clawed at his eyes for a second. Then he sighed.

He was ready to talk.

"Something wrong, General?" Wood asked.

Shifting his attention to the whiskers under his chin, Howard hummed uncertainly. "I've just been reading your report on Joseph and his band again, Henry. It's the third time in the last sixth months, and no matter how I read it, it always comes out the same way. You're absolutely right. Old Joseph never signed the 1863 treaty, which means the Wallowa was his to keep."

Wood shrugged. "You could argue that majority rules. Old Joseph accepted Lawyer's authority as head chief. That gave Lawyer the right to sign."

"But it didn't give him the right to sign away Old Joseph's land. Unless you stretch logic to the breaking point and say that all the lands were held in common, and if the majority agreed to the reduction of the 1855 boundaries, then Old Joseph was bound to go along."

"That's ice too thin to skate on, General."

"I know it is, Henry. I'm just trying to find some way I can do my job without compromising my principles."

"They're mutually exclusive, General. If you enforce the removal orders of Washington, then you'll be going against what you know to be justice, which very clearly sides with Joseph."

"I wish you were wrong, Henry, I truly do but, as God is my witness, I know you're not wrong."

"What are you going to do, General?"

"My duty, Henry. Just like I always do. And so will you . . ."

"I don't know, General. I've been thinking of asking for a transfer."

"Nothing doing, Henry. You're in this to the finish. Unless you want to go over my head to General Sherman."

"I don't know. I suppose I'll have to think about it."

Howard looked surprised and more than a little hurt. "I was counting on you, Henry. I really was. If we're going to get through this mess without serious difficulty, it will take more than a few cool heads. Besides mine, I was hoping yours would be in there, gears whirling, trying to find a way through this maze."

"Joseph's head is cooler than anyone's, General."

"I know that, Henry. And a good thing it is, too. I think I understand the man. And I think he understands me. I swear to you, I felt something that first time we met. He looked at me, and it was like he was looking right into my heart, as if he were measuring me somehow, trying to decide what I was made of. And I think he liked what he saw . . . or respected it, anyhow."

"It's going to take more than respect to solve this problem, General. I've never seen anything more intractable in my life, or a clearer case of might arrayed against right."

Howard bristled. "There's some right on our

side, too, Henry. Don't you forget that. We've offered the man a way out, but he won't take it. Hasn't yet, anyway. And I don't know whether he will, but I still hope he might."

"We'll see this afternoon, General."

"That we will, Henry. That we will. And if you have any spare time between now and the council, I'd appreciate it if you put in a good word with the Almighty."

"I haven't prayed since I was a boy, General."

"If ever there was a time to renew your acquaintance with the Good Lord, Henry, it's now."

Wood nodded, but made no promises. He walked outside and looked at the surrounding hills. The meadows were in full flower, and he could see a welter of bees shimmering like silk all the way up the slope, darting from blossom to blossom, their wings catching the light like thousands of tiny mirrors. Behind him, past the small encampment, the waters of the lake shimmered under the morning sun as if mimicking the reflected light from the beating wings.

It was no wonder, he thought, that Joseph loved this country as he did. It was beautiful to the point of Edenic tranquillity. Were he in Joseph's shoes, he doubted that he would be any more willing to surrender to what, he now realized, could only be characterized as the inevitable. For six months the troops had been present in the valley. And for six months they had been trying to convince Joseph, White Bird, Ollakot, and the other nontreaty chiefs that they had no choice but to accede to the recommendations of the presidential commission.

Those recommendations, Wood knew, were a

bitter disappointment to Joseph. The only question in Wood's mind was whether this would be the last enormous straw on the back of the frail and already overloaded camel. Joseph was a proud man and a logical one. He understood that justice was being denied him for reasons that ought to hold no weight in an evenhanded court. But there was nothing evenhanded in the white man's desire to have this last stronghold of Nez Percé independence for himself.

Wood walked up to the top of the hill, scattering bees with every step and smearing his trousers with pollen. When he reached the top, he pressed a clump of bunchgrass flat with his boots and sat down. Already, he could see the Indians approaching, and he knew that the time was almost here when Joseph would have to surrender the Wallowa or fight.

The Indians seemed to materialize out of the air. He could see a handful where, a moment before, there had been nothing in the valley below him. Then more and more appeared, and the small contingent he had first seen proceeded slowly uphill toward him on horseback.

As they drew closer he recognized Joseph and Ollakot. Both wore their hair in the fashion of the Dreamer cult, long braids on both sides with the front rolled up away from the forehead.

At first, Wood wondered whether he should run down to the camp to tell Howard that Joseph had arrived, then, realizing that if there was a single man in the valley to whom protocol mattered more than Howard, it was Joseph himself, he stayed where he was. As they drew close Joseph and Ollakot waved, and Wood got to his feet. Joseph dismounted when still a hundred and fifty yards from the hilltop. Wood swam through the grass toward him, and the young chief took his hand when it was offered.

"You're early," Wood said.

"No," Joseph said. "It is late, I hope not too late, but . . ."

"It's a beautiful day, isn't it?"

Joseph nodded. "I wish you could have seen this valley when the Nez Percé were the only ones here. There were no farms then, and horses were everywhere. The fish in the rivers were numberless and the deer in the forests were almost too many to count. It is all changing now. Now there are hardly any of us left in this valley."

"I understand, Joseph. Truly. And I wish we could have met under different circumstances."

"I wish that, too. But . . ." The chief didn't finish the thought, but there was no need.

"We will wait here for General Howard."

"I'll tell him."

Wood turned and started up to the top of the hill, turned once to wave, then went on down the far side to the camp. Howard was sitting in his tent, a Bible open on his lap. He looked up when Wood entered.

"He's here?"

Wood nodded. "Yes, sir, he is."

Howard got to his feet with a groan. "No point in putting this off, I guess." He set the book on the folding chair he'd just vacated and went outside without a word. He carried his hat in his hand and started up the hill. "Henry, get Captain Whipple and Lieutenant Andrews, will you please? You'll catch up."

Wood ran to get the officers named and raced after Howard, catching him while he was just below the crest of the hill. The four officers straightened their uniforms, the three junior officers doing so almost in unison after Howard himself shrugged his jacket into place, then clapped his hat on.

Ready, with a firm stride that belied the uncertainty he felt, General Howard crested the hill and started down the other side. He sensed that events were accumulating a similar downhill momentum, and that if a peaceful solution could not be be worked out in the next week or so, then war was inevitable.

Joseph introduced the other chiefs with him and then turned to an old Indian Howard had not met before, named Toohoolhoolzote, a medicine man. Like Joseph and Ollakot, he was a member of the Dreamer cult, as his hair clearly showed. Howard stiffened, expecting trouble. He was not disappointed.

"The other Indians may have sold their land or given it to you whites, but"—the old medicine man swept a hand broadly to take in Joseph and the other chiefs arrayed behind him—"we never did. The land is our mother and we cannot leave our mother."

"You know very well," Howard countered, "that a reservation has been created for you and that you must go there to live. Timothy has done so. He has a house and a farm at Alpowa. So can you."

"Where is the man who can divide the land? Where is the man who can make me stay on divided land?" Toohoolhoolzote snarled.

"I am that man," Howard told him. "Make no mistake about that."

The medicine man argued his case with logic that the general had to acknowledge was impeccable. But he was not there to hear a legal brief, but to enforce a military order, and whether he agreed with the order or not, it was an order and that was all he wanted or needed to know.

As Toohoolhoolzote became more belligerent Howard interrupted him. "Captain Whipple, please escort this gentleman to the guardhouse."

Whipple nodded to Lieutenant Andrews and stepped to the medicine man's side. Andrews moved to the old man's other side.

Howard looked at Joseph and said, "If we are to discuss this matter constructively, Toohoolhoolzote will have to stay out of it, Joseph." When the chief didn't object, Howard nodded, and the two officers escorted the shaman down toward the camp.

As Toohoolhoolzote was disappearing over the hill he turned and shouted at Howard: "You have brought a rifle to this council, a peace council. You give us thirty days to gather our stock and our belongings. You leave us no choice but to fight."

"Joseph," Howard said. "You and the other chiefs have seen the lands on the reservation where you are to live. Each of you has had his choice. I know it is not easy, but it is for your own protection. You saw what happened with Wilhautyah. Findley and McNall are not the only men of their kind here."

Joseph smiled bitterly. "You say it is for our protection, that you cannot stop men like Findley and McNall. You say there is the rule of law that cannot be disobeyed, and yet McNall and Findley disobey the law and nothing is done to them. Wilhautyah was my friend. He was respected by everyone in our tribe, and yet nothing is done to punish his

murderers. And I say that *we* can punish them. We
do not need the white man's protection against
their kind. But you say no, you must let us do it,
and you do nothing. That is your law. And that is
your protection."

"Joseph," Howard said, shaking his head. "The
land was sold by treaty. You know that. The
Wallowa is—"

"The Wallowa was never sold. It is as if someone came to me and said, 'You have fine horses
and I would like to buy them.' But I say no, I don't
wish to sell, and this man goes to someone else
and says, 'Here, take this money, I am buying
Joseph's horses.' If our land was sold, *that* is how
it was sold. We never did it."

"Joseph, I must have your answer. And I must
have it now. Will you go to the new reservation . . . ?"

The chief looked out over the lake far below,
squinting, almost as if he were looking for the
troops he knew were moving into the valley to
reinforce Howard's already impressive contingent.

He sighed. "Thirty days is not enough time."

"It is all the time I can give you, Joseph. Yes or
no?"

Joseph nodded sadly. "Yes," he said, his voice
husky. "Yes, we will go."

Chapter 28 ═══════════

As THE REALITY OF THEIR FORCED REMOVAL started to sink in, the Nez Percé were growing tense and irritable. Even under ordinary circumstances, the work would have been oppressive, but the knowledge that they would never again be able to call the Wallowa Valley home made it all but unbearable.

Joseph's wife, Tomah, was going into labor, and he pitched a small temporary camp on the banks of the Salmon River. The packing of their belongings and gathering of as much food as possible in the thirty days allotted them took every available waking minute. Most of the Wil-lam-wat-kin clan was on the far side of the Salmon. The women were gathering cowish roots and trying to prepare them for the trip, which required them to be spread in the sun to dry.

The traffic in and out of the makeshift camps was nonstop as people made trip after trip, packing everything they owned on horses and travois. On one of these transits, a young warrior named Wahlitits negotiated a patch of drying roots on horseback. His horse accidentally stepped on several, crushing them and making them worthless for food.

The women who had just finished spreading the roots glared at the young man, who seemed embarrassed, but said nothing.

The woman's husband was not about to let the accident pass unremarked. "Instead of going around undoing my wife's work and ruining our food," Yellow Grizzly Bear said, "why don't you go avenge the death of Eagle Robe? If you have nothing better to do, punishing the man who murdered your father should keep you out of the way."

Wahlitits, stung by the reminder of his father's murder, snarled something unintelligible at his tormentor, but nudged his horse on through the roots without further mishap.

He went on to the camp where his mother was working on her own supply of roots. Dismounting and walking on through the campsite to a small clump of trees, he flopped onto the ground and leaned back against a tree. One of his friends, Sarpsis Ilppilp, spotted him and left his own campsite to join him.

"I'm surprised you didn't fight with him," Sarpsis said as he lowered himself to the ground beside his friend.

"Fight with who?" Still stung by the insult, Wahlitits was barely paying attention.

"Yellow Grizzly Bear," Sarpsis said. "It's all over the camp."

"What is all over the camp? I don't understand."

"What he said to you."

That got the young warrior's full attention. He cursed quietly, and Sarpsis reached into his shirt. "This should make you feel better," he said as he pulled out a bottle of whiskey.

"He shouldn't have said that," Wahlitits said.

"I know it. And so does he," Sarpsis said. "Everyone's on edge. This is not a good thing that is happening."

But Wahlitits was not about to be distracted from the main theme. "He knows very well that Eagle Robe made me promise not to make trouble. He forgave his murderer and made me promise to do the same."

"We know that. No one thinks the less of you." He unscrewed the bottle, took a sip, and handed it to his friend. "Here, have some."

Wahlitits snatched the bottle angrily, tilted it back, and took a long pull on the cheap whiskey. It burned going down, but not as much as the remark of Yellow Grizzly Bear. "If it was up to me, I would have killed Ott myself with my bare hands when he killed Eagle Robe."

"But it wasn't up to you, Wahlitits. You might as well put it out of your mind. No one blames you for honoring your father's dying wish."

"Yes, they do." Wahlitits took another pull on the bottle. This time the rotgut didn't burn quite as much going down, and he took another quick sip before passing it back to Sarpsis.

"You know," Sarpsis said, taking a sip of his own, "it seems like the whites can get away with anything, and they make *us* move for our own safety. It's not us who kill the whites."

Wahlitits was lost in thought, his mind already a bit numbed by the whiskey. He grunted and reached for the bottle. "The chiefs are all old men. They are afraid of the whites," he mumbled.

Sarpsis shook his head. "I don't think so. They just know that if we start a war, we will lose it and maybe lose everything we have. That's what Joseph says, and White Bird, too. They all say the same thing."

"Not Toohoolhoolzote," Wahlitits pointed out. "He is willing to fight."

"He is the oldest of them all," Sarpsis pointed out. "How long do you think he would be able to wage war at his age?"

"I'm not an old man," Wahlitits said, taking one more swallow. "If it was up to me, I would make the whites pay for what they have done. It isn't just Ott. There are many others. How many of our people have been killed? And what punishment has been given to the murderers?" He stared idly at the bottle for a moment, and when Sarpsis said nothing, he answered his own questions. "I'll tell you— many and nothing."

"There is nothing we can do about it, Wahlitits. It is finished. The old ways are gone now. Now we are like squirrels in a tiny cage. We are told where to live. But that is how it will be from now on."

"Why?" Wahlitits upended the bottle, drained much of what was left, and handed the nearly dead soldier to his companion. "You might as well finish this," he said.

Sarpsis swallowed the last of the whiskey and let the bottle fall into the dirt beside his hip. "I can get another bottle. In fact, I think I will. Don't go away."

"Where would I go? There is nowhere *to* go. Not anymore." Even the slurring of his speech couldn't conceal the bitterness. He slid further along the tree and watched Sarpsis disappear into the milling throng. It wasn't good to brood this way. He knew that. But he knew, too, that no matter what Sarpsis said, some people did blame him for not avenging Eagle Robe. He blamed himself, he knew that. And if Eagle Robe had been someone else's father, he knew that he would blame the son who did nothing. It wasn't right to do nothing. It wasn't right that the killer still worked on his farm, on *Indian* land, while Eagle Robe was now just bones in a hole in the ground.

When he saw Sarpsis returning with a bottle in each hand, he smiled. His lips felt numb, but that was good. Better that he should be numb all over than feel the shame of Yellow Grizzly Bear's remark, and the sting of his own shame, of his own cowardice.

The two warriors sat there all afternoon, their backs no longer feeling the rough bark behind them. As the second bottle was dispatched after nightfall they started to get angry, and by the time the third was well on its way to empty, the anger had turned to outright rage. It was nearly sunup when Wahlitits said, "He's right, isn't he?"

"Who?" Sarpsis asked.

"Yellow Grizzly Bear. He's right, isn't he?"

"About what?"

"That I shouldn't be riding over people's food."

"Of course he is. No one should be that inconsiderate."

"No, not just that. I should avenge my father's death. If I don't, who will? Who will make the man who killed him pay for his crime? Who will make any of them pay? Joseph? White Bird? Looking Glass? Ollakot?" He shook his head after each term of the litany. And when he had reeled off the entire list of the Nez Percé leadership, he patted himself on the head. "No," he said. "They won't avenge Eagle Robe. *I* will avenge Eagle Robe. It is a son's duty to his father."

He got to his feet, wavering a little, but maintaining his balance. He started back toward the camp, with Sarpsis trailing along behind him. Stumbling once in a while, he managed to find the campsite. He put the small Nez Percé–styled saddle on his horse and went to the travois where his belongings were packed and took his gun and all the ammunition he had. Sarpsis was sitting by a nearly dead campfire as Wahlitits made his way through the sleeping Indians.

Wahlitits held his gun overhead and waved it. Sarpsis nodded and got to his feet. "Get Swan Necklace," Wahlitits said. "I'll meet you by the trees."

He threaded his way on through the sleeping camp and into the grass beyond, then moved to the trees. Fifteen minutes later, Sarpsis and Swan Necklace joined him, both having mounted their horses as soon as they were beyond the fringes of the camp. Wahlitits swung into the saddle and nudged his horse into a fast walk. Circling the camp, the three young warriors made their way to the bank of the Salmon River. They headed downstream, away from the camp where Joseph still sat awake, waiting for news of the impending birth.

Larry Ott lived several miles downstream, not far from the Salmon, and as soon as the young men were safe from the possibility of discovery, Wahlitits kicked his pony into a trot in the direction of Ott's place. His two friends fell in beside him, and all three rode without speaking for a long time. Not until the Ott homestead was within sight did Swan Necklace ask, "Where are we going?"

Wahlitits looked at him for a second, then turned away. "You'll see," he said.

Ott was already outside as the three warriors approached. He saw them coming and rushed into the barn as Wahlitits led a charge toward the homestead. Ott burst through the open barn door already in the saddle. He spurred his horse, a strong, loose-limbed Nez Percé Appaloosa, and cut across a plowed field, the animal's hooves kicking up clods of dried soil as it charged toward the tree line beyond the tillage.

Ott made it to the trees several hundred yards ahead of the warriors. His mount was fresh and theirs were tired. And he seemed to have some idea what they planned for him, because he rode like there was no tomorrow.

Once into the trees, he was home free. Wahlitits searched the edge of the woods for several minutes, then nudged his mount on into the trees. There wasn't much light in the woods, and the whiskey was still befuddling him. He gave up in disgust after ten minutes of fruitless looking.

"I guess we should go home," Swan Necklace said, uneasy now that their purpose was inescapably clear to him, even without either of the others having put it into words.

"No," Wahlitits snapped. "Eagle Robe is not the only Nez Percé the whites have killed. And Ott is not the only murderer who deserves to be punished. The man at Slate Creek, Devine, killed Da Koopin, didn't he? A crippled old woman, and he shot her for no reason. Shouldn't he be made to pay?"

"It is not for you to punish him, Wahlitits," Swan Necklace said.

"If not me, then who?" he asked.

Swan Necklace looked to Sarpsis for support. "Sarpsis? Tell him."

Sarpsis shook his head.

Before Swan Necklace could object, Wahlitits kicked his mount and they were off. The ride to Slate Creek took half an hour. And this time their quarry was at home. They thundered down on the house and burst inside. Richard Devine was just getting up from the rough-timbered table, a tin coffee cup in his hand.

Wahlitits fired his rifle without warning, and Devine sprawled across the table, the cup dangling for a second, spilling coffee onto the floor before it fell from his grasp and clattered into a corner.

Wahlitits spat at the twitching body and walked to the fireplace. He reached in for a brand, ignored the searing heat as his fingers came perilously close to the flames, and grasped the uncharred end of a small log. Jerking it out of the fire, he torched the faded curtains covering the only window in the room, then tossed the brand onto the floor and smashed a coal-oil lamp beside it. The splattered oil slowly pooled, then spread into a thin sheet and caught fire as its edge encircled the brand.

Swan Necklace stood in the open doorway, his jaw slack. "What are you doing?" he asked. "You can't—"

"Yes," Wahlitits said. "I can."

"But . . . the soldiers . . . they'll come and—"

"I don't care about the soldiers. I'm not afraid of them."

"But our people. They'll—"

"Go. You warn them. Tell them what you saw here. And tell them that those who want to join me will know where to find me. There are others who should die like this snake. We all know who they are. Joseph knows. Looking Glass knows. Tell them!"

And he burst through the door and ran for his horse. Swan Necklace looked at Sarpsis, who shrugged then ran for his own mount. Swan Necklace stumbled outside and stood on the porch as the two warriors rode away, only dimly aware of the tang of burning wood behind him. He looked once over his shoulder and saw that the flames had already spread to one wall, and he turned, uncertain whether to go inside and try to pull Devine out of the cabin. He took one tentative step into the cabin then backed out and did not turn around until he bumped into his pony.

As he galloped off he looked back once, just as flames burst through the roof of the cabin and a column of smoke spewed through the opening, showering sparks like fireflies as it rose. He kicked his pony harder, hoping he could reach Joseph before the whole Wallowa Valley went up in flames.

Chapter 29 ═══════════

White Bird Canyon—June 1877

WORD OF THE CARNAGE caught Joseph off guard. Exhausted from waiting for the birth of his child, a girl, he was stunned into silence when Swan Necklace told him what had happened. Now, he knew, there was almost no choice for the Nez Percé. And it would almost certainly have to be war. He knew General Howard well enough to understand that there was just the slimmest of chances to avert a catastrophe. And it was best to assume the worst.

He sent Swan Necklace as a messenger to the other chiefs and told them that he was moving his camp sixteen miles, to White Bird Canyon, where he would wait for them. Then he galvanized his people into action. Everything would have to be packed and moved as soon as possible. If it wasn't essential, it would have to be left behind.

Joseph's band was the first to arrive at White Bird Canyon, and while his people set up a minimal camp, keeping themselves ready to move on a moment's notice, Joseph rode the perimeter of the canyon. It was an ideal defensive position, one that would be all but impregnable if they had to fight.

Impregnable, that is, until there were enough soldiers to overwhelm them. It would at least give them time to decide what the next step should be.

When General Howard got word of the murders, now said to number fourteen or fifteen, with another dozen or so unconfirmed reports of still more deaths, he dispatched Captain David Perry at the head of Companies F and H of the First Cavalry. It was nearly seventy miles to the Salmon River, where Joseph had last been reported, and Perry made the trek nonstop in under twenty-four hours.

The troops arrived at White Bird Creek at midnight. Lieutenant Edward Theller, in command of one company, suggested that they camp for the night, then move up the creek in daylight.

"Lieutenant, if I do that, General Howard'll have my head. People are clamoring for retaliation. There are volunteers on the way, and if we don't move in, they'll just get in the way and possibly make this situation worse than it has to be."

"Can't get much worse than it already is, Captain."

"Maybe so, but there's no time to wait. We're going to move in and take up positions. As soon as we're ready, we'll let them know we're here."

"Yes, sir."

"And Lieutenant . . ."

"Yes, sir?"

"Pray, Lieutenant."

Theller snapped a salute without answering and raced back to his command. Perry dispatched scouts into the canyon, then started deploying his troops, reminding them that silence was paramount. Captain Joel Trimble directed the right flank, Lieutenant Theller the skirmish line at the center, and a small group of volunteers, supposedly the vanguard of a larger force just hours away, composed the left flank.

In the darkness, going was anything but easy. The canyon was rocky and its walls were precipitous. Smaller ravines ran off the canyon at odd angles, some of them large and some little more than holes in the wall. In the darkness, Nez Percé scouts occupied niches in the walls.

Joseph and Ollakot were in conference when a coyote call signaled to everyone in the camp that the soldiers were moving in. The brothers rushed toward the mouth of the canyon, taking cover behind jumbled boulders. As the sky slowly brightened, the rising light was accompanied by the sounds of men scrambling through the rocks, trying and failing to keep silent.

Just before dawn, it was light enough to see clearly and Joseph sent six warriors out with a white flag. He didn't know whether Howard was at the scene, but he wanted to make one last attempt at preventing the war. The six warriors moved cautiously, one waving the makeshift truce flag high overhead while the other five, their rifles cocked, scanned the walls and the crannies in the rocks.

They had gone no more than fifty yards when a rifle shot broke the morning stillness. The bullet, fired by one of the volunteers, missed the truce party, but as it whined away into silence Joseph knew that the last chance for peace had gone with it. The truce party abandoned the flag and scrambled into the rocks to work their way back to the Nez Percé lines.

The lodges had already been disassembled, and Joseph ordered the horses to be taken down the creek to the Salmon River, where they would be out of harm's way. As the horses started to move, a bugle sounded, and Perry's men started over the last ridge and into the canyon.

Shouting instructions, Joseph deployed his forces and steeled himself for the battle. Half his force raced to reach the buttes at the mouth of the canyon, where White Bird Creek flowed into flatland before meeting the Salmon. Joseph took command of one line of the remaining force, Ollakot a second, and Hasotoin the remainder. As the troops entered the canyon ragged volleys broke out, and the sounds of gunfire echoed off the canyon walls.

The Nez Percé only had fifty guns, and most of them were old. Ammunition was in short supply, and the warriors were instructed to make every shot count. Most of the warriors were armed only with bows.

The Indians held their ground, their ponies just behind them, reins loose, ready for mounting. Suddenly the atmosphere became very quiet. The canyon was several miles long and the Nez Percé had pulled back close to the Salmon. They were waiting patiently, Joseph still hoping that some way could be found to stop the war before it was too late.

Indian sentries sent word along the canyon, monitoring the approaching cavalry. The valley floor was full of willow clumps and brush, and dry creek beds zigzagged among the stones. White Bird Creek angled away behind some low buttes, and the troops left the water to enter a narrow ravine.

One side was flanked by a sheer wall, with the rounded buttes on the other. Lieutenant Theller's command was in the lead, Trimble fifty yards behind him, and Perry last, another fifty yards behind Trimble's men.

The ravine widened out now and became a V-shaped valley a quarter mile wide. Theller halted his men, wondering where the Indians were. They seemed to have vanished completely. His troops dismounted and started to advance cautiously when rifle fire exploded all around them.

Suddenly a line of Indians, ragged because of the profusion of rocks and boulders, materialized and opened fire. Bullets poured into Theller's line, scattering his troops as twenty warriors on horseback charged toward them in the wide stretch between the creek and the canyon wall.

Wahlitits and Sarpsis Ilppilp were among them, and as they charged, Wahlitits looked for Joseph, wondering if he would live long enough to apologize to the chief for the trouble he'd caused.

Perry advanced, deployed Trimble's men to low buttes to the left and right, then fell in behind Theller's command. The fire was thunderous and the canyon filled with gunsmoke, which drifted in clouds overhead, lowering like a thin fog. Joseph's warriors had good cover, and their fire halted the advance of the cavalry, but the Indians were outgunned, and for nearly an hour, the two sides exchanged shots incessantly but to little effect.

Some way had to be found to shatter the stalemate. Joseph hurriedly assembled a band of some sixty warriors and mixed them in with a herd of ponies, then sent horses and men up the canyon.

At the same time the cavalry was forced to dismount. The unceasing staccato rattle of the guns was making their horses skittish and unmanageable, and the unmanned mounts were sent back behind the lines.

As the mass of Indians and ponies exploded into view, the soldiers failed to spot the warriors until they were on top of their position. Suddenly the Nez Percé burst out of the stampeding ponies and opened fire. At the same time Ollakot led a flanking movement, trying to get around behind Perry's position. The superior firepower of the cavalry held off the assault, but the steady pressure of the Indians and their ear-shattering war cries were unnerving the troops, many of whom were green.

The small volunteer group was under heavy attack, and they had scattered, leaving their position on a low knoll and running for higher ground. Perry's line suddenly buckled as the raw recruits ran for their horses.

Joseph pressed the assault, seeing an opportunity to rout the cavalry that might buy his people some time. Both buglers in the command were down, and Perry's hoarse cries for order were all but inaudible. Theller's men, in the most forward position, saw Perry's men fleeing, and crumbled all at once, joining the general flight.

Helplessly, Captain Perry shouted commands he knew were inaudible in the tumult, then raced along the now shapeless line to find Trimble. The two officers managed to halt a few men long enough to re-form depleted companies, but the pressure of the Nez Percé was relentless. Seeing other troops on high ground, the men broke once more, fleeing for their lives as the Indians pressed their advantage.

Lieutenant Theller, seeing Perry and Trimble retreating, rallied eighteen men to form a rear guard, trying to delay the Nez Percé advance until his commander's men were in position to cover his own retreat. Theller ducked into a narrow canyon, his men backing deeper and deeper into it, firing at the Indians on the rocks above them and gathering around the mouth of the narrow defile.

Someone shouted and Theller turned to see one of his men trying to climb a sheer stone wall. The defile was a dead end. Indians swarmed along the top of the narrow ravine and Theller's men arrayed themselves in a circle. It was impossible to pick targets as the Indians bobbed up just long enough to fire, then disappeared. Another would pop up fifty yards away, then a third, then the first again, then a fourth.

In less than an hour, all nineteen men were dead, surrounded by spent cartridges in small, glittering mounds. The defile grew silent and the Indians backed away from the rim to rejoin the pursuit of Perry and Trimble.

For three hours the Nez Percé continued to assault the cavalry, chasing them fifteen miles before abandoning the pursuit. Rushing back to the canyon, they sifted through the debris of the battlefield, taking ammunition and guns, including some modern repeating rifles. There still were not enough guns for every warrior, and they had used a good deal of the ammunition they'd had on hand.

When the smoke cleared, the Nez Percé had sustained minimal casualties—none dead and only three wounded. Perry's command had lost thirty-four men. Some of the younger warriors were jubilant, but Joseph refused to join in their elation.

Wahlitits approached him, a sheepish grin on his face. "Maybe we can defeat the white soldiers after all," he said.

Joseph shook his head. "No, Wahlitits. All we can do is postpone our own defeat."

"We did well today."

"Today, yes. But there are many soldiers, more soldiers than there are of us."

"We are better fighters than they are."

"Maybe. But can you make a bullet?"

The young warrior stopped smiling. "No," he said.

"Neither can I."

Ollakot and White Bird joined him. "What should we do?" Ollakot asked.

"We should gather as many warriors as we can and attack the soldiers," White Bird said.

Joseph shook his head. "No. There is only one chance for us," he said. "We will have to go to the buffalo country, maybe even to Canada, where the Sioux Sitting Bull went after his war with the white soldiers."

"Canada is very far," White Bird said.

"Yes," Joseph said, "it is. We'd better begin the journey."

Chapter 30 ═══════════

Clearwater Valley—July 1877

GENERAL HOWARD, embarrassed that the Nez Percé had slipped through his fingers, began to mobilize forces from all over the northwest. He ordered troops to move from Walla Walla, Vancouver, Townsend, Klamath, and other, smaller military posts. At the same time volunteer companies were organized all over Oregon, Washington, and Idaho.

The citizens, as usual, clamored for more military might, and some packed their pockets with ammunition and their bellies with beer before going off to do battle, or so they told themselves.

Despite Joseph's concern for the defenseless women and children, the Indians were divided. Their normal military organization was only loosely structured, with chiefs appointed for battles by common consent. No warrior was compelled to follow his chief, and some elected to follow others, while some elected not to fight at all.

This indecision led to a temporary immobility, and nearly two weeks after the battle at White Bird Canyon, the majority of the nontreaty Nez Percé were still within shouting distance of the Salmon River. Howard himself had arrived to take command of the military, and his dispatches were hopeful that a quick end could be put to the troubles, despite the failure at White Bird.

In a spontaneous council, the Indians tried to decide what to do next. Joseph knew that peace was now a very slender reed, and placed little hope in it. But he was of two minds. Part of him wanted to run for Canada, while another, deeper part of him hoped that it would be possible to elude the soldiers long enough for passions to cool, when a return to the Wallowa might be possible.

The Nez Percé were getting intelligence from bands of their tribesmen who, so far, had not been involved in the hostilities. Even some of the treaty Nez Percé offered information, if not active participation. They knew that the military forces had grown from the hundred soldiers at White Bird Canyon to more than four hundred soldiers with another hundred volunteers. They had fewer than two hundred and fifty fighting men, and many of those were only lukewarm about additional combat.

At the council, White Bird wondered aloud, "Why should we fight if our village is not being attacked? We are not chasing the soldiers. They are chasing us."

Joseph, too, was in favor of avoiding engagement if at all possible. But on June 27, the decision was taken out of their hands. Howard's forces reached the Salmon River at a point almost directly across from the Nez Percé camp.

The river was still swollen to flood stage, and Howard realized then the justice of Joseph's position that thirty days had not been enough time to gather their belongings and reach the designated portions of the reservation. But that was all ancient history now, and, just or not, the position was irrelevant.

The troops had been spotted by scouts, and several warriors came to the riverbank to taunt the troopers, daring them to cross the river and fight. Howard sent two men across to scout the terrain on the far side, but the swim was a rough one, and getting fully loaded troops across could not be accomplished without rafts, boats, and ratlines for the infantry to cling to as they waded through the torrent.

It took three days for sufficient preparations to be made, and when Howard gave the command, his men started across. The rafts were sluggish and the few boats available held precious few men. But the Nez Percé elected to run rather than fight. Instead of lining the bluffs on the opposite bank and sniping at the soldiers, they packed their belongings and headed south.

At Greer's Ferry, the Nez Percé contingent, including nearly four hundred women and children, crossed the Salmon themselves and were now on the opposite side of the river once more. It was beginning to seem to Howard that the Indians were toying with him. Some of his men seemed to prefer it that way, whether because they sympathized with the Indians or were simply pleased to avoid the hazards of combat, the general wasn't sure.

He caught Major Wood with the ghost of a grin just dematerializing when it became apparent what had happened. "Henry," Howard snapped, "I'm starting to wonder just whose side you're on."

"I wondered, too, for a while, General."

"Does that mean you've now made up your mind?"

"Yes, sir."

"And what, if I may ask, was your decision?"

"Begging the general's pardon, sir, but I'd prefer not to answer."

"May I infer from that, Major, that I would not be pleased with your decision?"

"I'm sure I wouldn't know, sir. Not knowing where the general's own sympathies lie, it's not a question I could possibly answer."

"Should you ever resign your commission, Henry," Howard barked, "be sure you consider attorney as a possible profession."

"Yes, sir."

Despite Major Wood's evident sympathies, in which he was not alone, Howard pursued the fugitives the twenty-five miles to the ferry but, unable to get his men across, was forced to turn north again and recross at the mouth of White Bird Creek, the same point at which he had crossed initially. The Nez Percé had parlayed their maneuver into a two-day lead.

Howard was growing frustrated. After the recrossing, he sat up late with his adjutant and tried to decide on a course of action. "It looks as if Joseph doesn't really want to fight, Henry," he said.

Major Wood grunted. "He shouldn't have to, General. You know that as well as I do."

"No, I don't know any such thing, Henry. I have my orders, and so do you."

Wood sighed. "There are times when I regret that I'm a soldier, General."

"Forget you are for a moment, Henry. Man to man, what's on your mind?"

"Isn't there any way that a 'peaceful solution can be found? Joseph seems favorably disposed to some sort of compromise. There must be some way."

"No, there just isn't any way to compromise on this, Henry. Not now. Now that men have been killed, it's just . . ." The general shrugged. "I wish there were, but . . ."

"I regret the deaths of those men as much as anyone could, General. You know me well enough to know that. But I can't help but think their deaths were unnecessary. If we had just been more reasonable in the beginning. Joseph had agreed. He just said he needed more time. And we wouldn't give it to him. You saw that river this morning. How can you blame the man for wanting more time? He's not just moving military supplies, for God's sake. He's moving his whole life."

"Look, Henry. You may be right. I even think—and I'm talking as a man now, not as a military officer—that he should have been allowed to stay where he was. You know that. But then those young bucks went on their killing spree. Once that happened, it was just a matter of time before someone else got murdered, even if the guilty bucks were hanged. Some damn fool with a belly full of rotgut would go into a village toting a six-gun. Or a young warrior thinking he had something to prove would ride off and steal some horses. In the current situation, you can't have whites and Indians in the same valley any more than you can store fire and powder in the same keg. Either way, you get an explosion. And once it starts, who knows where it stops? I don't know now where it'll stop, Henry. And neither do you. For that matter, neither does Joseph. Events have a way of getting out of hand quicker than a wink. And war has a mind of its own, Henry."

"And whose fault is that?" Wood demanded.

"It's not up to me to decide that. I have my orders, and I mean to carry them out. I can't do anything else."

Wood got to his feet. "I think I'm going to turn in, General."

"I thought we were going to try to decide where Joseph would go next."

"I don't have a clue, General. And frankly, in the mood I'm in, I don't know if I'd tell you even if I knew."

"That's speaking as a man and not an officer, I assume?" Howard said, pursing his lips.

"I'm a man before I'm a soldier, General."

"Good night, Henry."

"Good night, General."

The following morning Howard made his next mistake. He sent a detachment to the camp of Looking Glass, who so far had not joined the hostilities. But there were rumors that he might, and Howard, hoping to forestall the possibility and possibly deal a blow to the morale of the fugitives, decided that having Looking Glass under lock and key was at the least prudent and perhaps even a necessity.

When the troops arrived at Looking Glass's camp, the officer in charge, Captain Stephen Whipple, deployed two Gatling guns and sent a scout in to bring the chief to him.

Sensing that something was wrong, Looking Glass sent an old man in his place, with instructions to tell the soldiers to leave. The old warrior, Kalowet, approached Whipple waving his arms. "What do you want with us? We are not making war. Leave us alone."

"I can't do that," Whipple said. "I have my orders. I must see Looking Glass."

Realizing that Whipple would not leave until he appeared, the chief walked to him and asked what he wanted.

"I have to place you under arrest," Whipple said.

"Why? I and my people have done nothing. We have been here, and we are on the reservation. That is what the white man wants us to do, stay on the reservation, and I have done that. Tell General Howard that I am not making war."

Before Whipple could reply, one of his men shot at a warrior in the camp. The Indians scattered, and Looking Glass darted away as the troopers opened fire. Whipple called for a cease-fire, but it was too late, and he knew it. He couldn't expect the chief to come with him now, not after an unprovoked attack on his camp.

In a matter of minutes the small camp was deserted as the Indians vanished into the hills beyond it. The troops burned the camp and everything in it, but succeeded only in adding a formidable chief and forty more warriors to the fugitive army.

It wasn't until July 11 that Howard finally caught up with Joseph again. Once more, the Nez Percé had established a temporary village, this time in a shallow valley surrounded by bluffs on all sides. Howard arrayed his troops on the high ground, but the slopes of the bluffs were precipitous, and there was considerable cover for the Indians below them.

Unable to charge without risking life and limb, the soldiers dug in and settled down to a full day of exchanging fire with the warriors, who were scattered among the clumps of brush and clusters of large boulders on the valley floor.

Because of the elevation of their position, the howitzers and Gatling guns of the soldiers could not be brought to bear on the village itself, tantalizingly evident to the gunners, who worked all day to excavate gun emplacements that would let them depress the muzzles enough for effective fire.

Joseph, Ollakot, White Bird, and Looking Glass were like apparitions, darting on horseback from place to place and exhorting their warriors. Even when the chiefs could not be seen, the soldiers could hear their war cries. They came to recognize the individual voices.

Three times the soldiers tried to assault the Indian positions, and three times the rugged terrain and the marksmanship of the warriors combined to drive them back.

Howard was getting impatient. His temper was short, and he was displeased with most of his commanders who seemed either reluctant to carry out his orders or were so dilatory in their execution that the Nez Percé always had time to react before an advantage could be gained.

And the Indians had control of the only source of water in the valley, a large spring. The sun was hammering the soldiers, and their canteens were empty, but there was no way they could get to the water without coming under the guns of sharpshooters strategically positioned around the spring.

The big guns started to pound the village, and the swirls of gunsmoke gradually blended into a thin haze that hung above the battlefield like low-lying clouds.

By nightfall the soldiers were desperate for water. Howard took advantage of the onset of darkness to devise a plan of attack for the following morning. He put every available man on the line and deployed two cavalry units for a charge to take place at sunrise.

In the meantime, the Indians were beginning to squabble among themselves. Several warriors slipped away during the night; weary of the fighting and convinced that the war would only end in their defeat, they decided to go to the reservation. The defections were not massive, but already outmanned and heavily outgunned, Joseph's forces could ill afford to lose a single man.

Only sporadic fire crackled during the night, mostly from the soldiers, who were easily spooked and, fearful of a full-scale assault, fired at the slightest sound beyond their lines.

At dawn Howard gave the order, and his line opened fire. The cavalry thundered around the bottom of a bluff and charged toward the spring. The attack seemed to take the warriors by surprise. They returned fire, but the attacking numbers were overwhelming and they were forced to fall back, yielding control of the spring to the army. From that point, it was inevitable that they would have to withdraw or risk being in the same desperate situation that had so dogged the soldiers the day before. There was not enough food for a long siege. But they fought fiercely, yielding as little ground as possible and charging the soldiers dearly for every yard.

Just past the spring, the ground was flat and favored the Indians, who were more mobile than the troopers and free to move or not on their own initiative. They darted like angry bees from boulder to brush and back, all but halting the advance of Howard's line.

The Indians kept up their resistance for twelve hours. The village lay behind them on the banks of the Clearwater River. It was heavily damaged by the howitzers, and lay in ruins. Lodges were sundered, their contents scattered in every direction. Food supplies were spilled everywhere, and mounds of buffalo robes lay abandoned as the Nez Percé once more had to take to their horses and run for their lives.

Captain Perry mounted another charge late in the afternoon, and drove his cavalry unit relentlessly ahead until he passed the village and reached the edge of the Clearwater behind it. He hesitated just long enough for the Nez Percé to make good their escape.

There was no clear winner, but Howard felt as if he had atoned somewhat for the defeat at White Bird Canyon.

Just before dark, the Indians, aware that Howard had pitched camp near their ruined village, camped on a bluff several miles south of the village. It was time to take stock, and the mood was grim.

The chiefs huddled together, trying to decide what their next move should be. No one argued for surrender, but the alternatives were few and equally difficult.

"I think," Looking Glass said, "we should take the Lolo Trail and cross into the buffalo country. We can join the Crows. They are like brothers. They will take us in, and if we join with them, we will be much stronger. I think the white soldiers will leave us alone there."

Toohoolhoolzote added, "The soldiers will not be able to bring their great guns over the mountains."

Joseph was not so sure. "You talk as if there are no soldiers on the other side of the mountains. Do you forget that that is where the whites came from in the first place? Or do you think they are all on our side of the mountains now?"

"What do you think we should do?" the old medicine man challenged.

"I think we should go to the Grandmother Country to join with Sitting Bull and the other Sioux."

"The Blackfeet are in Canada, do you forget?"

"I am less concerned about Blackfeet than I am about the soldiers. The Blackfeet do not have big cannons that can destroy a whole lodge with a single shot. You saw the village. You saw what we were forced to leave behind. I think now they will chase us until they catch us. But they can't chase us into Canada."

"We can go to the buffalo country," Looking Glass suggested by way of compromise, "and if the soldiers follow us there and will not let us be, then we can go to Canada."

"And bring our troubles to our brothers the Crows?" Joseph asked.

"We will not bring trouble. The soldiers will not follow us over the mountains. You will see."

Chapter 31 ═══════════

IN THE AFTERMATH of the Battle of the Clearwater, the Nez Percé were once again undecided about what their next step should be. The campaign was wearing them down, particularly since many of them were not wholeheartedly in favor of war to begin with. The pressures of the war were pulling them in several directions.

At a council the day after the battle, Joseph said, "We should take the Lolo Trail through the mountains. If we can get into Montana, we can leave the war behind. The Montana people are not our enemies. If we cross the mountains, we leave the war behind in Idaho."

Looking Glass was still in favor of linking up with the Crows, not in order to expand the fighting force available to them, but simply to find a place to live. There were simpler ways to get to Montana, routes that would make the passage easier, but Joseph believed that the least likely route would buy them some time, and even if Howard was able to follow them, it would take him some time, and the Nez Percé would certainly be able to cross the Bitterroots well ahead of the soldiers.

So far, the pursuit had been rather leisurely. Only one scouting party had come close to them,

and five warriors had been enough to turn the
scouts back. And a small raiding party had followed the scouts all the way back to the main contingent of Howard's command and recovered
several hundred horses, mounts that would be
absolutely indispensable for the grueling two-
hundred-and-fifty-mile climb through the Lolo
Pass, seven thousand feet above sea level.

The Lolo Trail, too, had another advantage. Even
Looking Glass agreed that the Flatheads, whose
country lay at the eastern end of the Lolo Trail,
would help them. The journey took eleven days.
The mountains were rugged, the route twisting and
turning through narrow defiles and more often than
not drenched in the shadows of massive pine
forests. The Nez Percé had used the trail for hundreds of years. It was one of their favorite routes to
the buffalo country.

But even their long acquaintance could not help
them carry their lives on their backs over fallen
trees, across deep mountain torrents, and through
fields littered with huge boulders, the gaps
between which often were barely wide enough to
permit passage of horses in single file.

But they made it through. Their hopes were
nearly dashed, though, when the Flatheads refused
to help. The Indians of western Montana had an
uneasy but persistently peaceful relationship with
white settlers. And the land was so vast and the
people, red and white alike, so few, that what con-
tact there had been had been pacific.

Pushing on, now headed for the Crows, Joseph
found his path blocked by a cavalry unit and detachment of volunteers headed by Captain Charles Rawn.

Joseph approached under a flag of truce, and Rawn, nervous but determined, walked into the middle of a meadow to meet him and Looking Glass.

"You'll have to turn back," Rawn said. "I cannot allow you to pass."

"We have no quarrel with you," Joseph said. "Our fight is not with the people of Montana. Our fight is with the people of Idaho, and we have left them behind us so that we will not have to fight again."

Rawn shook his head. "It's not that easy," he said. "I am a soldier, and I have my orders. The army here is the same army that pursues you from Idaho. The officers are different, but their purpose is the same. You'll have to go back. Either that, or you can surrender your weapons and ammunition and camp here until General Howard arrives."

"No," Joseph said, "we cannot give up our weapons. We will fight if we have to, but we do not want to. It would be better if you let us pass."

But Rawn was adamant. He was worried that one of the volunteers might get nervous and open fire. If that happened, Rawn knew, his chances of survival were slim. He had fewer than fifty men, and the Nez Percé numbered in the hundreds. Even if most of the Indians were not warriors, a quick estimate told Rawn that there would still be better than two hundred fighting men. And he knew they were fighting for their lives, a fact that would make them even more determined.

"We will have to think about your demands," Joseph said. "We will give you our answer in the morning."

But Rawn, fearful of a possible surprise attack during the night, countered with a demand that the answer be given no later than midnight. Joseph agreed, and he and Looking Glass returned to the waiting caravan.

Once more, the Indians were compelled to debate their future. Looking Glass was adamant that they should push on to the Crow country at any cost, even if it meant engaging Rawn's troops.

Wahlitits was troubled, partly because he was feeling guilty that his rash attack on Devine had been the cause of the war, and partly because he had had a vision. He had kept it to himself until the council, when he said, "I see myself dying in battle," he said. "There is smoke everywhere and women and children lying on the ground in rows like gutted salmon. I am afraid for our people."

"It is not the time to be afraid," Looking Glass said. "The white soldiers will not bother us. We are many and they are few. We should just tell them that if they block our way, we will fight them. They will not fight. They have no fight with us."

"You heard what the captain said," Joseph argued. "He said he cannot let us pass."

"We *will* pass," Looking Glass insisted. "The war is over. There will be no more fighting. Does Hin-mah-too-yah-lat-kekht think we should sit here and wait for General Howard?"

"No, I think we should go around the captain and his soldiers."

"But the way around is very difficult," Wahlitits said. "Looking Glass is right."

"Wahlitits," Joseph snapped, "do you want to see your vision become real? Do you want to see our women and children rotting in the sun like so many dead fish?"

"No, I . . ."

"Then we should go around. We should vote as
we always do, but you know my feeling now. The
captain is right. The army here is still the white
man's army. We cannot leave the war behind us."

Ollakot, like Joseph, was in favor of eluding
Rawn's men. White Bird, too, favored noncon-
frontational tactics. The irascible Toohoolhoolzote
was the only one on Looking Glass's side, and
unlike that war chief, he hoped there would be a
fight, and that Rawn would resist.

Joseph's prudence swayed them, and it was
decided to dispatch a small force of warriors to
confront Rawn without engaging him, keeping the
captain and his men occupied while the rest of the
tribe took a tortuous route through rocky draws and
up over steep ravine walls to get around behind the
makeshift fort Rawn and his men had constructed
out of logs and sod.

The stratagem worked, and when the warriors
fell back from the fort, they sprinted to catch the
caravan, leaving Rawn scratching his head. The
volunteer contingent, not especially disposed to
combat to begin with, took advantage of this opportunity to return to their homes, and Rawn was left
with too few men to pursue the Nez Percé, even if
he were so inclined.

Three days' march brought the tribe to the Big Hole
Basin, a half-moon-shaped valley, sixty miles long
and fifteen miles wide. It was a favorite camping
ground, not just for the Nez Percé but also for the
Crows and the Flatheads and even the Blackfeet. By
unwritten agreement, it was neutral ground, and even
warring tribes occasionally coexisted there peacefully.

Full of rich grassy meadows for the herds to graze on, and well watered by an interlacing network of streams that gradually flowed together to form the Big Hole River, it was an ideal place to rest and gather their resources. The fishing was good, enabling the foodstocks to be replenished, and deer and elk were plentiful, giving the Nez Percé the opportunity to eat fresh meat for the first time in weeks.

But General Howard had not abandoned his chase, and on August 8, he left the Lolo Trail, having spent nine grueling days in transit. He was still several days behind, but one of his officers, Colonel John Gibbon, was close enough to reach the village that evening.

Scouting the layout from a tall pine, Lieutenant James Bradley memorized the terrain and the configuration of the village, then returned to Gibbon's command.

"You're sure about that, Lieutenant?" Gibbon asked when Bradley had made his report.

"Yes, sir, I'm sure."

"It sounds like they're not expecting us," Gibbon said, stroking his beard. "Can they be that foolish?"

"Maybe it's a trap, sir," Bradley suggested.

"Did they see you, Lieutenant?"

"No, sir. I'm certain of that."

"Then how could it be a trap? As far as they know, General Howard is still on the Lolo Trail, days behind them. I don't understand, but this is an opportunity too good to waste. It'll take General Howard two days to reach us, but if we hit them hard and manage to take them by surprise, maybe we can force them to pack it in."

"I don't much like the idea of attacking a village full of women and children, Colonel," Bradley said.

"We didn't start this fight, Lieutenant, they did. But I'm God Almighty sure we're going to finish it, and this just might be the time to do it. We're going to bivouac now and get up at eleven o'clock tonight. That'll give us five hours to get in position before sunup. Then we'll hit them with everything we've got. We'll string our entire force in a line along one side of the V. Once we open fire, they'll be in our hip pocket."

Captain William Logan wrinkled his brow as Gibbon outlined his plan of attack. The colonel noticed, and frowned. "Something bothering you, Captain?"

"Begging your pardon, Colonel, but if we string our entire force in a single line, we have no reserves."

"Surprise is on our side, Captain. We won't need reserves."

"What about prisoners? We'll need a detachment to ride herd on the prisoners."

Gibbon shook his head. "There won't be any prisoners, Captain. And I want all of you officers to instruct your men. When we hit that village, I want them to fire into the lodges, and fire low. I don't want those Indians ducking under our volleys. Is that clear?"

"But there will be women and children in the line of fire, Colonel," Logan persisted.

"So be it, Captain. Now, get your men ready, all of you."

At eleven, instead of reveille, the troops were

awakened by their officers moving among the
bedrolls. By eleven-thirty, the column was on the
move. By three A.M., they were in position. Only
the river lay between the troops and the sleeping
village. At three-thirty, just as the sky began to turn
gray, Gibbon gave the order to move out. The men
were instructed to hold their fire unless and until
discovered. He wanted to get as close to the village
as possible before opening up. The closer the soldiers were, he knew, the greater would be the terror
as the disoriented and sleep-fogged warriors tried
to recover.

They got to within two hundred yards of the
river before an old man on horseback saw them. He
wasn't sure what it was he was seeing in the dim
light, leaned forward to get a better look, and was
blown out of the saddle by a flurry of rifle shots.
That turned the troopers loose, and they charged
headlong toward the river, splashed across the sluggish current and up the bank toward the lodges.

Awakened by the gunfire, people started to pour
out of the lodges. Most were women and children,
frightened by the noise. As the troopers reached the
lodges they bellowed at the top of their lungs and
sprayed a withering, indiscriminate fire through
the riverside leg of the V.

In the gloom, it wasn't possible to tell warrior
from woman, woman from child, but many of the
soldiers didn't seem to care. The least movement at
the entrance to a lodge brought a hail of bullets.
The troopers were among the lodges before the Nez
Percé could even think of returning fire. Most of
the warriors had to flee for their lives, leaving their
weapons behind. Those who had had the presence

of mind to grab bows or rifles had the daunting task of holding off the assault long enough for their brothers to regroup.

In small clusters, armed warriors led attacks back toward the line, pushing a dozen here and ten there back far enough and long enough for weapons to be recovered from the lodges.

Gradually, the chiefs and principal warriors took control of the panicked village. Joseph, Ollakot, Rainbow, and Looking Glass rallied warriors around them, and these small clusters of solidity acted like seed crystals. More and more warriors gathered around their leaders. Some managed to capture weapons from the troopers who either were killed or wounded, or who lost them in their haste to elude a sudden charge.

Equilibrium gradually returned, and the Nez Percé warriors started to push back the attackers.

Indian marksmen seemed to be everywhere then. Gunfire came from the willows along the river, from lodges, from clusters of boulders, and even from the low hills overlooking the village. As the troopers saw their comrades start to fall, they began to lose their momentum. One wing of the assault force left off its attack and tried to fire the lodges at one end of the village, but the damp hides and matting wouldn't catch fire.

This delay unbalanced the attacking line and enabled the warriors to turn it. The Nez Percé forces started to give ground now, gradually yielding the village to the assault force, but at the same time they sent a flanking movement around one end of Gibbon's line. In command of the village now, the soldiers were also caught in a cross fire as

Indian sharpshooters fired from all sides.

Joseph learned that one of his wives had been shot, and became like a man possessed. He seemed to fly from one end of the Indian line to the other, often charging in toward the village with Ollakot, whose own wife had been killed in the first moments of the assault.

The battle raged for five hours, until Gibbon, having lost several of his officers and seeing that there was no longer even the shadow of disciplined maneuvering among his troops, realized that he had to retreat or risk annihilation. As the Indians had regained their composure the troopers had begun to lose their own. Officerless groups of men whirled in circles, fearful of attack from all sides, and Gibbon, on the fringes, was unable to restore order. He had a horse shot out from under him and took a bullet in the thigh before managing to sound retreat.

The troopers fell back in disorder, following Gibbon's command to make for a low hill across the river and defend it at all cost. Even in retreat, the soldiers were under the muzzles of several marksmen, and the Indians seemed to pick their targets almost at will. Even their antiquated rifles were no hindrance as they dropped one trooper after another.

It was evident now that the entire attacking force had been beaten back, and annihilation was a real possibility, if the Nez Percé had wanted it. But Joseph, sensible of the need to rescue the women and children, deployed only thirty men, just enough to keep Gibbon's force pinned down on its hilltop while the rest of the adults made ready to escape.

As soon as they were under way, the rear guard started to fall back, and it soon became obvious that Gibbon was not in any condition to follow. Joseph also knew that Howard would not be far away, and any delay might give the general time to bring his own troops to bear, something Joseph wanted to avoid.

As they camped for the night it was evident that a severe blow had been delivered. Many of the best fighting warriors had been killed during the battle, including Rainbow, perhaps the single most proficient fighting man in the entire band. Wahlitits, too, was dead, his premonition all too sadly confirmed. And Sarpsis Ilppilp, fighting to avenge the death of his friend Wahlitits, had met his own death.

The casualties inflicted on Gibbon were significant. Several of his officers had been killed, including Lieutenant Bradley and Captain Logan, and his dead and wounded totaled nearly seventy men. But, as Joseph reminded the council, there were soldiers without limit, and every day, the number of Nez Percé grew smaller.

Chapter 32 ═══════════

THE CROWS WERE NOT HAPPY. At peace on the reservation, they viewed the fugitive Nez Percé as a liability. Looking Glass, despite his hope that the Crows would offer a refuge, was the first of the chiefs to concede that Canada was now their only hope. In an effort to elude Howard's column, still pressing hard on their trail, the Nez Percé headed south, then east through the newly opened Yellowstone National Park.

For the first time Joseph began to feel that their days were running out. The constant pressure of the pursuit, the burden of the wounded, and the exhausting need for constant vigilance all combined to wind the tribal nerves tight, then tighter still.

Angling back north, they sent out a small party of warriors to lay a false trail along the Shoshone River, then headed northeast along the Clark Fork. Howard wasn't convinced the Shoshone was the route, but he had no choice. He dispatched a substantial force under Colonel Samuel Sturgis to blockade the end of the valley along the Clark Fork, hoping to come in behind Joseph's band and squeeze it in a vise. But Sturgis, duped by the false trail, left the mouth of the

Clark Fork Canyon open, and the Nez Percé made it through without firing a shot.

For the next two months the flight wound its way through river bottoms, over rugged mountains, and across mile-high passes. The Nez Percé kept constant watch, leaving scouts behind and routing them in and out in order to keep themselves apprised of Howard's whereabouts.

The general, still smarting from the repeated victories of the fugitives and determined not to be outsmarted again, decided to make a feint of his own. Aware that the chiefs were not interested in fighting—they had avoided significant military engagement since leading a raid to recover their captured horses in early August—Howard decided to slow his pursuit, knowing the exhausted Indians would take advantage of the unexpected respite to hunt for food and rest their weary mounts. It would also give the wounded a chance to recover some of their strength.

But Joseph's fears had been almost prophetic. Unknown to the Nez Percé, Howard had another column, under the command of Colonel Nelson Miles, heading up the Missouri at a forced march. While the Indians slowed their pace, Miles was rapidly closing the gap.

In late September, advance scouts for Miles caught sight of the Nez Percé camp, just forty miles from the Canadian border. The village gave every evidence of being tranquil, possibly even permanent, and Miles pushed his men still harder in order to catch the fugitives before they escaped to Canada.

And Miles was anything but disinterested in the outcome of the pursuit. Ambitious to a fault, this

son-in-law of General Sherman was determined to
build a career for himself. Joseph was now the most
celebrated Indian leader in the country, and a man
for whom more than a few whites were actively
rooting, thanks to the extensive press coverage of
Howard's campaign and the widespread belief that
the Nez Percé were being victimized by a callous
and insensitive Indian policy. Despite this, Miles
knew that capturing Joseph would all but guarantee
his promotion to brigadier general.

He had three hundred and seventy-five men in
his command, both cavalry and infantry, and his
troops were armed with the most advanced
weapons the United States Army had in its arsenal.

The Nez Percé camp, located on the edge of the
Bear Paw Mountains, was clearly meant to be a
springboard for the final leg of the flight through
the pass between the Bear Paws and the northern-
most reaches of the Little Rockies range. The latter
mountains ran from northwest to southeast, and
screened Miles's approach toward the Bear Paws.
In order to ensure that his final approach was not
inadvertently revealed to the Nez Percé scouts, he
ordered his men to ignore the herds of deer, elk,
and bison grazing the rich grasslands that ran parallel to the Little Rockies.

And finally, at eight A.M. on the morning of
September 30, Miles got his first look at the Nez
Percé village, established on Snake Creek in a kid-
ney-shaped depression. A survey through field
glasses and the reports of his Cheyenne scouts made
it obvious to Miles that Joseph had chosen his
campsite carefully. The depression and the buttes
around it were riven with dry washes up to six feet

deep, fringed with brush and almost perfect as rifle pits. They were deep enough to offer the Indian defenders all the cover they needed, but not so deep as to pin them in should they have to move.

Any approaching attackers, on the other hand, would come under the Indian rifles well before they were close enough to swarm over the campsite. Knowing that subterfuge was pointless and stealth all but impossible, Miles ordered his column into a trot, even the infantry mounted on horseback.

As the soldiers charged the camp, led by Miles's Cheyenne and Sioux scouts, they fanned out into a long line and swept toward the still slumbering village. A small boy on horseback saw them and alerted the Indians, who swarmed out of their lodges and into the defensive positions, including a series of rifle pits they had been constructing at every camp since the near disaster at Big Hole Basin.

The defenders showed remarkable discipline, holding their fire even as the trot turned into a gallop and the thundering hooves kicked thick clouds of dust into the subfreezing air. Not until the attacking force was within a hundred yards of the advance line did the Nez Percé open fire. And their marksmanship immediately began to take its toll.

Soldier after soldier fell from the saddle, and the attackers were forced to dismount. Joseph and White Bird raced from defender to defender. They instructed the warriors to listen for the loud voices of the officers and to target their fire on the commanders. This tactic made effective control all but impossible for Miles, and the attackers were compelled first to fall back and then to dig in.

The infantrymen had charged on horseback, and they, too, had dismounted. They found cover in the brush and among the boulders, and their new, long-range rifles allowed them to lay down a withering fire that forced the Nez Percé to stay down. From time to time, one side or the other attempted an assault, but the marksmen on both sides were too skillful for any momentum to be developed, and a standoff developed.

The more adventurous of the Nez Percé were the principal war leaders, and they were therefore the most frequent targets. One by one, Looking Glass, Toohoolhoolzote and, finally, Ollakot fell to the army sharpshooters. For nearly four hours, the two sides exchanged fire, increasingly more sporadic as the survivors on each side grew more cautious.

Growing impatient, and fearful that Joseph might escape after nightfall, Miles ordered another assault shortly before one o'clock in the afternoon. By this time, the temperature had begun to fall rapidly, and the thickening gray of the sky seemed to be drifting slowly toward the earth. The weather might become an additional advantage for the Nez Percé, and Miles was determined to put an end to the battle before that could happen.

But this assault was turned back as readily as the first, and by evening, it had begun to snow. The winds had grown in force and swirled the snow so fiercely that visibility was all but eliminated.

All across the field of battle, soldiers and warriors lay, the dead immune to the cold, the wounded slowly freezing to death as the wind cut through their clothing and the snow accumulated in drifts against their numbed limbs.

The soldiers who had fallen within the Nez Percé lines were given water on Joseph's orders, but food was almost nonexistent in the Nez Percé camp and blankets at a premium.

During the night, Joseph and White Bird, each in his own way acceding to the inevitable, discussed their options.

"We can try to escape to Canada while the soldiers sleep," White Bird suggested.

"And what of our wounded?" Joseph asked. "They will not survive the trip and we cannot leave them. I have never heard of a wounded Indian who grew well again in the white man's hands. And our women and children are too weak to run. We cannot leave them to the soldiers."

"What will you do, Hin-mah-too-yah-lat-kekht?"

"In the morning I will speak to Colonel Miles and see if he will accept our surrender. I will ask if he will take us back to the reservation."

White Bird nodded. "I understand." The two warriors had been friends all their lives and White Bird could barely control himself as he spoke. "I wish you luck," he said. "We have ridden together for many years. I think, though, that we shall never ride together again."

"I want you to take my family with you," Joseph said.

"Of course."

"Please take care of them."

This time there were no words. White Bird simply nodded and turned away. During the night, with the wind howling and the snow swirling all around him, he led a contingent of more than one hundred from the camp and broke for the border.

At sunup, Joseph worked his way along the lines
of defense, telling each warrior in turn what he
proposed to do. Some wanted to continue fighting,
but Joseph painted the reality in such stark terms
that even the most belligerent were forced to accept
it. While Joseph continued his rounds the heavy
guns of Miles opened fire and the first few shells
landed in the center of the village, each explosion
echoing off the surrounding buttes as if to under-
line Joseph's grim assessment.

After he had spoken to all the fighting men, running up a flag of truce, he walked out between the
lines. Miles ordered the barrage halted and came
forward to meet him.

"If we surrender, what will happen to us?"
Joseph asked.

"I will see to it that you are treated well," Miles
assured him.

"The reservation . . . will we be allowed to go
there?"

"You have my word."

Joseph nodded sadly. "I will discuss it with my
people and will let you have my answer as soon as
we have decided."

For the next three days, the negotiations dragged
on. Some of the warriors did not trust Miles and
even those who did knew that his promises might
be worthless, no matter what his intentions might
be. Joseph knew this better than anyone, but he was
concerned for the wounded and the deteriorating
condition of the rest of the people, exposed to the
bitter cold and getting by on near-starvation rations.

On the evening of October 4, it began to snow
again, and at eight o'clock General Howard arrived.

Colonel Miles filled him in on the progress of the negotiations and said that Joseph had promised an answer the following day.

The two officers waited all morning. The weather stayed below freezing and they were beginning to fear for the Indians. But at two o'clock Joseph stepped from his lodge and mounted his horse. Accompanied by several warriors, he rode toward the army lines. Howard and Miles went out to meet him.

Dismounting, Joseph walked slowly forward then extended his arms and thrust his rifle at Howard, who deferred to Miles. And with the relinquishing of that rifle, Joseph brought to an end a remarkable journey that took nearly a thousand people, with all their earthly possessions, nearly one thousand eight hundred miles. In the course of their flight they had engaged or eluded more than two thousand soldiers and managed to come within forty miles, one day's journey, of their Canadian sanctuary.

Joseph looked over his shoulder then, at the village, and at the mountains beyond it for a long moment, then turned back to the commanders. He nodded, then began to speak. "Tell General Howard I know his heart. What he told me before I have in my heart. I am tired of fighting. Our chiefs are killed. Looking Glass is dead. Toohoolhoolzote is dead. The old men are all dead. It is the young men who say yes or no. He who led the young men is dead. It is cold and we have no blankets. The little children are freezing to death. My people, some of them, have run away to the hills and have no blankets, no food. No one knows where they are, perhaps freezing to death. I want time to look for

my children and see how many of them I can find.
Maybe I shall find them among the dead. Hear me,
my chiefs, I am tired. My heart is sick and sad.
From where the sun now stands, I will fight no
more forever."

Turning his back then, he pulled his blanket up
over his head and the war was over.

Afterword

AFTER THEIR SURRENDER, the surviving nontreaty Nez Percé were taken to Fort Keogh for the winter, except for the hundred or so who escaped to Canada with White Bird. Despite the assurances of Colonel Miles and General Howard that they would be allowed to return to the Nez Percé country and to the reservation at Lapwai, they were sent south. Generals Sherman and Sheridan were in favor of a stern policy that would, they believed, "serve as a warning" to other disaffected tribes in the northwest.

On the land set aside for them in Indian Territory, the present-day Oklahoma, they did not fare well. The climate was so different from their own, and diseases such as malaria so prevalent, that they died in significant numbers. Throughout the long ordeal of their exile, Joseph never stopped fighting for his people, and he did not have to fight alone. Several advocates for a return to the northwest came from their former adversaries in the military, including Howard, who was something of a humanitarian despite his foolish inflexibility at the eleventh hour when the war still might have been averted. Howard was instrumental in founding the university that today still bears his name. Surprisingly, the most vigorous advocate of them all was Colonel Nelson A. Miles.

Joseph made several trips to Washington during the long exile, where he proved to be an adept diplomat and advocate for his people. Eventually, the federal government relented, permitting a return to the northwest, and the Nez Percé were resettled on the Colville Reservation at Nespelem, Washington, in 1885.

Joseph continued to hope for an eventual return to the Wallowa Valley, but it was not to be. He saw his beloved valley only once more, in 1900, when he toured the Wallowa country during a "feasibility study" intended to explore the possibility of relocating the remainder of his band to their ancestral homeland. While there, he visited the grave of his father, which had been tended and fenced in by a white friend, but not before Old Joseph's body had been disinterred by a previous white owner of the land, its head removed and the skull put on display for a while in a dentist's office in Oregon. As late as 1903, Miles, by then a lieutenant general who had attained the position of chief-of-staff, was Joseph's host in Washington, D.C., and tried to help secure a return to the Wallowa.

On September 21, 1904, Joseph died, according to the agency physician, "of a broken heart."

I have tried hard to respect the facts of this story, although the requirements of fiction have led me on occasion to ignore a fact in favor of a truth which seems to me more significant or more dramatic. I hope such license, not lightly exercised, can be forgiven.

There is a considerable body of material available on Joseph and the final flight, but no study should begin without a reading of Alvin M. Josephy's monumental *The Nez Percé Indians and the Opening of the Northwest*. Other excellent studies have been written by Mark H. Brown, Helen Addison Howard, Merril D. Beal, and Francis Haines, all of which I have consulted in preparation of this novel, and all of which I commend to anyone who wants to explore the heartrending story of these heroic people. In addition, many of the military officers have left us memoirs, as have some of the Nez Percé themselves.